DRAWING
THE DEAD

DRAWING
THE DEAD

ROBERT J. MCCARTER

Little Hummingbird Publishing
Flagstaff, AZ

Drawing the Dead

Version 1.1, February, 2017
Version 1.0, April, 2013
ISBN: 978-0-9642096-4-0

Find out more about this book at: DrawingTheDead.com
Visit Robert's website at: RobertJMcCarter.com
Find out more about Barry Miller (BTBArtist), at: www.btbartist.co.uk

Published by:
Little Hummingbird Publishing
P.O. Box 23518
Flagstaff, AZ 86002
www.LittleHummingbird.com

Little Hummingbird Publishing is a division of Arapas, Inc. Find more about Arapas at: www.Arapas.com.

Dedicated to VTara...
we miss you over here on this side.

CHAPTER 1

Doubt filled their eyes, and hope and fear. But like all of Madam Valarka's clients, there was mostly desperation. The man and woman sat at the small round table across from her, their hands clutched tightly together as they watched her draw. It was to be expected. What followed would be either an amazing miracle or a huge disappointment. There was no middle ground.

A single light illuminated the silk festooned table in the otherwise dim room. The man and woman huddled close, leaning into the light as if afraid of the surrounding darkness. The room was silent and the air smelled of sage and sandalwood.

Madam Valarka paused, smiling at her clients, trying to put them at ease. Her heavy makeup, hoop earrings, jangling bracelets, and silks covering her slim body added to the mystical atmosphere. Valarka was a gypsy, and even though they sat in a small room above a bookstore in Sedona, Arizona, this was her domain.

A photograph of a smiling young man with unruly brown hair sat upside down to her left and in front of her was the portrait she was creating. Valarka always worked upside down. That way her clients could see their loved one clearly, but mostly because that was the way her grandmother taught her.

"It draws on a different part of the brain," the older woman had said. "I know it feels strange to do it this way, but it works."

She hadn't believed her grandmother, of course, and had tried drawing from a right-side-up portrait, but only once. That was all it took.

Valarka searched through her pastels finding the three shades of brown she needed for the hair. The silence wasn't good, so as she outlined and started filling in the hair, she asked, "Tell me more about Cole, what kind of child was he?"

"Oh…" the woman began, her shaking hand brushing at her hair. "He was such a boy. When he was just a toddler he would love to go outside and play in the dirt."

"And eat bugs," the man added with a thin chuckle. "That boy loved to eat bugs, he'd stick anything into his mouth."

They continued on, with occasional prompting, telling little stories and anecdotes about their son. Inevitably, each story would lead them back to the motorcycle accident and his death.

Each time she would prompt them again, taking them back to birthdays and vacations and other fond memories. Madam Valarka took these in as she worked the pastels, blending with her fingers, bringing the portrait to life. She moved from the hair, to the nose, to the lips, and finally back to the eyes.

She spent a lot of time on the eyes. They had to be perfect. They were brown, like his hair, soulful and expressive.

She worked hard, giving them depth and feeling, framing them with their heavy lids and long lashes.

The man and woman stopped talking, but she didn't prompt them to start again. She was almost done. She let her fingers guide her, choosing black, and began working it in around the face, filling in the blank portions of the paper. When she had first started drawing the dead she would have been scared by the choice. Black was often not good a sign. But, she had learned to trust. She had to trust.

"Okay," she said, putting her pastels away. "I think we are ready to try this."

"If... if it works. How much time will we get?" the woman asked.

"Just a few minutes," Valarka answered with a smile. "Just a few."

"That..." the woman said, tears forming, "that would be wonderful."

"Okay, I need each of you to place the fingers of your left hand on the bottom of the portrait, and I will do the same on the top. Only those touching the portrait will be able to see what happens."

Madam Valarka placed her hand so that her index finger touched the top of the young man's head.

"Now," she continued, "I want you to take a deep breath and see Cole on this page. See him alive and well and healthy."

She looked at them and saw they were holding their breaths. "Breathe, deeply," she continued. "See your son as smiling and happy, and alive." She led them, breathing deeply in and out, focusing her gaze on the portrait, feeling the energy build, feeling the portrait grow warm under her fingers.

When the moment was right, she leaned down and gently exhaled onto the drawing of Cole.

At first nothing changed, but slowly the picture began to look more three dimensional as the eyes came alive. The woman gasped and the man said, "Oh my God!" as the drawing began to move.

Fully alive on the paper, Cole's mouth opened and he said, "Mom? Dad?"

CHAPTER 2

Viki Dobos, known to her clients as Madam Valarka, sighed. Her clients left happy, having talked with their dead son, and she was exhausted. It took a lot to draw the dead.

She said a brief prayer of thanks that began the ritual that marked the close of her long work day. She felt grateful to have served and grateful that nothing untoward had happened.

The forces she dealt with were powerful, and things could go wrong... things had gone wrong.

After the prayer, she cleaned up. One step at a time, in the proper order, just as her grandmother had taught her.

First, she swept up all the stray pastel crumbs and put them into a jar. These she would dispose of in the desert in the way she had been taught.

Second, she folded up the colorful silk scarfs that covered the table, and packed them and the rest of her gear into her case, making sure each pastel, each piece of equipment was in place. She put the jar with the pastel crumbs in last, shut the case, fastened the hasps, and locked it. The tiny key she put in the heart-shaped locket around her neck.

She paused, a small smile on her lips, as her hand rubbed the old, stained leather of the antique, hard-sided cosmetic case. It had two brass hasps, a small lock, and a handle on the top.

The case, which she had inherited from her grandmother, had been customized to hold her gear. Something newer, something with wheels, might serve her better, but it connected her to her grandmother and rooted her in their tradition; connected her to her past.

Third, she cleaned the area, wiping down the table, and vacuuming the carpet and the chairs.

Fourth, she walked around the room clockwise four times, singing the Romani song her grandmother had taught her.

Lastly, she went into the little bathroom and attended to herself. She removed the silk from her head, the large hoop earrings, and slowly removed the heavy makeup—too heavy for her taste—from her face. She went in Madam Valarka and came out Viki.

Without her makeup, Viki no longer looked like a gypsy, but like a normal woman in her late thirties. She had a slim body, brown hair pulled into a ponytail, and hazel eyes. Her clients would not recognize her.

Case in hand, she was ready to go home for the night. She longed to draw a bath, light a candle, and immerse her body. She was about to leave when she saw the note slipped under the door.

"V, I know you are at your limit for the day, but please talk to the waiting gentleman. He doesn't want you to draw, he has an offer for you and has paid full price for the privilege of asking."

It was signed in a looping scrawl, "Reg."

Viki sighed, what now?

~~~

She opened the door and found what she could only describe as a "gentleman" waiting. He was tall and thin with long fingers, short grey hair, and brown eyes. He was impeccably dressed in an expensive suit.

"Ms. Dobos," he said in a genteel British accent as he rose and offered his hand. "My name is Alexander Wells. I am so grateful you have agreed to see me."

She hadn't agreed, but she couldn't refuse him. She felt fate nudging her along. She nodded and said, "Please come in, Mr. Wells."

She signaled for him to sit down as she unlocked and opened her case, pulled out a vibrant blue silk, and spread it on the table. She then retrieved a deck of cards from her case and sat across from him.

"I thought Mr. Anderson had explained," he said. "I don't require a reading, just a few minutes of your time."

"Yes, Reg did explain. But I need to find out who you are first."

"I am sorry, but there is some urgency to the situation."

She held up her hand. "Please, Mr. Wells. This won't take long. You have paid to see me—we will do at least this."

Viki had finished with her day, finished with clients; she needed something to bring her back to center so she could be present for his request.

She deftly shuffled the oversized cards and handed them over. "Pick one card." Alexander looked puzzled, his hands at his side. "They don't bite, I assure you, Mr. Wells. Just pick a card and we can get to what you came for."

He snatched the card on the top of the deck and handed

it to her. Viki nodded and smiled, and turned the card over. It was a simply, but elegantly, hand-drawn card with the word "Mercury" at the top. The card depicted a round orb with a figure of a man in front of it with winged shoes.

"Ahh..." Viki said. "Mercury, messenger of the gods. See, I do need to listen to you, Mr. Wells. Do you bring me a message from the gods?"

Alexander laughed briefly. "Well, sometimes he thinks..." He trailed off, cleared his throat, and continued. "Excuse me, Ms. Dobos. I didn't say that."

"I'm sorry? I missed that last part," Viki said with a grin. Alexander smiled. "Please, Mr. Wells, what is it you came here to talk to me about?"

"My employer would like to hire you for the next two weeks—"

"Ohh, I'm sorry, I have a lot of appointments, I can't just leave them."

"—for $2,000 per day."

Viki felt a cold sweat spring to her forehead as she put her hand over her mouth. This no longer seemed like a gentle nudge fate was giving her, but a giant push.

Chapter 3

"What the hell, Reg, what is this? Who is this guy?" Viki asked. She had excused herself, and left Alexander in her workroom and come downstairs.

Reginald Anderson stood behind the counter of the Sacred Vortex shop. He was a big man with long grey hair pulled back in a ponytail, sharp grey eyes, and wore a green silk shirt. "Calm down, V," he said, his voice deep and even.

"Calm down? Two grand a day? What is this?"

"Look, I've been checking his story out. He works for a very wealthy Russian named Mark Kosov. Kosov is one of those crazy-rich guys that made his money the old-fashioned way—by beating his competition to a pulp. Now he wants to give it all away. He's signed onto Bill Gates's and Warren Buffet's 'Giving Pledge.'"

"That's a lovely story, Reg. But if he is paying two grand a day, he is going to want something."

"The guy is for real. I can't find anything bad about him since he cleaned his act up about twelve years ago. Maybe you should talk to his man and find out more.

"Besides, two thousand a day for fourteen days is a lot of money. How can you turn that down?"

Viki inhaled, as if winding up to say more, but slowly exhaled and stomped back up the stairs.

~~~

"I apologize, Mr. Wells. It's just that the amount you have offered is a lot of money."

"I understand, Ms. Dobos, but the matter is urgent, and my employer thought it a reasonable compensation for the inconvenience."

"And what, exactly, does your employer, Mr. Kosov, I believe..." Alexander nodded. "What exactly does he want me to do?"

Alexander looked down at his steepled fingers before continuing. "To tell you the truth, Ms. Dobos, he didn't tell me exactly what he wants. All I know is that it involves your rather unique gift and your presence at his house in Hawaii."

"He wants me to draw for him? In Hawaii?"

"Yes."

"Why didn't he just come with you? I could draw for him here for a lot less money."

"I am sorry, but I am not sure. I do know that he has his reasons. He always has a reason."

Viki sighed and got up. "I am going to need to think about this. Can you come back in the morning?"

"I am sorry, Ms. Dobos, but the offer expires today. I have a plane waiting for us at the Sedona Airport and I was instructed to head back this evening with or without you."

~~~

Viki left Alexander Wells again and went outside to

think. The British man had been gracious about it, but she could tell he was agitated, he kept fidgeting and checking his watch. It was late January and cold. Viki pulled her sweater around her as she paced in front of the Sacred Vortex. She reflexively reached for a cigarette and silently cursed when she didn't find one. Five years later and the habit still wasn't totally gone. She missed Boston and how sure of herself she had been then. How with a few minutes with a cigarette her tension would fade.

The money was enticing, she had to admit it. It took a busy week for her to make two thousand dollars. Why not go to Hawaii for two weeks and make twenty-eight thousand? She could really get ahead, maybe start looking for a house. Not in Sedona, of course, she would never have enough money for a house in Sedona, but maybe down in the Verde Valley. That would be enough for a down payment on a small place. She could start a garden, or—

"V," Reg said as he sauntered out. "The butler is getting anxious, so what's it gonna be?"

"I don't know, Reg. The money is nice, but this doesn't feel right."

"Oh come one, V. You've barely left Sedona in the seven years since you got here. You've only been back to Boston once to visit your family. I know you and your mother aren't tight, but... she's your mother."

Viki's shoulders tensed at the mention of her mother. Memories of how they had fought flickered past. Fighting over her gift, over her lifestyle, over her lack of a husband, over her abortion. With her grandmother dead there was nothing left for her in Boston.

"Don't you think it's time for you to step out a little?"

Reg continued. "Have an adventure? And, God forbid, maybe some fun?"

"And what if I do? What if I lower my guard? What if it's like Boston all over again? What if someone dies?"

Reg frowned. "That wasn't your fault. You didn't know."

"Yeah, well maybe I should have. My gift should help people, not kill them."

"And what, just because you've got a gift, just because you're sometimes psychic, you think you should know everything? Be able to avoid every mistake? Is that what you're doing in that little room above my bookstore charging tourists a tenth of what your worth?"

"Reg, please..." Viki crossed her arms and looked down at her feet.

"No. I've got something to say and you need to listen. Remember when we met?"

"Yes," Viki replied. "You came to Boston, I drew your mother. You invited me to come draw at your bookstore."

"That reading changed my life, V. And the readings you do change lives every day. But back then you had started coming out of your shell, you wanted to find a way to help more people, even those you couldn't draw for. You weren't afraid. You weren't hiding then."

"I am not hiding," Viki said quietly, her gaze meeting Reg's.

Reg smiled thinly and shook his head. He gently touched her shoulder. "Yes you are. I do all the public stuff, and I am happy to, but this gift of yours could reach so many more people. Maybe this Kosov guy can be a start of something for you."

Viki turned, shrugging his touch off and walked several paces away.

"And make so much more money, you mean," Viki said.

"Yes, V, more money. And what the hell is wrong with that? You help more people, you earn more money. Sounds like karma to me."

"Mark Kosov, he's going to ask me to do something I shouldn't do. I can just feel it, Reg."

Reg shrugged. "So set your boundaries and go for it. If it doesn't look good once you get there, walk."

"But, my cat, who's going to take care of her?"

"I already called Jamie, she said she would be happy to look after Bast."

"But my appointments—"

"I'll reschedule."

Viki sighed and wrapped her arms around her chest, shivering at something other than the weather. Reg was right, she had been hiding, afraid to use her gift and afraid not to use it. Afraid to leave the safe little world she had created. What would her grandmother think? She felt change coming, and she knew she needed it.

More than anything she needed change.

"Okay, I'll do it. And, Reg, you'll get your usual twenty percent of this."

"Ahh... No need, V," Reg began, as he looked at his shoes. "I've arranged so my cut is separate from what they are paying you."

Viki laughed, "Of course it is."

She shook her head and walked back into the bookstore wondering about what was to come.

CHAPTER 4

The exodus had been frantic. A brief trip to her apartment to pack a bag, a drive up Airport Mesa, a quick walk through what passes for an airport in Sedona, and onto a four-seater Cessna.

"Yes, sir," Alexander said. He had been on his cell phone for the last five minutes. "I'll tell her." He closed the phone and turned to Viki. "Mr. Kosov sends his most sincere gratitude."

Viki smiled, looking closely at Alexander and ignoring everything else as the plane taxied down the small runway. She had never been in a plane so small. "What is he like?" she asked as she chewed on her thumbnail.

"Smart, demanding, perceptive. He is very driven and usually has an exceptionally clear vision of what he wants."

"And what he wants now is my ability?"

"Yes."

Viki shook her head. It's not that she didn't believe it possible. It was just—

"How did he find out about me?" she asked. Since Boston she had kept a very low profile, and even in Boston not many had known of her gift. What she did could be so easily misunderstood or misused, she had never sought publicity. She didn't advertise, didn't have a website, or a facebook page.

"You drew for some friends of his, some people he trusts."

"Oh."

"Believe me, this is not a normal avenue of investigation for Mr. Kosov."

Viki was about to reply when she felt the seat pushing against her as the plane rose. She felt the nausea and fear she always felt on takeoff, but it was quickly replaced with awe when she looked out the window next to her.

Spread out below her were the magnificent, towering red-rock formations of Sedona. With the airport being such a small and expensive point of departure, she had never seen Sedona from above. Tall red-rock spires, large mesas, winding streets dotted with homes. All of it bathed in the warm glow of the late afternoon sun.

Viki loved it. Her fear of flying forgotten, she stared out the window and watched the desert pass below her the whole way to Phoenix as the sun set.

~~~

In Phoenix, they traded the Cessna for a Gulfstream jet and took off for Maui.

Too wired to sleep, Viki dug into her case and pulled out her cards.

"Did you draw those yourself?" Alexander asked.

"Yes."

"What are they? If you don't mind me asking."

"No... no. It was part of how my grandmother trained me. Each card represents an archetype, a universal concept or symbol. She thought it important that I study and understand them. Having to design and draw the cards myself made that happen. I use them at the beginning of my time with clients. Sometimes when I draw, nothing happens. This way everyone gets at least a reading and a portrait from their time with me."

Alexander nodded. "And why are you pulling them out now?"

Viki smiled. "I am tired and confused. With the right attitude, cards like these can bring mental clarity."

Alexander smiled but did not comment.

"And, barring that, they will, at least, give me something to do."

Viki turned her attention back to the cards, shuffling them slowly. She didn't have room to spread them all out, so she divided them into two stacks and held her hand over both. She felt warmth over the stack on the right. She moved the left stack aside and divided the right one into two smaller stacks. She proceeded this way until there was just one card on the tray before her.

She slowly flipped it over. The card showed a hooded figure of indeterminate gender steeped in darkness. "Shadow."

Viki sighed. The Shadow represents that which is hidden in darkness, unknown, that which must be discovered. Was it something about herself that needed discovering or something about this Mark Kosov? Either way, it wasn't sounding like much of a vacation.

She put her cards away, put her seat back, closed her eyes, and after a time, slept. And she dreamed, dreamed of her grandmother.

~~~

"Ignore your mother," her grandmother said. "She has turned her back on her legacy, but not you, little one. In you I see the gift shining forth brightly."

Viki had been nine years old at the time. She knew what her grandmother did but she didn't comprehend it. "I don't understand, Gran. You draw pictures and the dead talk to the living. How does it work? Is it magic?"

Gran smiled. "It must be magic, because I have no idea how it works. I do as my mother taught me. I dress as she taught me; I use the pastels made by my own hand, as she taught me; I do the rituals, as she taught me, and it happens." She laughed, a deep throaty sound, and hugged her. "And it is how you will do it too, Little Sparrow."

Viki smiled and nodded. She still didn't understand, but she knew that she loved her grandmother and wanted nothing more than to please her.

"And listen to me now, child," the woman continued, holding her by the shoulders. "What I teach you, you must guard. The world won't understand it. The world will try to take it, the world will try to abuse it. You must—"

~~~

The jolt of the plane touching down woke Viki. She looked out the window, but it was dark and all she could see were the lights of an airport. "Where are we?" she asked.

"Kahului Airport, on Maui. It is about 11 p.m. local time," Alexander said.

Viki nodded and sat silently until the plane came to a stop and the door opened. She was contemplating her dream-memory, afraid of what was to come.

CHAPTER 5

Viki didn't see much on the way to the Kosov house in Kihei. She strained her eyes, peering into the darkness but only saw tantalizing flashes of vegetation once they left the confines of Kahului. She had long dreamed of visiting Hawaii, but seeing it would have to wait.

They soon stopped in front of ornate gates, the iron curled into the form of a griffin. The gates opened and they went down a long, palm-tree-lined driveway and came to rest in front of a house.

It was a large, beautiful home, but not the mansion she had imagined. She could hear the ocean and smell the saltwater.

Alexander showed her to her room. "Breakfast is at eight sharp." It was said as a simple statement of fact, but Viki knew what it was. A summons from her employer.

~~~

Viki burrowed her feet into the sand and stared out at the ocean. It was early, the sun had just started to kiss the sand she sat on. She marveled at the temperature, it was January and close to seventy degrees. Truly paradise.

Only a few people moved along the beach—joggers, young and old, and extremely tanned men walking steadily back and forth.

She had woken early, still on Arizona time, and made her way from her room across the well-manicured grass of the grounds and onto the beach.

To the north of her was a six-story hotel perched among black volcanic rocks, to the south of her was a series of beach homes, and further down, Wailea. The Kosov house was a bit larger than most of the surrounding houses, but not particularly big. She imagined it was chosen for the beach and the water, not for its size or stature.

Her roaming eye caught on a figure moving down the beach towards her. He was tall and slim, maybe sixty years old, with short grey hair, and a neat goatee. He was unusually dressed. Well, being dressed in anything but a bathing suit was unusual. He wore white pants with the cuffs rolled up, a loose long-sleeved linen shirt, and a white hat.

But more than that, it was the way he moved that caught her attention. Slowly, deliberately, carefully. He walked through the upper edges of where the surf came in, through the wet, firm sand. He moved like a man unsure of how to walk. Moving slowly, pausing between each step, a look of concentration on his face.

When the man came in line with the house, he turned sharply and started moving through the dry sand, his walking process even slower and more deliberate.

Realizing who she was watching and getting a glimmer of what was going on, Viki rose, walked up to the man, and extended her hand.

"Hello, Mr. Kosov," she said. "My name is Viki Dobos."

Mark Kosov smiled and gave her a small nod. His face

formed a smile, but his blue eyes did not. "Thank you for coming."

His voice was low and smooth with just a trace of an accent, the way he chewed on his vowels. "You must be hungry, let's see if we can't get Alexander to serve breakfast a bit early."

Viki smiled at him as they turned towards the house. Mark wobbled unsteadily and Viki reached out and took his arm, and held it until they went through the small gate where Mark retrieved his cane. To someone passing it looked like she was leaning on him, not the other way around.

~~~

After breakfast and pleasantries—the weather, Maui, the home they were in—Viki said what was on her mind. "You are dying, aren't you?"

Mark smiled, this time his eyes joining in. "Yes. Is being psychic one of your gifts?"

Viki shrugged noncommittally. "Sometimes, maybe. But I didn't need to be psychic to see that."

Mark poured them more coffee—100 percent Kona, of course—and gestured for her to continue.

"There had to be a good reason for you to bring me here in the first place. That and your appearance." Viki saw in the way his flesh lay on his cheeks that he had lost weight recently. The dark smudges under his eyes, his sallow complexion, and the way he walked all added to the picture. She saw a man that was frail, but not used to being frail.

"And..." Mark prompted.

"And you want me to draw for you, you want to talk to your loved ones that have already passed. You brought me here instead of coming to Sedona because of your condition and your means."

Mark smiled again, his blue eyes distant, and nodded at Viki.

She could tell that she had missed something. He wasn't telling her something important.

CHAPTER 6

They sat outside on a second-story, ocean-facing lanai. Viki's things were arrayed on the round table, with Alexander and Mark sitting across from her. She smelled the tang of the salt air and heard the whisper of the palm trees and the crashing of the waves behind her as she prepared to draw.

Mark Kosov had told her it was a test run. He wanted to see a demonstration of her abilities before she drew for him.

Viki had passed the day pleasantly, walking along the beach, resting, reading. She would have drawn earlier, but business kept Mark for most of the day.

She looked at the photograph in front of her. Blue eyes, dull with age; grey hair, wispy and curly, framing a round face; thin lips pulled into a reluctant smile; deep folds and wrinkles adding character; arched eyebrows sitting above those wise eyes.

Alexander's mother.

Viki was dubious anything would happen, the woman had been gone for fifteen years. She had explained this, but her client wanted her to start here. If nothing else, Alexander would get a portrait of his mother.

Viki worked quickly, pulling the pastels from her case without looking. The picture and the portrait both faced Alexander and Mark. She worked upside down as she always did.

First she drew the eyes, lightly sketching them in. The eyes first and the eyes last. Then she lightly filled in the outline of the head and the hair. Then the nose and the ears, until there was a delicate sketch of the woman. Helen, her name was Helen.

She didn't look up from her work, but she could feel her clients. Alexander was quiet, internal, and sad. Mark was focused, intent, and a bit aggressive. Or perhaps eager would be a better word. His need unsettled her.

Around she went, filling in the details of the face, bringing in depth, and dimension, and character. She didn't draw everything, just what mattered most. The traces of dimples. The mole to the right of her nose. The waves of wrinkles on her forehead. The wispy feel of her hair.

She ended on the eyes, making them as real as possible.

Nearly done, she closed her eyes and felt for the background. This was important, almost predictive. A mostly white background generally indicated a peaceful death, a dark background, not so much. She reached, she felt, she let her hands work. The background was a light blue, which boded well.

"I think we're ready," she said, looking up and smiling at the men across from her. Alexander nodded. Mark met her eyes but she could not read anything but his need.

"Both of you put your fingers on the portrait, right at the bottom as I will do the same at the top."

Alexander complied, but Mark's hands remained in his lap.

"Please, Mr. Kosov, you need to put your hand on it if you are going to experience it."

"I have to be touching the drawing to see it come alive?" Mark asked.

Viki nodded and Mark delicately laid his fingers on the drawing next to Alexander's.

Viki gathered the energies, said her prayers, and leaned down, blowing a gentle breath across the page.

She waited. One breath, two breaths, three breaths, but nothing happened.

"I'm sorry, Alexander," she said. "It has just been too long. Your mother is at peace, I can feel that."

Her eyes met Mark's. She saw doubt—that she expected—but she saw something else. Fear. He was counting on her gift being real and afraid that it wasn't. What did he want from her?

~~~

Viki Dobos sat on the large lanai watching the sun set through the veil of tall palm trees that ringed the ocean side of Mark Kosov's property. A few clouds lay heavy on the horizon and the sun, caught behind them, was throwing an orange glow over the ocean.

When she was younger, a failure like this would have worried her. Not now. She knew from experience, from thousands of readings, that some were beyond her ability to reach. It wasn't the best first impression, but there was nothing to be done about it.

The sun peaked out from below the clouds, scattering a yellow light to mix with the orange, as it started to lower itself into the ocean.

She turned when she heard a scuffing noise behind her. Mark stood there holding a book. The color of the sunset reflecting off his face added warmth to the paleness, making him appear healthier, stronger.

She studied his face, hoping to see his secret, but she couldn't.

He carefully laid the book down on the table and said, "I want you to draw this man."

Viki cocked her head, eyebrow raised. "The author? Has he passed?"

"He was dead when he wrote it."

Puzzled, Viki picked up the book: *Shuffled Off: A Ghost's Memoir.*

"At the University of Arizona," Mark began, "they created a kind of typewriter that this fellow used to write his story."

"I…"

"It's pretty convincing; there are witness interviews, documented events, descriptions of the technology used. The fellow, JJ Lynch, didn't seem to be in a hurry to move on. He should be reachable and open to it."

Viki opened the book and began idly flipping through the pages. At the end of the book was a black and white photograph of the "author."

"There's your picture," Mark said.

Viki shook her head. "I don't know. It's always been a friend or a relative I drew. Someone they know."

"Read it, I think you'll find he's open. I want you to draw him for Alexander and me tomorrow afternoon."

With that Mark got started walking away.

"Wait," Viki said, "I need a color picture. I've never tried with black and white."

"I'll have one for you," Mark said as he left.

CHAPTER 7

Warm sugar sand, blue water, crashing waves, bright yellow sun, swaying palm trees... It wasn't a bad way to spend the day, but Viki felt nervous, her feet carrying her up and down the beach. Why did Mark want her to draw a stranger, to prove herself?

"Did you read the book?" Reg asked Viki, drawing her attention back to their phone conversation.

"Yeah. Very interesting," Viki answered.

"And do you think the ghost would be open to being drawn as Mark suggested?"

"I guess."

"Then what's the problem?" Reg asked.

"It's just not right. There must be a loved one he wants to talk to, otherwise, why am I here?"

"Ahh... V, you're there to have a vacation and make a ton of money."

"He's going to ask me to do something I don't want to, I can just feel it."

"So have a Mai Tai, chill out, get paid. And when he

asks you to do something you don't want to, walk. What's the big deal?"

Viki laughed, it was always so simple for Reg. She took a deep breath, relaxing her shoulders as she exhaled. "Okay, Reg, okay. I'm gonna chill."

"Good girl."

"They said they have a car I can use. Maybe I could go see the island."

"There you go, and don't forget the Mai Tai. A little rum will do you good."

~ ~ ~

As promised, Mark produced a color picture of JJ Lynch for her to draw. Because of the hot sun they worked inside, the crashing of the waves a mere whisper.

Viki had been distracted all day, worried about Mark and what he wanted. Concerned about where this time in Hawaii was taking her. She had barely been able to eat, her stomach rebellious. But, the butterflies melted like ice on a hot Sedona summer day as soon as she laid pastel to paper. The process took over and took her deep, as it always did.

This time when she breathed on the paper, the blue-green eyes of JJ Lynch came to life, but it was not what she expected.

His eyes were wide and wild, his face pinched.

"What! Who... Who are you?" he exclaimed.

~ ~ ~

"I don't understand why this works, Gran," Viki said, looking at the picture she had touched, the picture drawn in vivid pastels that had come alive. She was eleven years old and had just talked to her cousin, six months dead from leukemia.

Her grandmother's eyes sparkled. Viki thought she was so old, but her eyes were so young. Maybe not young, but alive, her eyes were so alive. They were a deep brown, mahogany, that seemed to have a light of their own. They danced and shined.

"'Why' does not matter, as long as you know how," her grandmother said.

Young Viki took a deep breath and wiped the tears from her eyes. She missed her cousin horribly, and talking to her had been a joy, and when that talking ended it had turned to sorrow.

"Why? Why did you have me draw Sandy?" she wiped her nose again, holding back another round of tears.

"Because, my little V, you need to know, you need to understand."

"Understand what?"

"What it feels like to talk to the dead. It is not what you thought it would be, is it?"

Viki shook her head, her ponytail swishing back and forth.

~~~

"I think I've finally lost it," JJ muttered, his face alive on the page.

Mark roused himself, eyes wide, but he didn't say anything.

"I apologize, JJ. My name is Viki Dobos, and I have a gift."

JJ paused, surrounded by inky blackness. "You're real? I... I am not imagining this?"

"No," Viki said. "No, you are not. I can assure you this is quite real."

"Okay. And you do what?"

"I am a medium. I draw the dead and the drawing comes to life and the dead talk to the living."

"You know, this is not a great time. I'm... I'm kinda going through something right now. I came up here for privacy, not to get on some mystical skype call."

"Please, Mr. Lynch," Mark said. "Can you confirm you wrote this book?" He held the book up above the paper and the image of JJ's face.

JJ squinted. "*Shuffled Off...* Nice title, Banquo's gonna love that. If you are asking, did I use the facilities at U of A to write a memoir of my life and death, then yes. Can I go now?"

Viki looked up at Mark who gave a small nod.

"Sorry to bother you, JJ," Viki said as she breathed on the paper again, lifting her hand, signaling the men across from her to do the same.

The image of JJ melted back into the page, and it became the mere drawing they had started with.

~~~

Alexander brought the wine—Up Country Gold, a local vintage—poured for Mark and her, and left. Viki wished he had stayed; she appreciated his calm presence. It was a balm to Mark's urgency and blatant need.

There was also something she couldn't quite perceive going on between Alexander and Mark. When Alexander looked at his employer, she saw caring and concern, but something else. Something she couldn't quite put her finger on.

They watched the sunset through the palm trees that guarded the western edge of Mark's property. They were tall, all leaning towards the ocean, their fronds whispering in the wind.

Mark's face was drawn, from the illness, from fatigue, and he looked deep in thought. It made him look even more sickly.

He sighed, his eyes coming back, sniffed his wine and sipped it. "I guess it is time," he said, his voice bland.

"Time?"

"Time to tell you why you are here."

"I am here to draw, obviously. But you haven't told me something, that too is obvious."

"And it is time to tell," Mark said, but then his eyes lost their focus again. Some minutes passed until Mark spoke again. "I want you to draw for me..."

"Okay," Viki began, "I have been drawing for you."

Mark shifted away from the setting sun and looked directly at Viki. "I want you to draw *me*."

Viki blinked, sure she must have misunderstood him. "Excuse me?"

"I brought you here to draw me."

Viki swallowed, her face turning white. She looked at the wine glass in her hand and saw that she was suddenly gripping it tightly. She brought the glass to her lips and drained the contents. She turned to face Mark squarely. "I don't draw the living."

Mark nodded his head. "I understand, but my circumstances are different. I am dying."

Viki poured herself more wine and took another large swallow. "I don't do that." Her hands were shaking.

"I only have months to live," Mark said gently. "I... I need to know..."

"What?" Viki said, the word coming out much louder

than she intended. "What do you need to know? That there is an afterlife? I think you have your proof of that. I think..." Viki trailed off, drinking more wine and turning away from Mark.

"I *need* you to draw me. Please."

Viki looked back at him, compassion replacing the fear on her face. "If I do, you will die."

CHAPTER 8

The sun had set, and purple and salmon light was kissing the waves. Viki stood there, sinking her heels into the wet sand, letting the water wash over her feet.

She didn't draw the living—ever. It was forbidden, it was obviously something you should never do. If her skill connected the living to the dead, what would happen if she drew the living?

She, unfortunately, knew what would happen. It hadn't been intentional, but she had drawn a living person before. That was back in Boston, before Sedona, before—

The two feet that deliberately placed themselves next to hers on the sand brought her up short. It was Mark, she didn't need to look up. The fine linen pants and the radiating need made it obvious.

"Can you tell me what happened?" Mark asked, his voice gentle.

Viki turned and looked at him, her words coming out harsher than she intended. "What? Are you the psychic now?"

Mark managed the barest of smiles. "Your reaction was

strong enough that even a Neanderthal like me could tell there was something deeper."

Viki nodded, turning her attention back to the water.

"Can you tell me?" Mark asked again.

Viki nodded. "I guess you deserve at least that," she said, launching into her story.

~ ~ ~

I was born in Boston. I learned to draw in Boston from my grandmother. I made my practice in Boston.

I never advertised, even back then. Once trained, my grandmother started sharing her practice with me, and once she passed, I took it over. There were always people to draw for. They all came by word of mouth.

Eight years ago, I drew for two college students and I shouldn't have. My gut told me to turn them away, but I didn't. They smelled of alcohol and laughed too much, but they had cash and they were referred by one of my older, trusted clients.

I drew a close friend of theirs. One they said had been depressed and had recently committed suicide. It was a believable story. Harvard has a few of them every year or so.

He was an affable-looking young man, bright green eyes and red hair. The act of drawing him was easy, and bringing him to life was even easier—in retrospect, too easy.

When the drawing came to life, he looked around and screamed. A blood curdling scream. The boys, his friends, went white, ripped their hands away from the paper and ran out.

At first I thought the red-headed boy had been in a bad place. It happens. They had told me he had committed suicide, so it kind of made sense.

Later that week I was reading the obituaries. I know, I know, a bit morbid but I'm in the business, you know. Anyway, I found the obituary for this young man. It was dated two days after I drew him.

I freaked out. I didn't know what to do. I was terrified of what I might have done by drawing him when he was alive.

After a few sleepless nights, I went to his funeral. I wanted to confront the two who had me draw him, but they weren't there.

After more bad nights, I got up before dawn and drew my grandmother. She came... actually it was the last time she came. As her death had grown more distant, she had gotten harder and harder to reach, and she stayed for less and less time.

I told her, very quickly, what had happened. I will never forget what she said. "You did your best, Little Sparrow, don't give up your gift. Don't let it die. You must find a way to pass it on. I love you." And then she was gone.

It wasn't what I was looking for, it wasn't what I needed. I considered drawing the red-headed boy again, but I couldn't bring myself to risk it. What if he was in a bad place after his death, what if I had put him there?

I eventually did track down the two boys I drew for. It wasn't easy. The first two times I found them, they ran. I eventually found out where they lived and kept going by every morning until they talked to me.

What they told me didn't help much. They thought what they were doing was a joke—a joke on me. They were convinced that I was a charlatan, and by doing this they would expose me.

They had one of those tiny cameras and filmed the whole

thing. They were planning on uploading it to the Internet and exposing me.

Except it worked.

The red-headed boy saw things, saw things that scared him. They didn't know the details, but they said he started acting very strangely after the incident.

Two days later he was found dead in his room.

~~~

"What was the cause of death?" Mark asked.

Viki shrugged. "I don't know. I was never able to obtain that information. The family didn't release it."

Mark was quiet, nodding and rubbing his goatee. "And what of the video they shot?"

"The video shows me drawing and that's it. It doesn't show him coming to life—cameras never see that. The experience is limited to those who are touching the paper."

Mark's eyes narrowed as he looked at Viki. He held her gaze for several long breaths before turning and walking away without a word.

Viki stayed on the beach as darkness came, feeling the guilt of her past press in around her.

CHAPTER 9

Viki loved the beach. It called to her every morning, relentlessly. The song of the breeze, the whisper of the crashing waves, the beckoning of the swaying palm trees.

She was on Arizona time and woke before dawn every day. Starting on her second day in Hawaii, at first light, she made her way onto the beach and walked with the other early-morning ocean goers. There were old, over-tanned men, bare-shirted and big bellied. There were dog walkers and joggers. There were natives fishing and other early-rising tourists walking.

Actually, walking is probably the wrong word for what many of them did. It wasn't walking, it wasn't exercising, it was meditating. It was sinking down and becoming the ocean and the breeze and the palm trees.

To Viki it was glorious and a wonderful respite to what was going on with Mark Kosov.

At first she headed south down the long beach, which quickly took her to Wailea and some of the big hotels—The Grand Wailea and The Four Seasons. She didn't do this often because she found the vibe of it interfered with her meditative state. So much money, so much entitlement.

She then turned her walks north, which briefly required sandals, as she passed an expanse of lava rocks that took her off the beach, past the Kihei boat ramp, and over some black rock cliffs before she came into the sandy part of Kihei. Three long beaches all named Kamaole—III, II, and I in the direction she walked.

She felt more at home. Not that there wasn't money there, not that there weren't entitled people there, but it wasn't so much as to take over the restfully restless energy of the ocean.

So she walked there every morning and began to identify some of the characters that populated those beaches.

There was a man, probably in his seventies, named Howard. His skin was as brown as a coconut, his hair as white as a cloud, and his belly as big as a cantaloupe. He wore a white hat with a small bill and smiled at her every time their paths crossed. He would bob his head and say, "Beautiful morning, Viki." She would bob her head in agreement and say, "Indeed, Howard. Indeed." If felt to her like they were two birds strutting down the beach doing a ritual greeting that involved a lot of head bobbing. At first they didn't know each other's names, but on the second day he stopped and asked, so he could "greet her beauty properly."

There was Baxter, the dog. He was a yellow lab who came and greeted her with doggish enthusiasm every time they passed. He would run into the receding surf, and dash out as the waves crashed just past him, and rocket to Viki, shaking salty water all over her. She would laugh and pet him, and tell him he was a good boy.

Baxter was tended by a young woman. She was petite

with long black hair, and dancing brown eyes, but Viki could not remember her name. Baxter left her little room to attend to anything else when he was near.

There was another older man, maybe sixty, that Viki thought of as "Ex-Pat Businessman." She imagined he had exiled himself from New York or Chicago to Maui. They never spoke, but he was there every morning with overly tanned skin, his belly as big as a watermelon walking to and fro. He was very focused on his walking and would generally pass Viki twice as he power-walked up and down Kamaole II. He didn't leave his beach, which would have required him walking up and over to the next beach, or threading around through a lava strewn area, but instead marched back and forth, back and forth at his best pace.

And there was a father and a daughter playing on the beach every morning. He was slim with blond hair and angular features. She was around nine with brown skin and black hair. Viki's attention was drawn to them as they threw a ball back and forth, or as the girl played in the surf and he watched.

As the man watched his daughter, his arms folded, his stance stiff, Viki saw something, felt something. She found herself drawn to the ocean, wanted to be in the ocean, but he stood distant, on vigil, as if he didn't trust the ocean, as if it might attack at any time.

He was clearly the girl's father, but at first Viki thought that she was adopted. He was a white man and she looked like a light-skinned Hawaiian girl. Her mind changed when she noticed the hint of his angular features on the girl's face.

On her third day walking the beaches, the morning after she drew JJ Lynch, they met.

Viki was distracted, saying good morning to Howard, when the girl ran right into her, knocking her to the ground. The girl had been running, watching the ball her father had thrown.

Viki laid there on her back, stunned. First she saw Howard's tanned face. "Are you okay, Viki?" he asked.

Then she heard the father's voice.

"Anela!" And then she saw his face. She hadn't seen him this close up before. He wore a baseball cap, and his face had only the barest of tans. His eyes were blue and he had deep lines forming on his forehead, exacerbated by the concern on his face. "I am so sorry. Are you okay?" He was much handsomer than she had thought.

The third face was the brown face of the daughter, Anela. She had her father's sharp nose and a frown on her face. She knelt down next to Viki, small hands patting at Viki's shoulder, voice pitched high. "Are you okay, lady? I am so sorry, I didn't see you. Are you okay, lady?"

Viki shook her head, trying to clear it, and tried to sit up. She felt the man's strong hands support her from behind. "Yeah, I think I'm okay, just got the wind knocked out of me."

She saw Howard with a phone in his hand. She was puzzled as to where he hid that as he walked down the beach in a bathing suit. "Should I call 911?" he asked, looking from Viki to the father.

"No. No," Viki said. "I just need a minute."

"Where are you staying?" the man asked from behind her.

"Umm..." Viki began. "I am staying in a house down the beach." She vaguely pointed south. "About a mile."

"I don't think you are in any condition to walk that far," the man said.

"Oh, I'll be fine."

"Please," he said. "Let us help you." He gestured to a three-story building facing the beach. "I live here. You can just sit. Have some juice, get your legs back underneath you."

She was about to say "no," when she saw Anela's face. It was a face only a young girl can make. It held innocence and intent, desire and guilelessness. The girl had taken her hand and was tugging it gently.

"I can vouch for Tim here," Howard said. "He's helped me out a time or two." With Howard on her left side, and Tim on her right, they got her up and walking, headed towards the stairs that led to Tim and Anela's place.

~~~

"Fresh papaya," Tim said, laying the bowl containing the fruit in front of Viki. "English muffin with jam, Kona coffee with cream. Can I get you anything else?"

Viki looked up and smiled. "No. Really, I am fine. You didn't have to do this." She gazed out from the third-story lanai past the lone palm tree to the ocean and the beach below. The sun was rising behind them and direct sunlight was just starting to touch the beach.

"It's the least we can do," he said. "I feel bad, Anela feels bad. Don't you, Anela?"

The girl looked up from the paper she was drawing on with crayons at the table across from Viki. "Yes, Father. I am so sorry, Miss Viki, I should be looking where I am going."

Her head wasn't up long, soon her face was down and she was drawing again. Carefully picking through the brown crayons and eyeing them closely before choosing one and making long strokes on the page with it.

Viki looked down at what the girl was drawing and caught her breath. It was the face of a woman with hazel eyes, arching eyebrows, thin lips, and brown hair pulled back in a ponytail. Viki realized that Anela was drawing her.

"You draw well," Viki said. The proportions of the face were close, much closer than girls her age usually managed. The ears aligned with the top of the eyes and the bottom of the nose, the eyes were halfway down the head, the distance between the eyes was the breadth of the nose. The girl had even included a small dot representing the mole between Viki's nose and upper lip.

"Thank you, Miss Viki," the girl answered.

"Who taught you?"

Anela stopped drawing and looked up, her eyes first meeting her father's and then Viki's. "Mama did. She is dead now."

~~~

"I'm sorry," Viki said as Tim walked her down to the beach.

"No. Really, it's okay." Tim's face darkened, his mouth forming a frown. "It's been a while, almost two years now since Tess died. Anela is in this phase where she needs to be really blunt about it."

Viki nodded. "I think it's healthy that she can speak of it."

"And about our little accident... I am really sorry."

"Stop apologizing," Viki said with a laugh. "I just had the wind knocked out of me. No lasting damage. And I got breakfast out of the deal."

Tim brightened, his eyes connecting with her. "Well, maybe we'll see you tomorrow."

"Maybe," Viki said with a smile, feeling her heartbeat quicken as she walked down the beach towards Mark Kosov's house.

CHAPTER 10

"What if..." Mark began over dinner on the lanai. "What if the death of that young man had nothing to do with you? Had nothing to do with you drawing him. Would that make a difference?"

Viki looked up at him, lost in thought, her mind straying down the beach to Anela and Tim. Hearing the girl's high voice, seeing her bright eyes, feeling Tim's strong hands against her back. "What?"

"I am investigating that young man's death. Evan O'Claire. I don't have full details yet, but it sounds like he had problems, serious problems, before you drew him. Would that make a difference?"

Viki met Mark's blue eyes, they were steady, unwavering, expressing his need. "No, it wouldn't make a difference. I draw the dead, not the living."

She saw anger rise on his face, which he quickly covered with his napkin. His chair scraped noisily against the lanai's deck as he stood. "Excuse me for a moment."

"Is he all right?" Viki asked Alexander as he began clearing the table.

Alexander smiled shyly and said, "Mr. Kosov is used to getting what he wants."

After Alexander left with the dishes, Viki sat alone on the lanai and watched the stars brighten and listened to the surf. On one hand she had a rich, demanding man whom she didn't understand, and on the other she had a father and a daughter she felt strangely attracted to. She felt homesick. At least in Sedona she understood Reg, she understood his motives and his needs. She was about to pull out her cell phone and call him when she felt the presence of Mark Kosov.

She closed her eyes and focused on her feeling of him. His presence was large and angular with spikes radiating forth. It was red with hints of indigo and blue. It was loud and insistent. She heard him breathing but he didn't say a thing. She let the moment stretch out. In truth, she was testing him. He had displayed some sensitivity to her needs, and she needed a bit of silence and wanted to see if he was capable of giving her that.

He was.

When she let out a deep breath, opened her eyes and looked, he was leaning on the railing of the lanai, looking out over the ocean and the night. He looked relaxed and casual, and in the dim light, healthy. In the silence, his need had dissipated to a less invasive level.

Viki rose and went to the railing next to him. Through the palm trees, the ocean was its ever restfully restless self. The moon was rising behind them, casting a silver glow on the sand. A couple walked by slowly, hand in hand.

"You have told me what you want, Mr. Kosov," Viki began, her voice quiet and gentle. "But you haven't told me why."

Mark didn't move but sighed.

"I need to know why," Viki said.

Mark turned to her, the intensity returning. "I am dying, Ms. Dobos, is that not reason enough?"

"No, it is not. There is more."

A smile crept onto Mark's lips. "Are you being psychic now?"

Viki shrugged, "Maybe. But there is more, you haven't denied it."

"No, no I haven't."

"So tell me why."

"If I do, will you draw me?"

Viki paused, her eyes on the ocean. She wanted to acquiesce to this dying man's need, but she couldn't. It was too much to ask. "Probably not," she said finally.

"Excellent!" Mark exclaimed, pushing himself from the railing and moving towards the house.

"Excellent? What do you mean excellent?"

Mark turned and flashed a broad smile. "Probably not, is much better than no. It means there is hope, Ms. Dobos, it means there is hope."

Viki was left wondering what there was to hope for. Hope for an early demise when Viki drew him instead of waiting for the cancer to take him?

CHAPTER 11

The next morning on Kamaole Beach II, Viki watched Tim and Anela as she approached. Anela played in the water, darting in as the waves receded and running away laughing after the waves broke and the foamy water reached for her. Tim stood, stiffly, watching the proceedings, his arms crossed. Like before, he was dressed in shorts, a polo shirt, and a baseball cap. Unlike everyone else on the beach, he wasn't wearing a bathing suit.

When Viki approached, Tim looked over, smiled, and said, "Good morning. How are you feeling today?"

"Wonderful," she said.

"Really?" Tim asked.

"Stop it," Viki said. "I mean it. I'm fine."

Tim nodded as he returned to his vigil, his eyes on his daughter. "So, umm... what do you do for a living?"

Viki paused, as she always did when confronted with the dreaded question. She had yet to come up with a good answer that would satisfy the listener and be even remotely honest. "I..." she began. "I... Well, it's complicated."

Tim nodded.

"What do you do?" she asked.

He looked at her, his face serious. "It's complicated."

"Are you mocking me?"

He gave her a sharp nod and smiled. "A little. Actually, it is a bit complicated. I'm a lawyer—"

"That's complicated?" Viki asked, cutting him off.

"A bit, yes. But I also manage some of those condos," he added, pointing to the building behind him, "and do repairs."

Anela came running up and stopped, panting in front of Viki. "Wait!" she said. "I have something for you." And turning to her father, she asked, "Can I go get it?"

Tim nodded, handing her a key, and she raced off, her feet kicking up sand.

Viki looked at Tim, a question on her face.

He shrugged and said, "Just wait and see. It's complicated."

Viki laughed. "Now I know you are mocking me."

Tim smiled. "Well, I can always provide breakfast in compensation for any slight delivered by me or my daughter."

"Wait a minute," Viki said, her brow furrowed. "You're a lawyer."

Tim nodded in answer.

"All that taking care of me yesterday, was that some legal defense? You know, in case I was really hurt and decided to sue or something?"

Tim's face fell, his eyes darkening as he said, "No." Viki waited, expecting more, but more didn't come. The "no" was sharp and final and didn't invite more discussion.

They had lapsed into an uncomfortable silence when Anela returned, her feet again kicking up the sand, her breath coming in ragged gasps, a piece of paper flapping in her hand.

"Here!" she said, handing Viki the paper.

It was the finished portrait of her. It was obviously a child's hand, and done in crayons, but Viki could see the talent, clear and bright. She had captured the sadness that Viki often saw in her own eyes when she looked in the mirror.

"Anela, this is beautiful," Viki said as the girl embraced her in a wet hug. She knelt down, putting her free hand on the girl's shoulder. "You are an artist, Anela. Never stop drawing." The girl's face shone brightly as she looked up to her father.

"Come on, Angel," he said, "say good-bye to Viki. We have to go."

"I'm sorry I knocked you down," she called to Viki as they walked away.

Viki wasn't, but she worried that her lawyer comment had turned what might have been another breakfast invitation into an awkward situation.

She felt drawn to Tim and Anela. She wondered if they were really why she was here, and hoped she got the chance to find out.

~~~

Later that day, Viki knocked tentatively on Tim's door. She heard a dull buzzing sound coming from behind it. She knocked again, slightly louder. She wasn't sure why she was here. What did it matter if this man she hardly knew was insulted by her question? What did it matter if his feelings were hurt?

She had liked to think that maybe she was developing a friendship on this island. Her time with Mark Kosov was difficult. He was a customer, not a friend. What he wanted from her was bringing up the past, a past she did not want to confront. If she were being honest, she needed a friend, even if that friend was a lawyer.

The thought made her smile, and she knocked again, louder this time, and rang the doorbell.

And then she thought of Anela—so young, but not so young. She had been through a lot for a girl her age. Viki went through a lot herself at that age. Her parents divorcing, her father growing distant, her mother and her beginning to fight over her gift. She saw herself in Anela and wanted to help the girl if she could.

She rang and knocked again. This time the buzzing sound stopped. She heard the shuffling of feet and the door opened.

Tim stood there, his face a question, wearing worn jeans, a ripped T-shirt, covered in sweat and dust. Viki found his musky scent distracting.

She looked down. "Can I come in? I have something I'd like to say."

Tim nodded mutely and opened the door for her.

This time, as Viki looked around, the signs of renovation were clear. She was dazed her first time here and somehow hadn't put it together. There were paint cans in one corner, a freshly painted wall devoid of artwork, and plastic hanging in front of one of the bedroom doors.

"We can talk on the lanai," Tim said. "Can I get you some tea?"

Viki nodded and made her way to the small lanai, sat and took in the view of the sand and the ocean, watching the families down below playing, or sitting, or talking.

Tim returned with two glasses of iced tea. He put one down in front of her and sat.

"I'm sorry," Viki said with a sigh. "I should not have questioned your motives. You have been nothing but kind."

Tim nodded.

"My family hasn't had the best luck with lawyers."

He watched her, but his face was impassive and he didn't speak.

"But," Viki said, looking at his sweat-stained shirt and the white dust in his hair, "you are clearly not your average lawyer."

Tim nodded again, a small smile finding his lips.

"Oh," Viki said, "I have something for Anela. Is she here?"

"School," Tim said.

"Of course." Viki pulled the items out of her bag and put them on the table. It was a box of colored pencils and a small pad of good quality drawing paper.

"Thank you," Tim said. "That's very thoughtful."

"She is very talented. I would be happy to show her a few things if you, and she, liked."

Tim's eyes narrowed and he frowned deeply. "That's a bit complicated. Can I let you know?"

Viki nodded and got up. She was having a hard time reading him. She wasn't sure if her apology had been accepted. "I need to get back."

"Of course," Tim said as he got up and showed her out.

CHAPTER 12

That evening, Mark Kosov placed a folder in front of Viki. It was thick with papers and pictures. "You don't need to read the whole thing," he began, his voice loud and bristling. "The top page is the private detective's summary. It gets right to the point."

Viki looked closely at the folder and stiffened, a rush of air catching in her throat. On the tab of the folder was written "Evan O'Claire." She pushed herself back into the couch and folded her arms across her chest.

"It wasn't your fault," Mark said, his voice quieter and gentler. "Listen to me, Viki. It wasn't your fault."

Viki looked up at him and gazed into his eyes. She saw his need, but she saw other things—compassion and certitude. He believed what he was saying. He was, in his way, trying to help her.

Viki sighed, her shoulders relaxing, her arms still folded across her chest. "Explain it to me," she said.

Mark eased himself into a chair across from her. He held his cane just in front of him with both hands and leaned forward. "The boy had mental problems, from a young age.

He was diagnosed manic-depressive and bipolar. He had gone off his meds; he was off them when you drew him."

Viki nodded, slowly unfolding her arms, but still leaning away from the folder. "So, he was mentaly ill, and being drawn had no effect?"

Mark paused, licking his lips and shaking his head slowly. "I am not saying that. It was obviously an experience, an intense experience, but it wasn't the cause of his death."

"How can you be so sure?"

Mark slowly pushed himself up to a standing position and gestured at the folder. "If you don't believe me, read it. He was subject to hallucinations when he was off his meds. The night you drew him, was just one of many experiences he was having. You didn't kill him." With that Mark left the room, walking slowly and leaning heavily on his cane.

Viki slowly reached for the folder, at first touching it gingerly, as if its touch might cause pain. She opened it slowly. Paper-clipped to the left side was a picture of the red-headed boy. One at a time she took out each page and slowly read it, tears rolling down her cheeks.

~~~

"I want to believe it, Reg, but I don't know," Viki said on the phone the next morning as she paced the beach. "It seems too easy, too convenient, too perfect for what Mark Kosov wants." She let the morning sun warm her face as she paced in front of Mark Kosov's house.

"Then bail, V," Reg said. "Take the money you've earned and run. You don't want to draw him, you don't draw him."

"But... The man is searching, he needs something, and he is dying. Can I turn my back on him?"

"And he's paying you two grand a day, let's not forget that."

"Reg!"

"Don't be too holy about this. You're there because a rich man is paying you a ton of dough for what is mostly a vacation. I hear the surf in the background. You're on the beach right now."

Viki sighed, but didn't answer.

"And as a bonus he is lifting a huge weight of guilt from you—if you will let him. Do you have any idea what laws he bent or broke to get that information so quickly? Do you have any idea how much money he spent?"

"I... No, Reg. I have no idea." Viki's voice rose in anger. She had called him because she needed a friend to talk to, someone she understood, someone she could rely on. "Do you?"

"Not exactly, no. But let's say it's a lot. Let's say it cost him many times what he has paid you. Do you want to know what I would do?" There was a playful lilt in his voice.

Viki had a good idea what was coming, but asked anyway. "What would you do?"

"I would ask for more money and draw the man," he said, his big laugh rumbling.

"Of course you would."

"And I would get a rock solid contract that held me blameless. In case... you know, just in case."

~~~

"Beautiful morning, Viki," Howard said as Viki passed him on the beach, his head bobbing.

"Indeed, Howard. Indeed," she said as she bobbed her head in response.

Viki heard the pause of Howard's feet on the beach and instinctively turned and saw him looking at her. His white hair contrasting with his deeply brown skin reminded Viki of a chocolate cupcake with white frosting. She was hungry and found herself smiling at him.

"He's a good egg you know," Howard said.

"Who?" Viki asked. She knew who he was talking about but wanted to cover her surprise.

Howard just smiled and repeated, "He's a good egg. Just been through a lot." He turned and resumed his walk down the beach.

Thinking of Tim and Anela, Viki smiled and felt her mood brighten, thoughts of Mark forgotten. She played with Baxter briefly and waved to the dog's person. When she got to Kamaole Beach II, she even tried to engage the Ex-Pat Businessman. He grunted and she smiled.

As she moved up the beach, her mood evaporated. She didn't see Tim and Anela. She looked up at their third-story lanai, but the shades were drawn. She stood there on the beach for some time wondering. Wondering if he was avoiding her. Wondering about the widower that watched the ocean like a man watched an enemy. Wondering at the man who took such easy offense. Wondering at the brown-skinned little girl with a gift that reminded Viki of herself when she was a girl.

She ended up sitting on the beach for a good hour. Maybe their timing was just off; maybe they would be down soon.

She left after the hour angry with herself. Why was she waiting for them anyway? What was he to her?

~~~

Dinner was quiet and subdued. Viki picked at her food, but didn't eat much. Mark ate daintily and consumed little, but for different reasons, Viki suspected.

Alexander cleared the table and brought them coffee. Viki perked up at the rich scent of the dark brew. She smiled, wrapping her hands around the warm mug.

"Did you read the file?" Mark asked casually.

"Yes," Viki said, her tone even as she blew on her beverage.

"Are you convinced?" he asked.

Viki nodded. "More or less." Mark gave her a questioning look, so she continued. "I played a part, but I was not the only part. How big a part is hard to say."

"Yes, but he didn't fall over dead the moment you drew him. That much is clear. He died several days later in his sleep."

"Then why did he die, exactly?"

Mark shrugged. "The autopsy wasn't conclusive, but did suggest a cardiac incident of some sort."

"And how do you know that won't happen if I draw you? Several days later you have a 'cardiac incident.'"

"I don't know. This life is mine and it is a risk I must take."

"And what about me?" Viki asked, her voice rising and her face reddening. "What about the risk to me, Mark? If you die from what I do, I have to live with that. What about that risk?"

Mark was quiet, his gaze sweeping across the palm trees and the ocean. When his eyes finally found Viki again, he said, "I acknowledge your risk. What do you need?"

Viki could hear Reg in her head saying, "I need more money. Risk should equal reward," but that is not what she said. "I need two things. Legal protection in case the worst happens and I need to know why." Mark looked away, his hand reaching for his cane. "I need to know why, Mark. I need to know."

As Mark walked away, he said, "I'll have contracts for you in the morning."

CHAPTER 13

Viki started her day with a few simple stretches. She was bending down to touch her toes when she saw the large manila envelope. It had been slipped under her door sometime in the night. Attached to it was a brief handwritten note.

"Ms. Dobos, please see attached contract indemnifying you from any harm that might come to me as a result of your services. Also see the bonus for each drawing of myself you do. I trust this will allay your concerns. Sincerely, Mark Kosov."

She sat on the bed and read the contract several times, but kept getting lost in the wording. What was clear was that she would receive a bonus of ten thousand dollars each time she drew Mark. The amount took her breath away. Which, she was sure, was the intent.

She got her phone out and called Reg.

"Do you know what time it is?" he asked, his voice sleepy.

"Yeah," she replied. "It's about 6:30 here and 9:30 there. Late enough for me to call."

Reg began to object, but Viki cut him off, telling him about the contract and the bonus.

"Good job, V! Didn't know you were such a good negotiator."

"I didn't ask for more money, Reg."

"Yes, but you made it clear that you were taking a risk. A man like that understands risk and reward."

"What should I do?"

"Draw the man, just draw him." Viki could hear the exasperation in his voice. "Come on, V, this is just not that complicated."

"But I don't really understand the contract. It's total legalese."

"Then hire a lawyer, change the contract. This is a negotiation. Make sure you get what you want."

She felt fate, or maybe destiny, pushing her along again. She needed a lawyer... Tim was a lawyer... Viki grabbed the envelope and headed onto the beach. The usual morning crowd was there, but she hardly saw them.

~~~

Viki barely mumbled a greeting when she passed Howard, her eyes searching the beach for a father and daughter.

When she got to Kamaole Beach II, she didn't see them and she felt her heart sink and then chided herself for it. She had no right to feel disappointed, she barely knew these people. She took a deep breath, dismissing the thoughts and looked again. She spotted them throwing a ball back and forth on the beach.

She breathed a sigh of relief and quickened her pace, reaching Tim first. "I need to hire you," she said, the envelope clutched to her chest.

Tim's right eyebrow raised as he turned and yelled to his daughter, "Look who's here, Anela!"

The girl, seeing Viki, ran and embraced her in another wet hug. "Thank you, Miss Viki. Thank you! I love my fancy drawing kit."

"You're welcome, Anela," Viki said, wiping the sand off the envelope.

"I would have thanked you sooner, but I spent the weekend with my grandparents." Viki nodded, relieved to understand their absence. "Daddy says you might be willing to show me some things. Will you?" The girl's brown eyes sparkled in the morning light.

"Sure," Viki replied looking up at Tim, "if it's okay with your father."

"Dad?" the girl asked.

Tim nodded. "It seems Viki and I have some business to discuss anyway." He turned to Viki. "Breakfast?"

Viki smiled as Anela took her hand and pulled her across the beach towards their condo.

~~~

"Keep your pencils sharp," Viki said to Anela. They sat at the kitchen table, pieces of paper and colored pencils strewn about. "Hold the pencil up for a thin line, and lean it on its side for a thick one." Viki demonstrated as Anela watched closely, attempting to copy every move.

Viki glanced at Tim who sat in the living room, his feet propped up on a five gallon bucket of paint. He wore reading glasses, his eyes quickly scanning the contract. She could tell little about what he was thinking, his expression gave nothing away.

"Like this, Miss Viki?" Anela asked as she leaned an indigo colored pencil on its side and ran it across the paper.

"Just like that, Anela. Just like that."

Anela smiled. "Show me something else!"

"Okay, so draw a thin line in a circle, like this." Anela copied her, taking a fresh piece of paper and drawing a large circle. "Now tilt you pencil and gently move it back and forth inside the circle, filling the color in. Do it more on one side and it will look more three dimensional, more real."

Anela smiled and began filling in her indigo circle. "Practice that," Viki said, "I'll be right back."

She walked over to Tim and sat next to him. "Well?"

Tim looked over glasses at her, his blue eyes serious and intense. "What, exactly, is it that you do, Viki Dobos?"

Viki sighed, her hands coming together and pressing against her chin and lower lip. She met Tim's eyes. "Are you my lawyer, Tim Unger? Is our conversation confidential?"

Tim nodded. "Yes I am, and yes it is."

Viki took a deep breath, letting it out slowly, and told him exactly what she did.

~ ~ ~

Viki had expected doubt, she had expected fear, she had expected that look she had gotten so many times in her life. The look that said, "You need help, you need medication, you need a padded cell." But that is not what she got.

After she told Tim, as succinctly as possible, what she did, he asked, "Will you draw for Anela and I?"

Viki had taken a deep breath, ready to expel it rapidly in defense of herself, but instead she let out a long, weary sigh. "Tim?"

He glanced over at his daughter, her face intent as she

moved the pencil slowly back and forth in the circle. "It happened so quickly. Anela never got a chance to say good-bye." He pulled off his glasses and jabbed at his eyes. It was clear to Viki that his request wasn't just for Anela.

"Understand that it doesn't always... often doesn't work. Not all souls are reachable."

Tim's eyes widened, but he nodded slowly. "You draw for us, I will help you with this contract. It's not good enough, not by half."

"I can pay you," Viki said.

Tim rubbed at his eyes again, wiping away the tears that were forming. "If you can do this, if you can reach Tess, that would mean so much... Please," he added, his eyes meeting hers. "Please try."

Viki swallowed hard and nodded, brushing away the tears forming at the corners of her own eyes.

She couldn't deny Tim's need. Just like Mark, he had an intense need, but his she understood, his she could help with. His called to her heart. She understood grief, and his need was the need of all of her clients. His desperation was the kind she understood all too well.

CHAPTER 14

The sun was high when she returned to Tim Unger's condo. She had walked back to Mark Kosov's house, gotten her kit, and drove the little red Mini Cooper put at her disposal back to the Hale Pau Hana where Tim and Anela lived. She had told Alexander that she was going to meet with a lawyer. His eyebrows had risen at the sight of Viki carrying her case, but he didn't say anything.

Viki felt nervous as she knocked, her belly tight. She was anxious about doing this drawing. She wanted this to go well for them, but that was out of her control.

Tim opened the door and gave her a smile. It was small and shy, not a smile she had seen on his face before. When she walked in she found Anela staring at her, her brown eyes wide and intense, her face betraying a trace of fear. Tim must have told her what she did.

Tim closed the door and stood with his hands in his pockets. "Umm, where... how..." he stammered.

She smiled at him trying to put him at ease. "We need a table," she said, pointing to the kitchen table, "and a few chairs. And three glasses of water."

As Tim moved into the kitchen, she put her case down and squatted in front of Anela. "Hi, honey."

"Miss Viki," Anela said, her voice shaking, tears threatening, "can my mama really talk through your drawing?"

"Maybe," Viki said. "Sometimes it doesn't work. If she's close though, she will come and talk to you."

As Viki felt the tears running down her own cheeks, she saw them mirrored on the little girl's face. Anela grabbed her and held her in a fierce, wordless hug.

She preferred drawing for strangers. It made it easier to be detached, easier to focus. But Tim and Anela were no longer strangers and she felt the extra stress, the extra need to succeed.

She spread the silks out on the table, and Tim and Anela sat across from her. She pulled out her cards and shuffled them quickly. The cards would help, they always helped.

"Before I draw," she began, seeing the question forming on Tim's face, "I will need each of you to take a card. This will help us all focus; this will help set the energies. This will show us what you need to know about Tess right now." She handed the deck to Tim. "Think of Tess, think of your love for her, and draw a card. Leave it face down."

Tim's face was tight, his brow furrowed as he fumbled with the cards and quickly drew one. He placed it in front of him and quickly handed the deck back to Viki as if he didn't like the touch of them, as if they could hurt him.

Viki handed the deck to Anela. "Think of your mama and pick a card."

"How do I know what card to draw?" the girl asked.

"You can't draw the wrong one, Anela. Whichever one you pick will be perfect."

The girl, serious and intent, slowly went through the deck two times before picking a card.

Viki leaned across the table and turned Tim's card over. The card showed a small girl playing in a rain puddle with "Child" written at the bottom. Anela snickered, Viki smiled, and Tim frowned.

"The Child," Viki began, "represents the playful innocence in all of us. Typically, when an adult draws the Child it is because they need more play in their lives."

Anela looked up at her dad and nodded.

Viki reached across the table and turned the girl's card over, "The Fool." Anela frowned and stuck her tongue out at the card.

"The Fool," Viki said looking at the girl, "is a very important card. It is the part of us that will try new things, that will boldly go into the unknown, that is innocent and wise at the same time." The girl smiled. "When it comes to what we are about to do, we all need to be the Fool."

Viki set the deck aside and brought out her case. She took out a clean sheet of drawing paper and took the eight-by-ten picture of Tess from Tim. She took a deep breath before looking up at them. "I am going to start drawing now. I need you to talk about Tess, to share your memories of her. It will help me draw... it will help me find her. Share the pleasant memories, share what you loved about her."

She paused, staring at the picture, which lay upside down to her and faced Tim and Anela. The woman's face was round with brown skin and dark brown eyes. Her nose was slightly upturned, one ear a tad higher than the other. Her black hair was long and pulled back in a ponytail. Her eyes held a trace of sadness; her lips were full and expressive.

Viki's hand reached into the case and pulled out a brown

pastel. Start with the eyes and end with the eyes. She held it poised, the silence stopping her.

She looked up, both the man and the child looked fearful. She smiled. "Breathe, and speak, you must speak of her, of how you loved her, of why you loved her, or I can't do this."

Viki knew that wasn't quite the truth. She had just drawn JJ Lynch with no one knowing him, but she also knew that they needed to talk about her. They needed to express these things, and whether the drawing came to life or not, they would come away with something of value.

"Mama loved the water," Anela began. "She swam every day, every chance she got." As the girl started speaking, Viki's hand started moving, sketching in the eyes.

"Mama drowned... the ocean took her."

Viki's hand paused and she was about to say something when Tim said, "Let's talk about the best parts of your mama, okay?" She could feel the girl nodding as Tim starting talking. "She was born on this island and loved it dearly. She was an amazing cook; she could take whatever happened to be in the refrigerator and make something delicious out of it. She was..."

As they spoke, Viki sketched the round form of the face, the outline of the nose, the eyebrows, the tracing of wrinkles in the forehead, the ears, the hair. Her hand moved swiftly, pulling each pastel as needed without looking.

"Mama was going to teach me to surf when I turned nine. She was a good surfer..."

Filling in the face.

"...she was a lawyer, but a mother first and foremost..."

Outlining the hair.

"...took me to Disneyland for my sixth birthday..."

Delicately outlining the lips.

"...we wanted to learn to tango, never got to that..."

The drawing came swiftly and Viki ended on the eyes, catching the trace of sadness there. Her hand moved, filling in the hint of epicanthic folds, detailing the long lashes.

And finally the background, her hand found several shades of blue as she quickly sketched in a multi-toned blue background.

The man and child had gone quiet. Viki put away her pastels and said gently, "I think we are ready to try this. If it works, you won't have much time, so..." she trailed off. She wanted to tell them to say what most needed to be said, to use the time as efficiently as possible, and that made logical sense, but never held up in the moment.

She had them touch the bottom of the drawing with their left hands as she rested her left hand touching the top of the woman's head. She gathered the energies, took a long, deep breath, and blew on the picture.

The woman came to life, her eyes widening, her mouth opening only to emit a burbling scream. The blue around her turned to water, churning and turbulent. She was drowning.

"Mama!" Anela screamed.

"What the..." Tim gasped.

"Stay calm," Viki said, although her own heart raced. "Stay calm, keep your hands on the paper and talk to her, send her your love."

"Where is she?" Tim asked. "What's going on?"

"She's trapped in a dream," Viki said. "We need to wake her up." She took another deep breath, her eyes closing as she reached out to the presence she had summoned. She sent love, she sent peace to it, beckoning it to come to her, to wake up.

"Mama," the girl began, grasping Viki's instructions before her father. "Mama, it's me, Anela. Wake up, Mama, you are just having a bad dream. Wake up, Mama."

The woman on the paper continued to struggle, blind to those around her.

"Tess, my love. Tess. It's okay, please wake up, please," Tim said, his voice strangled.

"I miss you, Mama, I need you," Anela continued, tears flowing down her face. "I need you..."

Viki felt the energy shifting, felt the woman gaining consciousness so she opened her eyes. She saw a flash of recognition in Tess's eyes, and her fright lessen just a touch. But at the same moment, Tim surged up from the table, breaking his connection as he rushed out onto the lanai.

"Mama, Mama!" Anela intoned, her left hand touching the bottom of the paper while her right hand patted at her mother's now animated face. Tess's eyes focused for a moment on Anela, a hint of a smile on her face before the terror came back and the picture turned back into a flat lifeless drawing.

Anela looked up at her and asked, "What's wrong with Mama?" Viki watched as tears rolled down the girl's frightened face.

CHAPTER 15

"I'm so sorry, Tim. I am so sorry," Viki said. They sat on the lanai watching the beach-goers below. Viki looked at him, his face was stony, his lips pressed tightly together.

He nodded but said nothing.

"Is Anela okay?"

Tim shrugged. "She's sleeping. I think." He was silent for a long minute, standing at the railing watching the ocean, his shoulders high, his back straight. Finally he asked, "Does this happen often?"

"No. But it does happen. Not this exactly, but this kind of thing. Sometimes the dead seem to be trapped in a dream, a bad dream. Tess is trapped in the dream of her death, the dream of her drowning."

Tim nodded.

It all made sense, the way Tim seemed to try to guard his daughter against the ocean, never getting in, never in a bathing suit.

"We almost reached her," Viki said. "I think we can in one or two more sessions. We can help her out of that place."

Tim turned and stared at her, his face still stony, but

his eyes tortured. "I don't think I can. I..." He looked away. "I don't think I can subject Anela to that again. It is just too much. This was a mistake. I shouldn't have subjected my daughter to this."

"But—"

"It's too much," Tim said cutting her off. He turned and walked back into the condo. "I'll have a revised contract for you in the morning. Please let yourself out."

Viki nodded, feeling spent, and slowly rose. She gathered her things and left. In the parking lot she got in the Mini Cooper and sat there. She thought for a long time. Could she reach this woman without her picture, without her family? She had never attempted it, but having drawn the face she knew it. Maybe on her own she could help Tess wake from the nightmare of her death. Maybe she could do something to make this right.

Just as she was about to turn the key on the Mini, there was a quiet tapping on the window. Viki jumped, her adrenaline spiking before she saw Tim. She stared at him mute; she didn't know what to say. She saw in his face the stress and the grief of what had just happened, but there was something else. Dread? Another layer of fear? No, it looked like concern, deep concern.

"I need to show you something," he said, his voice barely above a whisper. Viki got out of the car and followed him slowly up the stairs. He walked carefully as if he didn't want to make a sound. Viki followed as quietly as she could.

He opened the door slowly and tiptoed through the condo and pointed at a crack in the door to Anela's room.

Viki took a slow breath, steeling herself for the sight of a grieving child, but that is not what she saw.

Anela sat at a small desk with a piece of paper in front

of her and her new colored pencils arrayed before her. Next to her was the picture that Viki had just drawn from. It was upside down. Anela was drawing her mother.

She stood there transfixed watching the girl. Tim's head was close to hers as he watched too. His breath smelled of coffee, his skin of soap. She also felt his need. His need for his daughter to be okay. His need for his dead wife to be at rest. She found his presence distracting as she watched the girl.

Anela drew carefully, emulating Viki's flow, ending on the eyes before filling in a blue background. Then Viki's breath caught as the girl inhaled deeply and blew on the picture, just as Viki had done.

Viki held her breath for five seconds... ten seconds... fifteen seconds... But nothing happened, the drawing remained inert. A sob escaped the girl's throat as she tore up the paper and threw it to the ground.

She wanted to go to her, to comfort her. She was about to, but she felt Tim's hand on her arm, gently pulling her away. He led her to the lanai and gestured for her to sit down.

"Listen, Tim. This doesn't happen often. I am so sorry."

Tim nodded, his eyes glistened, but tears did not flow. "What now?"

"We draw her, and we keep drawing her until we get through."

Tim nodded again. "But it may not work?"

Viki nodded in agreement, her eyes downcast. She longed to talk to her grandmother, she would know what to do, she would know how to reach this woman. But it had been years since she had been able to contact her grandmother. She was convinced that her grandmother had moved on. Then she remembered the book Mark had given her and the man she had drawn for him.

She rose from her chair. "I have an idea. I have to go get something. I'll be back as soon as I can."

~~~

Viki drove down South Kihei Street as fast as she could. At first that wasn't fast at all. The south end of Kihei had plenty of tourists, but she soon moved past them and into a long stretch of condos as the properties became more and more expensive. It was only about two miles to the Kosov house, but it felt like it took forever. She wanted to pass the blue rental car that was going so slowly, but she didn't. She just breathed and calmed herself.

She triggered the iron gate with the sweeping image of a griffin on it, parked and ran into the house. It was early afternoon and she expected the house to be quiet, to be empty. It usually was this time of day.

Instead, she found a pacing Mark Kosov. As she entered the house, she got a glimpse of him through the hallway in the great room that faced the ocean. His pace was slow as he leaned heavily on his cane. His need was sharper and more obvious than usual.

She wanted to turn and leave. She wanted desperately to help Anela and Tim, but she couldn't. This man was her employer, this man needed something too, and she was sure it had to be about her, it had to be about her drawing him.

She took a deep breath, wiped away the remnants of tears from around her eyes, and walked into the great room.

At first Mark didn't change his slow path. Back and forth, back and forth, back and forth... Viki searched the room with her eyes for what she needed. And she found it, but didn't move. Mark's path had finally changed and he ended up in front of her, his ocean-blue eyes searching her face.

"Are you okay?" he asked.

Viki was surprised. She hadn't expected him to sense her state, much less be empathetic about it. She gave a sharp nod. "How can I help you, Mark?"

"Draw me."

"I have a lawyer looking over the contract right now. I..." she hesitated, she wasn't about to tell a lie but she was going to omit the salient facts. It didn't feel good, but she didn't have time, and really didn't think it was any of his business. "I need to get some things and meet with him now."

Mark paused as he continued to search her face. "Does that mean you will draw me?" he finally asked.

"If three conditions are met." Viki could see that standing was tiring him out. "Can we sit?" she asked. He was a proud man and she couldn't help but admire his spirit.

He nodded and moved slowly to the couch and sat heavily with an involuntary grunt.

"And, what are your conditions?"

"One. We come to terms on the legal matters. I will want a few changes."

Mark nodded matter of factly.

"Two. You loan me the *Shuffled Off* book and let me have the color picture of JJ Lynch."

Mark's eyebrow raised and she could see he had questions, but he nodded. "Three?"

"You tell me why you want to do this."

Mark didn't nod this time, his hand rubbing his face as his head came down and rested on his chest. He inhaled deeply and sighed. "When the time comes," he said. "When the time comes… The book is over there." He pointed at the bookshelf where Viki had already spotted it. "The picture is in the top drawer of that cabinet." He indicated a dark wood cabinet. "Help yourself. When can I expect the contract?"

"Tomorrow some time."

"Then I expect we will start tomorrow night." He nodded his head slowly up and down. "Good. Good." He got up and left, leaving Viki alone.

CHAPTER 16

Viki gave the book to Tim, opening it to the picture of JJ Lynch. "He can help." In answer to Tim's puzzled look, she added, "Mark had me draw him to prove myself. He has experience with this kind of thing."

Tim, still puzzled, flipped through the book and looked back to Viki. "Haven't you dealt with this kind of thing before?"

Viki nodded. "I have, but it has been a while. My grandmother was better at this—it can be tricky. And I... I don't want to take any chances." Viki turned and began, once again, transforming the kitchen table into her work space. As she laid down an orange silk, she asked, "How is Anela?"

"She's still trying," he said, glancing towards her bedroom.

Viki stopped her activity and looked up at Tim. "How long are you just going to let her go on? Shouldn't you intervene?"

Tim's sad face turned cold. "Why don't you just—" he said loudly before cutting himself off.

Viki tightened her grip on her case and stared at Tim. She felt both embarrassed by her comment and upset by his anger. She understood he was stressed, she had empathy for what he was going through, but—

"Excuse me," he said as he rubbed his forehead. "I know you are just trying to help. Anela is a lot like her mother. When she is like this it is best to let her find her own way, or exhaust herself, whichever comes first."

Viki went to the table and started setting up her work space. "Well, go get her. I think she should be here for this."

~~~

Short brown hair, blue-green eyes, a look of determination. Viki quickly drew JJ Lynch, finding it easier the second time around.

Across from her Tim and Anela sat, the girl watching her every move with a laser-like focus, her eyebrows occasionally rising as she seemed to glean some insight from the activity.

Viki caught her doing this, the two of them sharing a smile, before she turned her attention back to the drawing. It gave her hope that in the midst of all this Anela had not lost her sense of wonder.

When the time came, she had them place their hands on the bottom of the drawing while she placed her hand on the top. After a long, slow inhale, she gently blew on the drawing and JJ Lynch came to life.

"Hey, it's the lady that skypes the dead," JJ said, a smile on his face. He waved and said, "Come on, guys, check it out."

"Hello, Mr. Lynch," Viki began, "please excuse the intrusion. I hope this is a better time."

"'Mr. Lynch,' seriously? Please call me JJ. And yeah, now is fine. We're just hanging out." The drawing of JJ turned and spoke to someone else, someone where JJ was. "Do you see anything? You guys look kind of dim to me... It's this kind of double vision; I mostly see them and the room they are in... Sure, why not, give it a shot."

Viki gasped as she watched the image of JJ shrink and three more faces appeared on the page.

To the left of JJ was a brown-skinned man with a big mustache. Right next to him was a petite woman with striking blue eyes. To JJ's right was an older bald man. They all looked up in amazement.

"Can you see them?" JJ asked.

Viki, Tim, and Anela all nodded.

"Nice. Okay," JJ said, nodding to his left. "This is Jesus, my best dead-friend." He pronounced the name as Hey-Zeus.

The Mexican man nodded and gave a big grin "Thank you, JJ."

"Sure, bro," JJ continued. "To his left is Lela, Jesus's... What should I call you two?"

Lela smiled and said, "You haven't figured that out yet, huh?"

JJ smiled and said, "This is Jesus's significant other." He then nodded to his right and added, "And this is my friend and mentor, Banquo."

Banquo nodded his bald head deeply in what looked like a mini bow.

"You must be Ms. Dobos," Banquo said, his voice deep and resonate. "JJ told us all about your first encounter."

Viki nodded and said quickly, "It's nice to meet you all. I don't mean to be rude, but I have an important matter I am hoping you can help with and these connections don't usually last very long."

Banquo smiled as he looked around, his neck craning far to the right. "I think we can do something about that." He turned to JJ, Jesus, and Lela and said, "Do you see that? That halo of energy around JJ?"

Jesus and Lela nodded and JJ said, "What? What halo, I don't see anything?"

"It's okay, JJ, take a moment and look carefully," Banquo said. "Jesus and Lela, focus on the halo, feel it, make it stronger."

Viki's mouth opened as the drawing grew sharper and felt the drain on her own energy fade. "That seems to be working," she said.

"I don't see any damn halo!" JJ said, his head swiveling.

"That may be because you are the focus of the energy," Banquo said gently. "Just focus on Ms. Dobos, try to make her as clear as you can."

Viki gasped, not because the four of them became even clearer but because of the energy. It was unlike anything she had felt before. Warmth flowed through her fingers into her body. If Tim's and Anela's expressions were any indication, they felt it too.

After a moment of silence, Banquo asked, "Better?"

Viki nodded. "Yes. That is amazing. How do you—"

"One thing at a time, my dear," Banquo said with a smile. "You needed JJ for something. How can we help?"

Viki bit her lip, looking up at Tim and Anela. Anela's eyes were wide, her lips slightly parted as she stared at the animated faces of the four ghosts on the paper. Tim looked up, his eyes meeting hers as he gave her a small nod.

"With me is Tim and his daughter Anela. I just drew Tim's wife, Anela's mother, and..." Viki faltered, she felt her center slipping away, which was putting the connection at risk. If she didn't stay calm she would lose them, despite their efforts. She closed her eyes for a moment and continued, "She is in what you would call a bardo state, reliving her death over and over. She drowned."

JJ's face grew pinched, Jesus shook his head slowly back and forth, and Banquo nodded.

"How long has she been dead?" Jesus asked.

Viki looked to Tim who replied, "Almost two years."

"Please help my mama," Anela said, her eyes red and watery.

"I'm sorry," JJ said, his head hung low. "I can't, not again..."

"I don't understand," Viki said.

"My dear," Banquo said, "as you know, the bardo is one's own personal hell, a place ghosts sometimes get trapped in. JJ has recently had a very long and very difficult encounter with it. None of us go there willingly."

"Then you won't help?" Viki asked.

Viki felt the connection waver and threw her energy into keeping it open.

"Focus now," Banquo said, "we are not done here yet."

The four faces came back into sharp focus as JJ met her eyes again. "Reaching someone in the bardo is very difficult. You," he said looking at Tim and Anela, "have the best chance. You knew her, you loved her, you are the ones that can reach her."

"How?" Viki asked.

"Simple, my dear," Banquo said. "You have to find something more important to her than her suffering."

"While it may be simple," Jesus added with a kind smile, "it's not easy. Not easy at all."

CHAPTER 17

Viki felt raw, ragged, and drained. Before her sat three drawings of Tess. Since talking to JJ, Jesus, Lela, and Banquo, she had drawn Tess three times, and three times they had failed to reach her.

They had tried everything they could think of. Tim had talked to her, cajoled her, begged her. Anela had tried, but mostly cried, often too incoherent to be understood. Viki had tried too, telling her what this was doing to her family. All to no avail.

Tim had put Anela to bed. He had to remove all her drawing implements from her room and yell at her before she got into bed and cried herself to sleep.

On a good day, Viki would draw for her clients a total of three times; four was the max she had ever attempted. Each drawing took a lot out of her. Today she had drawn five times. The first time with Tess, then JJ, then three more times with Tess. She felt frail and delicate, but she felt a resolve burning in her. She had to help them, she had to reach Tess.

She looked over at Tim. He was slumped on the couch,

his head resting on his chest. She listened carefully and could hear no sound from Anela's room.

She slowly pulled out a new piece of paper and started drawing Tess. Her hands moved quickly. Tess was close, and she had drawn her so many times she barely needed the picture.

When she was finished, she felt the energies gathering and looked around one more time. Tim was still and the house was quiet. She took a deep breath and blew on the paper, bringing the screaming woman, who was still experiencing her drowning, to life.

She leaned close to the paper, her eyes fixed on the wide, terrified eyes of Tess Unger. What was more important to her than her suffering? Apparently not the pleadings of her husband or her child. But maybe...

"Tess," she whispered, a smile creeping onto her face, "I have something wonderful to tell you." The blue of the water swirled around Tess's face as the woman struggled for a life that was long past. "Tess, today is the best day of my life. Anela, sweet, beautiful Anela, she called me Mama today."

Viki was not surprised by the words, she had felt them coming, but she was surprised by the emotion that accompanied them. Tears flowed down her face as she felt what it would feel like. She knew it was a lie, but she found herself wishing it wasn't.

Tess's eyes snapped into focus, and her struggling decreased. "That's right, Tess," Viki continued. "Anela, your Anela, is finally healing. She has let me into her life, and I just wanted to thank you for her." Viki paused, her tears becoming profuse. It was a lie, but the longer she told it, the clearer it became she didn't want it to be. Tess's struggling had stopped, and her eyes looked almost normal.

"Tess, you must understand. This is the happiest day of my life. I never thought anyone would call me Mama."

Tess's face grew hard and her eyes sparked. "Anela is *my* girl," she said looking around. "She calls *me* Mama. Who are you?"

"Tim!" Viki cried. "Get Anela, Tess has come around." When she saw Tim rouse himself, rubbing his face, she turned back to the drawing. "Do you want to see Anela, Tess? Do you want to talk to her?"

Tess nodded. "Where am I, what happened? Who are you? Why... Why would my Anela call you—"

"Tim and Anela are coming, Tess. Just keep focusing on my face, make it as clear as you can." Viki's left hand resting on the paper began to shake. She placed her right hand on top of it, trying to steady it. She was past her limit, but she had to keep going. She dug deeper and Tess's face came into sharper focus. Whether from her efforts or Tess's she didn't know.

Tess was confused, but Viki did her best to distract her, talking about the weather and the beach, keeping her engaged.

It was only a minute or two before Tim and Anela put their left hands on the bottom of the drawing, but it felt like a month to Viki. The room was starting to sway, but she held on.

"Mama!" Anela cried as soon as her hand touched the drawing and she could see Tess.

"My little angel," Tess said, pastel tears running down the drawing of her face. "Oh my, how you have grown." She turned to Tim and asked, "What happened?"

~~~

During a normal session, Viki's clients got to talk to their loved ones for two, maybe three, minutes. It wasn't long enough, but no matter how long she held it open it wouldn't be long enough.

During her recent drawing of JJ and his friends, that connection had stayed open about ten minutes. But, she had had their help, and she had learned something from that help.

Before, her sense of the energy connecting the living to the dead was a complicated thing with her focus split between the drawing, the clients, and the distant spirit. Now, she just focused on keeping the drawing of the dead sharp and alive. It was easier, but it wasn't easy.

The minutes ticked by as she held the connection open between Tim, Anela, and Tess.

She held it steady while Tim told her how she had gone swimming one morning and never returned. How her body had never been found.

She held the connection open while Anela cried and patted the image of her mother with her right hand telling her how desperately she had missed her.

She held strong while Tess told Anela that she would watch over her, that now that she had awakened from the terrible dream of her death she would always be there.

She held firm while Tim told Tess how much he missed her and how there would never be anyone else for him, and while Tess told Tim that he needed to move on.

After three minutes Viki felt the connection slipping away, but she dug deeper and held it steady, pulling the wavering image of Tess back into focus.

After five minutes her breath caught and her lungs burned as if she had been on a long run. The image wavered, and seeing the raw look of desperation on Tim's face as he glanced at her, she dug even deeper.

After ten minutes the room began to spin around her and her mouth went dry. She couldn't quite hear what they were saying anymore. All her world was the moist brown eyes of Tess as she told Anela the things a mother needs to tell her daughter.

After twelve minutes, Viki couldn't see properly and felt a sharp pain in her chest. Her breath was ragged and her pulse raced. Still she held on.

At thirteen minutes, she clutched her chest and the world went black.

Chapter 18

The old lady was elegant with long fingers, a slender waist, and an air of certainty. The little girl stared up at her from her sick bed. The girl's fever had receded, and the evil dreams of her stuffed toys attacking her were fading.

"Gran," little Viki asked, "why do we die?"

The old lady smiled, showing white teeth that lined her mouth irregularly, but somehow didn't take away from the air of elegance. "Why do you ask, Little Sparrow?"

"I was real sick, right?"

The old lady smiled and nodded as she held the back of her hand to Viki's forehead.

"I could have died, right?"

Again the old lady smiled, and nodded. "I won't lie to you, Viki. We all die. Someday, something will take our lives. Accident, disease, time. Something. It is not to be feared."

"But *why* do we die, Gran?"

The smile slowly faded from the old lady's face as her eyes grew distant. She leaned down and whispered something in the little girl's ear. The girl smiled, grabbed the black teddy bear, which was her favorite, and closed her eyes.

~~~

Viki opened her eyes and quickly closed them again. The light hurt. She smelled the tang of antiseptic and heard a sharp beeping sound. She felt a squeeze of her left hand and heard, "Viki, thank God you're okay. Viki."

She kept her eyes closed, enjoying the warmth of the hand that held hers, resting in the glow of a dream-time visit from her grandmother. She didn't want to wake up, she didn't want to return to reality. But—

"Viki," the voice said again, quieter this time, "please be okay."

She inhaled deeply, letting the air fill her lungs and said slowly, "I. Am. Okay. What. Happened?"

She felt her hand squeezed again and heard a rush of air released. It sounded as if her companion had been holding it for a very long time. Still with her eyes closed, she reached and felt him. His concern was there, and guilt, and need. But there was something else, something quietly brewing in the background. "Tim," she said, her eyes slowly opening to confirm her impressions.

Tim Unger sat clutching her left hand, his face forming a weak smile, dark smudges under his eyes, his clothes wrinkled and his hair unkempt. "You passed out while you were..."

Viki nodded, the memory flooding back. The memory of Tim's wife locked in the bardo reliving her death. How she had pulled her out of it by making her jealous, making her think that she had taken her place.

"Anela?" Viki asked.

"She is with her grandparents. When they came and got her she was talking a mile a minute about what you can do and what you did..." Tim trailed off with a lopsided grin on his face. She wasn't too worried. People always talked about what Viki did, but most did not believe it. Not until they needed her gift.

"Is she okay?"

Tim smiled, fully this time. "She is more than okay. She..." Tim trailed off as tears formed and silently ran down his cheeks. "Thank you for helping us. I... How... I don't think I can ever repay you. But why? Why did you hurt yourself doing it?"

Viki's attempt at a shrug was ineffectual with the hospital gown and the blankets around her. "I just had to. You... Anela... I couldn't allow your suffering to continue if I could..." Viki sighed and squeezed Tim's hand, which still gripped hers. "I just had to."

Tim smiled, pulling his hand from hers, as if surprised it had been there. "Thank you," he whispered. It looked as if he might have said more, but a doctor entered the room.

Dr. Metcalf was in her thirties, with a kind, plain face. She explained to Viki that she had been severely dehydrated and her electrolytes were imbalanced. She had questions, but Viki brushed them off saying she had forgotten to drink water all day—she hadn't. The doctor also told her she had a heart condition called "Long QT Syndrome."

"It's a genetic defect; in most cases the cause is an inherited genetic condition," she told Viki as blandly as if she was reading a grocery list. "Your heart doesn't recharge in between beats as quickly as a normal heart. The dehydration put stress on your system which, combined with the long QT, led to an arrhythmia—an irregular heartbeat—and a syncopal episode."

"Syncopal?" Viki asked.

"You passed out. You need to see your primary care physician as soon as possible. They'll refer you to a cardiologist. Avoid dehydration at all costs. If not treated it can cause things much worse than fainting."

"Like what?"

"Seizures and death."

Viki blinked rapidly, having trouble processing the information. Her mind jumped to the mundane and she asked, "How long have I been here?"

Looking at the chart, the doctor said, "Twenty-seven hours." Dr. Metcalf excused herself after telling Viki she wanted to keep her another night to make sure the arrhythmia had subsided and her electrolytes had returned to normal.

After the doctor left, Viki said, "Where is my phone? I need to call Mark Kosov."

"No need," Tim said. "I called him yesterday. He was in for a few hours. He knows."

Viki nodded. She first felt scared by what the doctor had told her, then guilty about her client, the one that was paying her. Her worry didn't last long, as she was soon asleep.

~~~

When Viki next awoke, she felt the need of the person sitting next to her, but didn't feel the warmth of a hand in hers. She kept her eyes closed for a minute to better sort out what she was sensing. The need was sharp, and she could faintly smell the acidic tinge of his breath. Mark Kosov.

"I really expected our roles here to be reversed," Mark said when she opened her eyes.

"What?"

"Well, I expected it to be me in the hospital bed with you attending to me."

Viki's smile was sheepish. "I am sorry, Mark. I—"

"No need. Tim seems a good sort. He told me what you did for them." Mark paused and Viki had trouble reading his expression. Wistful, regretful, maybe jealous. "It's helpful really," he added, his face returning to its normal bland mask. "More confirmation of the validity of your gift and what it can do."

"But I have cost you time. I am so sorry, I didn't mean for this to happen."

Mark nodded. "I have been putting something off, something I need to do before the end. You need time to recover, so I am going to go on a trip."

"A trip?"

"Yes. I was going to do this after we were done, but our current circumstance lends itself to me doing this first."

"How long will you be gone?"

"Five days, maybe a week," he said.

"A week?"

"Don't worry. You can stay at my house. Rest up. Get our legal agreement in order."

"But..." Viki began.

"I will continue to pay you the agreed-upon rate."

"No. Not that, I have appointments in Sedona. I have a life there."

"Oh. Alexander already spoke with your Reginald. He says he has everything under control and your cat—Bast, I believe—is doing well."

Mark rose slowly, leaning heavily on his cane. "So stay. Rest. Alexander will take care of you." As he was about to leave, he turned and added, "And please, Ms. Dobos, be ready to draw me when I return."

Viki knew Mark was avoiding telling her why he wanted to be drawn, but she didn't feel she had the strength to fight him about it anymore.

~~~

When she awoke next, she had the nurse get her phone and she called Reg.

"Bast is fine!" he said as greeting.

Viki chuckled weakly. "Well, that is at least something."

"So how's your Hawaii adventure going?"

Viki sighed. "Well, it has been interesting to say the least."

"So kiddo, what happened?"

Viki told him everything, including the dream about her grandmother. He listened carefully with an occasional "um-huh" and "ahh-huh" but didn't ask questions, letting Viki find her way through the story.

When she was done, he was silent for several breaths, which surprised Viki. Not much kept Reg from talking. When he finally spoke, his voice was low and conspiratorial. "Sounds like you really care about this Tim and his girl."

"Well... I..." she stammered as the reality of what Reg said sunk in.

"You knew what you were doing, V. You knew where it would likely end up. Still you did it; still you pushed yourself farther than you ever have. You don't do more than three or four minutes for our clients. So, you must really care about Tim and Anela."

"I guess I do," Viki said slowly. "I do."

"Are you okay, V?" Reg asked.

"I think so... Yeah, I'm fine, Reg."

"So what did your grandmother tell you about why people die?" he asked

"Oh... She whispered, 'To make room.'" Viki chuckled, remembering the warm tickle of her grandmother's breath. "It's one of my favorite memories of her. For some reason it always makes me smile."

After the call, she laid there wondering if it would be her turn to "make room" soon.

CHAPTER 19

Viki held the drawing and studied it carefully, a grave expression on her face. Tim pushed her in a wheelchair, Alexander walked in front of her, and the artist—Anela—walked beside her. Viki was happy to be getting out of the hospital; she didn't find it relaxing at all, the place being filled with death and full of potential clients. She had felt silly about the wheelchair, but gave in when hospital regulations were cited.

The picture showed four people on the beach. A girl holding hands with a man and a transparent woman and a second woman standing on the other side of the man.

Viki smiled. Anela had drawn herself holding hands with her living father and her ghost mother. She had also put Viki in the picture. "It's beautiful, Anela, just beautiful."

"Thank you, Miss Viki," Anela said, her smile bright.

"Is this for me?" Viki asked.

Anela nodded vigorously. "Yes, Miss Viki. You saved my mama."

"I couldn't have done it without you, Anela."

~ ~ ~

In the morning, Viki resumed her ritual of walking the beach at sunrise. When she made it to Kamaole II, both Tim and Anela ran up to her.

The girl reached her first and embraced her. "That's from Mama, she wanted me to say thank you."

She looked up at Tim who gave her a conspiratorial nod. "Are you well?" Tim asked. "Do you need to rest? Something to drink? I can call a cab later to take you back."

Viki laughed and showed him the water bottle she had in her bag. In truth she was feeling the walk much more than she had before her trip to the hospital, but she was glad to be outside. "I'm fine, Tim, just fine."

"Well, you should at least come in for breakfast. I have been reviewing the contract and need your input."

Viki nodded, and Anela soon pulled her into a game of catch as they headed towards the condo.

~~~

Tim looked up from the spread of papers in front of him. He and Viki sat at the dining room table. He had reading glasses on and Viki watched as he made notes with a red pen on the copy of the contract Mark had given her. He looked different. Gone was the handyman that Viki had seen so often. Gone was the man guarding his daughter against the ocean. Gone was the man deeply worried about his daughter and dead wife. This Tim was somehow more elemental, more focused, and despite the glasses, fierce. He spoke in short, direct sentences cutting through the legalese and explaining things clearly.

"The indemnification is clear, but I think you might want more," he said, his red pen stabbing at a section of the contract.

"More?" Viki asked.

"Yes. Tell me what your worst fear is."

Viki shrugged. "That's easy. That drawing him while alive will kill him." She had shared what had happened with the red-headed college student in Boston. "I really have no idea how it will affect him."

"Well, then," Tim said, "let's have medical personnel on site. A crash cart and other resuscitation gear."

"We can ask for that?"

Tim smiled, reminding Viki a bit of a wolf. "This is a contract, so we can ask for anything."

Viki nodded. "That sounds good. And one other thing. I want a witness there. Someone I trust."

Tim nodded and wrote some notes on a yellow legal pad. His writing was slow and precise. "That's not a problem."

"I want you there, Tim."

Tim paused and he lowered his glasses and looked over them at her, smiling gently. "Of course." He slid his glasses back into place and added, "Let's video the whole thing too, so there is no question about what happens."

Viki's mind wandered as Tim made more notes. She was feeling something. She wasn't sure what it was, but she was sure it was scaring her. Tim looked at her differently since they had reached Tess. He seemed tender. She didn't know if that was because he felt he needed to take care of her after the trip to the hospital or because—

The sound of soft words coming from Anela's room interrupted Viki's train of thought. "And these are the pencils that Miss Viki gave me... Yes, that *was* very nice of her... She showed me some things, she taught me how to shade... Yes, Mama, I would love to learn more."

Tim's eyes met hers and followed them to Anela's room and back. "She talks to her mom all the time now," Tim said.

Viki smiled. "This is new behavior?"

"Yes," Tim said. "Do you... Do you think she is really talking to her?"

In answer, Viki smiled and closed her eyes. She focused on what she could feel, not with her five senses, but with something deeper. She felt Tim next to her, he looked like a wolf defending her. She felt Anela in her room, she felt like a dolphin, swimming and playing. And she sensed a third presence, a stately and graceful heron.

"I do, Tim," Viki said when she opened her eyes. "I feel a presence in there with her. A great graceful bird, a heron, with black feathers on its head."

Tim blinked and took his glasses off and rubbed at the tears forming in his eyes.

"What?" Viki asked.

"That's the Aukuu, the Black-crowned Night Heron."

"Okay..."

"When Anela was six and we were here on an extended vacation, we came across an injured Aukuu on a hike near Hana. Tess was crazy about that bird and she took it in, and she and Anela nursed it back to health. Tess loved that bird." Tim paused rubbing at his eyes again. "It has to be her."

CHAPTER 20

Viki spent the rest of the day enjoying the beach, and in the evening, she read about and tried to understand what Long QT Syndrome was. She eventually gave up when the information overloaded and depressed her. All she knew was that her heart could have trouble beating at times, especially at times of stress. And, in extreme cases, the condition causes a "lethal arrhythmia."

In the morning when she went out to the beach in front of the Kosov house for her morning walk, Tim was waiting for her, pacing back and forth on the wet sand.

"Tim? Is there a problem?"

"Huh?" He replied as if pulling himself from somewhere deep. "No, no problem. I just have something I need to ask you."

"Where's Anela?"

"A friend is watching her, so I... so we..." He rubbed his hands together, took a deep breath and sighed. "I hope you don't mind the intrusion."

In fact, she did mind. She had come to treasure her morning solitude and felt she needed it this morning more than most. But she didn't say anything, and just smiled in answer.

As Viki started her slow walk down the beach, Tim matched her pace, keeping himself between her and the ocean, his hands thrust into the pockets of his shorts.

"So?" she asked after about a hundred yards.

"Huh?" Tim said, again seeming to be far away.

"What is your question?"

"Oh. Well... You see..." Tim stammered.

"It's about what I said to Tess, isn't it?" Viki asked. "What I told her to wake her up."

Tim didn't answer, just nodded, pushing his hands deeper into his pockets.

"What do you want to know?"

"Why? Why did you tell her that? She was quite confused when we first started talking to her, worried that she had been replaced."

Viki stopped and then walked towards the water so that each wave coming to shore rolled over her feet. Tim pulled the hat down on his head, crossed his arms, and faced her.

"I will do my best to answer that question, but I have two conditions." Tim nodded, so she continued. "First. I suspect you are looking for a clear-cut logical answer to your question." Tim nodded again. "I can't give you that. It is not the way my mind works, but, I'll try. And second, I would like to know more about you and Tess."

Tim nodded his head at the beach, signaling that he wanted to continue walking and Viki reluctantly pulled her feet out of the wet sand. The water had eroded the sand around them and she had sunk in several inches. She liked the feeling of being connected, being on the boundary of land and water.

As they started walking again, he began speaking.

"Tess and I, we were both born on Maui. I was born in Kihei and Tess up the mountain in Pukalani. But we didn't meet here, we met at UC Davis in law school." Tim paused, looking out at the ocean without the guarded look he usually had, but with what looked to Viki like longing. "It was the ocean that brought us together."

"The ocean?" Viki asked.

"Yeah. Law school is pretty intense. Sacramento is inland a bit, so we both missed the ocean and ended up on some trips together to some surfing spots near San Francisco. When we discovered we had Maui in common, we hit if off quickly.

"We got married right out of law school and both got jobs in the Bay Area. A few years later Anela was born. Tess took mothering seriously and quit her job to stay home and take care of her. She taught some online courses, but being a mom was what she wanted.

"We were out here on vacation a few years ago. Tess went out swimming early in the morning, something she always did when we were here. She never came back. I moved Anela back here to be close to her grandparents."

They walked in silence for a time before Viki asked, "And is that why you don't go in the ocean anymore? Why you seem to be guarding Anela as she plays in it?"

Tim nodded. "The ocean has taken too much from me. My father died in a diving accident."

Viki wanted to say she was sorry, to say something that would make a difference. But she knew from her own experience that words didn't offer much succor to grief. "Thank you for telling me, Tim."

Tim nodded.

They walked in silence past the Kihei boat ramp, then up along the path that traced the black volcanic cliff until they reached Kamaole Beach III. Viki took her sandals off, picked them up and dug her feet into the sand.

"I was desperate," she began without preamble. "You and Anela had failed to get through to Tess, and I was desperate to reach her. My gift usually makes things better for people, but seeing the state she was in caused both of you so much suffering."

Tim walked, not making eye contact, his head down.

"I felt like I was running out of time. Mark wanted me to draw him in the morning and after that I would probably be leaving.

"I didn't think it through; it just came to me. If Anela's pleas couldn't reach her, then maybe the thought of her being replaced would. I know it was a shock, and I'm sorry for that, but it worked."

Viki kept glancing at Tim, trying to see a reaction, but he was closed. She almost said more, she almost said that she would be honored if Anela called her Mama. That she found herself missing the girl's smile and her bright brown eyes when they were apart. She almost said that she found herself caring for both Anela and Tim more than she should.

Before she knew it their feet had carried them to Kamaole II and they were at the steps leading to Tim's condo.

"Breakfast?" he asked. "I finished the contract; we should go over it."

Viki's smile was forced as she nodded in agreement and started up the steps.

CHAPTER 21

Viki and Tim sat on the lanai, their breakfast and the contract done. Tim sat with his coffee, staring out into the ocean. Viki stole glances at him while he brooded.

"Have I done something to insult you?" Viki asked, and immediately regretted it. She hadn't meant to say it.

Tim, mid-sip of his coffee, snorted it out, getting the brown fluid all over his clean white shorts.

"I'm sorry," she said grabbing her napkin, leaning in as he leaned down. Their heads came together with an audible clunk.

"Sorry," Tim said with a grimace.

"No, no. My fault," Viki said holding her head with her hand and handing the napkin to him.

Tim got up saying, "I think I need to change," and quickly left, leaving Viki alone with her thoughts.

She couldn't sort out her feelings. Why had she told Tess, lost in her death, that Anela had called her Mama? Did she really want that? And if she was a mother to Anela, what would she be to Tim?

She took a deep breath and blew it out noisily. Her

relationship with her own mother had soured her on the prospect of children. And, in truth, while there had been romances, they were short and far apart. Her work kept her distant. She couldn't do what she did and be normal enough for most men.

And if she was going to have children, she was almost out of time. She was thirty-seven, and while women were having children later in life, she knew the risk went up at forty.

And while Tim didn't seem normal, and he had a unique perspective on her gift, his communication style was entirely male-normal. Too few words, all logic, no emotion. Clearly he felt emotions, but he was woefully inadequate at expressing them. If only he could—

"That's better," Tim said as he sat back down.

"I am sorry, Tim," Viki said. "Maybe I should go."

"Please," he said, his hand resting briefly on hers, "don't. Stay."

His hand was warm, which she liked. It brought her back to the moment when she woke up in the hospital and he was there, his hand holding hers, his concern evident. She liked the feeling, but his hand only stayed a moment.

"Just talk to me, Tim. Please. I... I would like to think we're friends."

Tim nodded and smiled. "I'll try, but it's complicated."

Viki smiled back. "Isn't it always?"

Silence stretched out as they sipped coffee and watched the people below on the beach. Swimming, sunbathing, playing in the gentle waves. It was mesmerizing.

"You've done nothing to insult me," Tim began finally. "In fact, you've done more for me and Anela than I could have asked or expected."

Viki nodded, trying to meet his eyes, but they were trained on the ocean below.

"And I can't thank you enough for the interest you have taken in Anela. How you have encouraged her art like... like her mother used to."

Viki breathed slowly and quietly—she didn't want to miss a word. This, she could tell, was difficult for him.

"And we are friends, Viki. And, I think if we had met under different circumstances there would be a chance for..." His voice trailed off, his eyes briefly meeting hers before he rose, gripping the railing of the lanai. "Talking to Tess the other night... I feel like I am experiencing her death all over again."

"Tim. I—"

Still facing away from her, he held his hand up cutting her off. He turned slowly and met her eyes. "Don't you see, Viki? You have freed Anela, and for that... for that I can never repay you. That is such a gift. But me, I am right back in it. Feeling it all like it happened yesterday."

~~~

Viki tried to talk with him more about it, but he wouldn't do it. He gave her a manila envelope with the contract in it, told her to call him when she was going to draw Mark Kosov, and asked her to leave.

On the beach, she slowly walked as tears rolled down her face. She felt sad and confused and frustrated. As they passed, people stared at her, but she didn't care. Her grandmother had taught her that tears were not a sign of weakness but a sign of strength. Her ability to feel made her who she was, allowed her to do what she did.

She didn't understand men. So many rules, so many conditions. Why can't they just follow their hearts?

Her thoughts went back to Sedona and Reg. Now there's a man she understood. He had his rules and his logic, but they were simple rules and simple logic. She understood them, and she understood him.

She fished out her phone from the small bag she carried and called him.

"Yo, V. How you doing?" he said as a greeting.

"Not good, Reg, not good at all."

"What's wrong, honey?"

"I've made a real mess of things here, Reg. I don't know what to do."

"Okay," Reg began, "I can help. Where are you right now?"

"I'm on the beach walking back to Mark Kosov's house."

"Okay. Here's what you do, hightail it back there. I have a surprise for you. I am going to call Alexander and he'll have it ready by the time you get back."

"What are you up to?"

"You'll like this surprise, I promise." He laughed and Viki felt her heart lighten a bit. "Just get back here ASAP and call me."

~ ~ ~

As she walked, Viki talked to her grandmother. It wasn't the kind of conversation she wanted to have. She wanted to draw her and have her portrait come to life, and have no doubts about the fact that she was talking to her.

But, that was not an option. So she talked to her grandmother and listened carefully to her replies. It was something she counseled her clients to do, whether their drawing was successful or not. She advised them to talk to their dead loved ones and listen to what they had to say. She counseled them to not get caught up in whether it was real or not but to listen to their hearts. Their loved ones were still there and what came from their heart would be what they needed to hear.

"I'm so confused, Gran," she said softly.

"What's wrong, Little Sparrow," she heard her grand-mother whisper back.

"I don't understand men. They are just so... so..."

She heard her grandmother's throaty chuckle. "Join the club, dear. I never really understood them either. And you know what? They don't understand us either."

"How can that be?" Viki asked. "How stupid is that?"

She sensed her shrugging as her heart-grandmother said, "Fortunately, Little Sparrow, the most important thing is not understanding."

"It's not?"

"No, it's not. The world is full of people that think differently and act differently. We can, and should, strive for understanding, but it is not paramount."

"What is, Gran?"

"Love, my dear, love and tolerance. If you feel love for this man and his daughter, then follow your heart. There is nothing else to do. There is never anything else to do."

Viki smiled and quickened her pace, eager to see what surprise Reg had in store for her.

CHAPTER 22

Reginald Anderson stood on the edge of the lanai looking out through the palm trees at the ocean when Viki saw
him. He was wearing a loud Hawaiian print shirt, shorts,
and sandals. A squeal of delight escaped her when she saw
him. As she ran to him, he turned and swept her up in a
big bear hug.

"Good surprise, V?" Reg asked.

"The best, Reg, the best." He set her down and Viki
asked, "How? Why?"

"How? The usual way, on an airplane. Why? Because
you need me, V." Reg's smile was big and his eyes bright,
but Viki sensed he was withholding something.

"Reg..." she said, letting his name draw out and her
voice deepen as if she were talking to a recalcitrant child.

"What, V? Me being here is not enough?"

"I am delighted you are here, but you haven't told me
the whole story. You never leave the store, except for the
gem and mineral show. And you hate to spend money when
you don't have to. A last-minute ticket to Hawaii is expensive." As she mentioned the ticket, Reg started studying his

sandals. "You didn't buy a ticket, did you? Mark flew you out here, didn't he? In the private jet."

"Guilty," he said, briefly meeting her eyes.

"Spit it out, Reg, all of it."

"Mr. Kosov called me after your little trip to the hospital. He was worried that you wouldn't be able to, or would be unwilling to, draw him. So, I... I gave him some assurances and told him if I were here I could help things along..."

Reg's head was still down so he missed the smile that came upon Viki's face, but he could not miss her laughter. "Oh, Reg," she said, "you are so predictable, so reliable, and that is why I love you."

"You're not mad?"

"Not at all. I know somewhere in your black heart you came here to help me as well as yourself. No, I'm not mad. I am so glad you're here."

Reg returned her smile and pulled out a chair for her. "Great, then let me help. Start at the beginning, tell me everything, and don't leave anything out."

~ ~ ~

They sat on the lanai watching the afternoon slowly turn to evening as Viki recounted her tale. She was happy to have someone to talk to, and Reg was an attentive listener. When the tale was done, she felt better about everything.

Reg was silent for some minutes before he said, "Mind if I comment?"

"No," Viki answered, "of course not."

He scooted his chair so he was facing Viki, took a deep breath, and said, "So, you located probably the kindest and the most wounded man on the beach. You immediately fell for his daughter and have had trouble sorting out your feelings for him. You then showed him that his wife, dead for two years, was in a living hell, experiencing her death over and over. You then put yourself into the hospital rescuing her from said living hell and discovered you had an undiagnosed heart condition. You are now put out because the man is having some trouble sorting his feelings out and, quite predictably, is back in the grief of the loss of his wife."

Viki stared at him gape jawed but didn't say anything.

"Was that a fair assessment?"

"Reginald Mathew Anderson. You come all this way just to make fun of me? Just to—"

"Hey," Reg said, his voice rising. "Don't use that maternal middle name crap on me. I am quite immune."

"You can be a real shit sometimes, Reg. That hurt!"

"That's better. I know it hurt, V, but was it fair?"

Viki stood, feeling the sting of tears on her cheeks as she stared at the ocean. She said, ever so quietly, "Yes."

"What was that?" Reg asked, coming to stand next to her. "I couldn't quite hear you."

"Yes!" Viki yelled. "Yes, goddamn it. That was fair."

Reg pulled her into a side hug. "I'm sorry, honey."

"What should I do, Reg?" she asked.

"Just give him a couple days. He said you were friends, right?"

Viki nodded.

"Well give him a couple of days and take him at his word. Act like his friend."

"And then?"

"Hell if I know," Reg said laughing. "You're the psychic, my dear, not me."

Viki nodded, wiping her eyes. "Any other *brilliant* words of wisdom?"

"Yup! Three to be exact. Let's. Get. Drunk."

~~~

The three of them, Reg, Alexander, and Viki, ended up a mere thirty minutes later at Moose McGillycuddy's. The selection process had been quick. Reg found Alexander and asked, "Where's the nearest bar where you don't have to be a rich son of a bitch or have a stick up your ass to have a good time?"

Alexander had driven them, which hardly seemed necessary—it was a three-minute drive to the southern end of Kihei. Moose McGillycuddy's, Viki was somewhat horrified to discover, was right across the street from Hale Pua Hana, where Tim and Anela lived.

When they got there, Alexander said he would wait in the car, but Reg would have nothing of it. He insisted that the Englishman join them in their celebration. The butler had demurred but quickly gave in under Reg's insistence.

Moose McGillycuddy's was on the second floor with a large bar in the middle of the restaurant and tables along the edges. There were no windows, just open wooden panels that let the sea breeze in. From their second floor vantage, they had a fine view of the beach across the street.

Viki sat facing south, so she could see the beach, but not the third-story door to Tim's condo.

"A toast," Reg said, raising his glass. "To good friends, old and new." They raised their glasses, touching them together and drinking.

Viki sipped her white wine and let the alcohol do its work. She didn't drink often, so it didn't take long for her to feel it. She liked the wine, although she didn't know enough to comment on its qualities beyond liking it. Alexander had recommended it. It was a local wine made "just up the hill," as he put it. The winery was above them on the volcano. A long drive, but really not far away.

Both Alexander and Reg were drinking dark beer, a coconut porter that Reg kept raving about.

"Well, since you are here," Alexander said, "you should have the best the islands have to offer."

"I'll drink to that," Reg said, raising his glass, his eyes scanning the bar.

"So where is Mark?" Viki asked after the second round of drinks came and conversation had slowed.

Alexander looked surprised by the question. "He went home. He's getting some experimental treatments and visiting some relatives."

"Home? Russia?"

Alexander nodded. "Well, Kazakhstan to be exact."

"Family?" Viki asked.

He shook his head. "No, no. His parents died many years ago, and Mr. Kosov is an only child. He has an uncle alive and a few cousins."

"Is this okay? Me asking these questions?"

"Sure, fine," Alexander said, but she could see there was something underneath, something else going on with him.

"Why hasn't Mark asked me to draw his parents or any deceased loved ones?" It had been on her mind for days, but she hadn't felt quite right asking it. Perhaps it was the wine that gave her the courage.

Alexander shrugged and took a drink of his beer. "He is a very private man. I..." he faltered and looked at the sun setting over the water, his eyes far away. "I don't understand him nearly as well as I would like."

"So," Reg said, clearly bored by the line of questioning,

"how did the man make his money? I read it was dot-com money before the bust in 2000."

Alexander looked relieved at the change in subject. "Yes, but it's more complicated than that. After the fall of the Soviet Union, when government controlled industries were going private, he was in the right place at the right time. He and some partners managed to get control of a significant portion of the wheat crop. They made a lot of money. When he got bored with that, he and one of his business partners sold out and came to America. He was an angel investor in some small companies, mostly retail technology. He got out of these before the bust, and he became truly wealthy."

"Well, I'll drink to that," Reg said, raising his glass again as the other two followed.

"So, V," Reg said, his eyes narrowing. "Before you get too far into your cups, perhaps you can do an old friend a favor." He nodded towards the bar where two women sat talking.

"Seriously, Reg? Those girls are at least twenty years your junior. You're old enough to be their father."

"Hush. Don't say the 'f' word. Not nice. Besides, for what I have in mind, the age difference doesn't matter."

"Really?"

"Please, V. I just want to sample the best the islands have to offer, like our friend Alexander here said."

Viki rolled her eyes, put her glass down, and studied the two women, a blonde and a brunette. They were in their late twenties and appeared to be alone. "The blonde," Viki said, her voice low. She hated herself for doing it, but she couldn't say no to Reg.

"Why?" Reg asked with a grin.

"Look at her left hand. There was recently a ring there. She's trying to get over someone. And see how she looks at the other girl? She thinks her friend is the pretty one. If you focus your attention on her you might have a chance."

"You're the best, V!" Reg said as he drained his glass. "There's two, are you in, Alex?"

Alexander shook his head and stared into his beer. Viki noticed a trace of red on his cheeks.

"Well, I'm off. Don't wait up for me, kids."

~~~

Viki and Alexander walked along the beach, the moon lighting their way. After it became clear that Reg wasn't coming back, Viki had declared her intentions of walking back, and Alexander had insisted on walking with her, saying he would come back and get the car later.

"You really don't have to walk me," Viki said as they started south. Viki was careful not to look back at the building Tim and Anela lived in.

"Really I do," Alexander said. "I must make sure nothing untoward happens to you before Mr. Kosov gets back."

Viki nodded, an idea forming in her mind and taking root as she looked at Alexander, a question she didn't really know she had finally coming clear. "You really should tell him, you know."

"What?" Alexander asked.

"Mark, you should tell him."

"I'm sorry. I don't understand what you are getting at."

Viki took his arm and gently squeezed it. "You should tell Mark how you feel about him."

"I..." Alexander began, his face visibly turning red even in the moonlight. "How?"

Viki laughed, a gentle sound that merged with the crashing of the waves. "Watching people is part of my business,

Alexander. And, you know, some people think I'm a bit psychic."

Alexander nodded, but didn't reply.

"He's dying, you really should tell him. It would be better for you not to leave something that big unsaid."

The man sighed and rubbed his face. "I'm afraid of what... And he's not..."

"He's not gay? Is that what you're saying?"

Alexander nodded.

"This isn't about starting a long-term relationship, or sex, or anything like that. It's about saying what you need to say while there is still time. Besides, I have a good feeling about this."

As they walked, Viki heard her words echo back to her. What wasn't she saying that needed to be said? What was she holding back because circumstances weren't right?

They didn't speak again until they were almost back at Mark Kosov's house. "I..." Alexander began. "Thank you. Thank you for the talk. I have a lot to think about."

Viki nodded, she did too.

CHAPTER 23

Viki got up in the morning, pre-dawn as usual. She had heard Reg come in late and didn't bother him. She knew he wasn't an early riser and didn't think the time difference would have an effect.

She walked out onto the beach and started her walk north. She wanted to see Tim and Anela but didn't know if it was the right thing to do. Reg had said, "Give him a couple of days and take him at his word. Act like his friend," and it had only been a day.

These thoughts bounced around her head as she walked down the beach. She said good morning to Howard and climbed up the spit of land separating Kamaole III from Kamaole II and stopped. She stared down the beach and saw them. Father standing guard while daughter darted in and ran from the crashing waves.

She breathed deeply and tried to feel, feel what she was feeling. She longed for a hug from Anela and a smile from Tim. She felt love and tenderness and a desire to nurture when she thought of Anela. She felt... She felt... She was having trouble closing in on what she felt for Tim and it made her mad. "Just follow your heart, Little Sparrow," she could almost hear grandmother saying. Nice advice, but not easy.

What was she feeling? She was fond of him, confused by him, and yes, attracted to him. But what was she, some junior high girl with a crush who had never been kissed? Was she some wallflower at a high school dance waiting for some boy—any boy—to ask her to dance?

Anger flared up and she took a decisive step forward, determined to act like this was any other day. But she came to a shuddering halt after one step, turned on her heal and headed back down the beach the way she had come.

The fact was she didn't know her heart and since she didn't, she was going to follow Reg's advice and give him some time.

All was quiet when she got back to the house. Well, the house was quiet, but her mind wasn't. She got a bath towel, spread it out on the beautiful green grass behind the Kosov house and started doing yoga.

She hadn't done yoga since she came to Hawaii, using her beach time instead to calm and center her. But today her walk had done anything but. So she began her routine hoping that breathing and stretching and sweating would quiet her mind so she could hear her heart.

~~~

That afternoon, once Reg had gotten up, they made the trek up to Haleakala Crater. Alexander drove and seemed to be happy to show off the sites, and Reg kept up a constant campaign of distraction with Viki.

He had her retell the story of how, with her grandmother's guidance, she had learned to draw the dead. Reg insisted that Alexander should know the story, and he kept insisting on more detail so the story took up most of the trip.

Once they arrived at the crater, she needed no distractions. She was awestruck.

They were in the small visitor's center at the top, with a large glassed wall that overlooked the vast crater.

"It looks... It looks like pastels," Viki said.

"What?" Reg asked. "Pastels?"

"It looks like it was drawn with pastels. The softness of it, the vividness of it—how the blacks merge with the reds, and the reds merge with the browns. It looks like it's made of pastels."

Despite the cold temperature and fierce winds, Viki insisted on going outside to view the crater. She had to have nothing between her and the color.

She stood shivering. Not just from the cold and the wind. She felt like she had found something essential, something primal, something important.

Alexander came out with a coat he had bought at the gift store. It was blue with a patch on it that said "Haleakala Crater." He held it for Viki as she put it on.

"Thank you, Alexander."

"Think nothing of it," the Englishman said. "It is amazing, but more so for you, I think. What are you seeing? Can you describe it?"

She looked at him briefly, searching for the words to match her feelings, before turning her gaze back to the crater. "When you draw with pastels, the result has a certain feel to it. A vibrant softness. It is very distinctive. What we are looking at here," she gestured, encompassing the wide crater, "has that same feel, that same vibrant softness. It's as if God drew this using the same kind of tools I use."

"You can hike down in, you know."

"You can?" Viki asked, her voice rising like a little girl's.

"Yes. I've done it quite a few times."

"Well, let's go!" Viki said, looking around for a trail.

"Hold on," Alexander said with a laugh. "We are not prepared. I have the proper gear at the house. We can come back tomorrow, and I can take you on whatever length hike you would like."

Viki threw her arms around Alexander and hugged him fiercely while happy tears ran down her cheeks. "You have no idea what this means to me."

She lingered, staring at the crater below, only leaving reluctantly when the sun started to go down. She felt like she belonged there.

That night Viki dreamed of soft and vibrant colors that flowed all around her. She was living in a world drawn in pastel.

CHAPTER 24

In the morning, Viki went on her usual walk, and again paused on the piece of land between Kamaole III and Kamaole II. Again she saw Tim and Anela doing their usual morning activity.

"Take him at his word," she mumbled to herself as she took a step forward.

"Take him at his word," she said again but didn't move.

Last night before they went to bed, she had asked Reg about it. Asked him why she should "take him at his word."

"Because it is respectful," Reg had said. Viki cocked her head but didn't say anything. "It is a sign of respect. That you believe him... that you trust him, that you don't need to read between the lines. He said you are friends, so act like his friend. Take him at his word."

"C'mon Viki, get it moving," she whispered to herself. She took a step forward, and then another, and then another.

Soon she found herself walking down Kamaole II. She nodded to the Ex-Pat Businessman, and then stopped and shared a few words with Howard.

"Take him at his word," she whispered one more time as she approached Tim and Anela.

Anela was digging in the sand, her back to Viki, and didn't see her approach, but Tim did.

"Good morning," Viki said with a shy smile.

"Good morning," Tim said with a nod.

"How are things?" she asked, cringing at the awkwardness.

"Fine, and you?"

"Umm. Good. Things are good. I've..." Viki trailed off.

Tim turned to his daughter and said, "Look who's here, Angel."

The girl's face brightened and she got up and gave the woman a hug. Viki had squatted down for it and Anela leaned close and whispered in her ear, "Mama told me to tell Daddy to be nicer to you, so I did! He promised!"

Like many children, Anela's whisper was loud and carried farther than an adult's whisper. When Viki looked up, she saw Tim's cheeks reddening and felt a flush on her own cheeks.

"Well," Viki said, standing and brushing sand off. "I came to ask you two something."

Tim nodded, seemingly glad for the change of subject.

"My friend Reg is in town, and Alexander, Mark Kosov's butler, took us up to Haleakala yesterday. Today Alexander is going to take me hiking in the crater. Would you two like to go?" Viki held her breath. She was taking Tim at his word, treating him as a friend.

Anela's face lit up and she turned to her father. Tim didn't say anything, his gaze going to the sea.

"It's Saturday, Anela doesn't have school," Viki offered.

Tim nodded. "She is to be with her grandparents today."

"Please, Daddy, please. I want to go hiking with Miss Viki. I can go see Gran and Papa after."

Viki couldn't quite tell what was going on with Tim as he weighed his options. "Tell you what, sweetie. Let's go call your grandparents and see what they think. I can't say yes unless they do."

Anela grabbed her father's hand and began tugging him towards their condo. "They'll say yes. I'll ask nice."

"We're leaving at nine," Viki said as they walked away. "Please call me either way."

Tim nodded and waved as he allowed his daughter to pull him up the beach.

~~~

The sun was high in the sky as they stood at the trail-head—Alexander, Tim, Anela, and Viki. Reg had insisted he had a date, but Viki suspected he just didn't want to hike.

Alexander had them equipped with fanny packs, water bottles, coats, and walking sticks. He had briefed them that conditions could sometimes be harsh with high winds, cold temperatures, and difficult footing. They were poised at the Pa Ka'oao trailhead. It wasn't the most difficult or spectacular trail, but it would get them down into the crater.

Viki was rapt, swept away looking at the landscape. They stood taller than the clouds, the sky bright blue above, and the rest of Maui seemingly asleep beneath the thick white blanket of clouds below. Every once in a while a patch of shimmering blue ocean or a peek of the big island of Hawaii to the south appeared before hiding beneath the clouds.

The crater, once again, reminded her of a pastel drawing with the textures and smooth transitions of color. To the north, at the lowest portion of the crater, at a place called the Ko'olau Gap, clouds slowly spilled over the edge and moved into the crater only to evaporate before they made their way very far in.

"Everyone ready?" Alexander asked.

There were nods and yeses and one enthusiastic "Ready!" from Anela.

The little girl gripped Viki's hand and whispered a thank you as they headed down the trail.

From a distance it might look like a pastel drawing, but up close it was different. Cinders, it was all cinders, the small jagged rocks evidence of when this volcano, that they were walking into, was active.

Not far to the south on the big island of Hawaii there was an active volcano. Viki felt the earth as she walked down the trail. It felt primal and alive, as if only napping briefly.

Viki enjoyed the silence, hearing only the wind and the crunch of their shoes on the trail. She was locked in her own thoughts and guessed the rest probably were too. Alexander had told them on the drive up that Mark had accepted her contract, and he would be returning to Hawaii late that night. He expected to be drawn tomorrow evening.

"Have you been down here before?" Viki asked Tim after they had left the rim of the crater behind. It was a friendly question to ask. Taking him at his word, she was.

"Yes," he said. "But not for years. Not since I was a kid with my parents."

"It reminds me a bit of the Grand Canyon, only..." She was at a loss for the words. "I mean it's big like the Grand Canyon, and beautiful, but less complicated, more primal. It doesn't have all the layers the canyon has."

Tim nodded. "Tess and I did a tour of the southwest for our honeymoon. We went to the canyon and hiked in a bit."

"It is spectacular," Viki offered. "I've been down to the bottom a few times."

Their conversation continued in that vein—friendly and companionable—but it also seemed hollow to Viki. What weren't they talking about? And was that the kind of things that friends talked about?

CHAPTER 25

In the morning, Viki took her usual walk along the beach, but it was not a usual day. Late the previous night she had heard the return of Mark Kosov.

Today she would draw a living man. No, today was not normal at all.

She stopped on Kamaole III briefly and spoke with Howard who doffed his hat to her as an addition to their bird-like greeting.

"What's that about, Howard?" she asked.

"Seems only appropriate," he said with a small twitch of his lips.

"Appropriate? Why?"

Howard's lips twitched again as he straightened his hat. "The beach is always brighter with your presence." With that, Howard resumed his walk.

Viki thought there was something more, but didn't have time for anything more than a shouted, "Thank you!"

On the piece of land between the two beaches, Viki looked for Tim and Anela. It took a bit longer than usual because of the lack of movement. It appeared that today was sand castle day.

Viki took a deep breath and trotted down the little hill onto the beach. When she got close, Anela spotted her and ran to her, giving her a hug.

"Come see," the girl said as she took Viki's hand and pulled her forth.

The structure Anela had been working on was not a sand castle, but a sand volcano. The large mound of sand had a deep bowl shape very much like the crater they had just hiked.

"Haleakala," Viki said. "That is beautiful, Anela."

"Daddy helped too." Tim smiled at her from his sitting position as he packed wet sand in. "Do you want to help, Miss Viki?"

With a girlish nod of her head, Viki sat and began adding sand as directed by Anela.

After a time, Viki asked, "Wait, it's Sunday. Why aren't you with your grandparents, Anela?"

"Going later," Anela said, intent on her project.

"She's going to spend a few days with them this week. I need to be free for business." When he said "business," his eyebrow raised and he nodded at Viki. "So, I get a rare Sunday morning with my angel."

Viki felt her heart beating in her chest, doing her best to cover it by keeping her head down and patting the sand. When she felt calmer, she said, "Thank you, Tim. I really appreciate you being there for this."

"Of course."

When Anela was off with her bucket getting more water from the ocean, Viki asked, "How is she doing with her mom?"

"Still talking to her, all the time. She draws her every morning and talks to the picture throughout the day."

"Picture?"

Tim nodded. "She draws her upside down, the same way you did, from the same picture you did."

"Does it..." Viki said.

"Come alive? No... I... Well, I don't know. I am not touching it. But, how could she?"

Viki shrugged. "I'm sure it's not that. She's just a girl who draws and talks to her dead mother. Completely normal. Nothing to worry about," Viki ended with a smile.

Tim rubbed his chin with his hand leaving a trail of wet sand. "Your gift. It is passed from mother to daughter, right?"

Viki ignored the question, reaching out and brushing the sand off Tim's chin. She wanted to touch him and assured herself it was something a friend would do.

As she pulled her hand away, Tim grabbed it, holding it tightly. "She can't have your gift, can she?" His eyes were wide.

"Tim, I..." Viki became caught between the feeling of his warm hand and his wild eyes. "I don't think so. I don't know. There's no rule book or anything."

Locked in conversation, they hadn't noticed Anela return. She carefully put her bucket down and patted her father's hand which still held Viki's tightly. "Mama said that you would be nice to Viki. Mama knows things."

Tim let go of Viki's hand, his hand going again to his chin and leaving another trail of sand. Viki wanted to wipe it off again but didn't have a chance.

Tim surged to his feet. "We have to go, Anela. Get your things."

"But Daddy, we are not done making Haleakala."

"No, Anela!" he said, his voice rising. He turned to Viki and added, "I'll come by the Kosov house at six, right?"

~~~

Viki sat there for some minutes staring at the sand volcano. She went over in her mind what had happened, trying to sort it out. Was Tim actually afraid that his daughter might have her gift? Should a parent be afraid that a child could talk to the dead?

Viki laughed as she stood, brushing herself off. The laughter was a little too loud, a little too high pitched. It caused some people to stare at her.

"Of course!" she said aloud. Of course a parent should be scared if their child could do what Viki could do. If their child was a freak. Viki's own mother was terrified of the gift, so much so that she rejected it herself and did everything she could to get her daughter to turn her back on it.

Of course.

The fractured view she had been having of Tim suddenly came together. His fears were clear and apparent. The man guarded his daughter when they were at the ocean because he had lost so much to it. He kept Viki at arm's length to protect himself and his daughter. He freaked at the first hint that his daughter might be exceptional in a way that was different and frightening, because he was a father being protective of his daughter.

"Of course!" she shouted again as her fist rose to the sky. "Of course!" She drew stares and mutters this time, but she didn't care. She was a freak and she knew it. While it hurt to be reminded of it, it was nothing new.

Men weren't complicated, not once you understood what they feared, what their wound was.

Pain avoidance, pure and simple. Nothing to it.

Viki's stride quickened to a trot and then a run as she kicked up sand. There was energy burning through her that had to be expressed. She couldn't be still, she couldn't be placid, she had to move.

She ran down the beach, over the little hill to Kamaole III, up onto the lava cliffs, past the Kihei boat ramp, past the hotel and to the beach on which Mark Kosov's house sat.

She pushed hard as she ran, letting the low elevation oxygen power her. She pushed back the pain, she wasn't much of a runner, and kept going. She pushed down thoughts of how difficult it was to be different, how horrible it was not to be understood, and ran. She pulled up her mental image of Tim and found the part of her that had a crush on him. That little girl inside that drew "Tim + Viki" in a heart, and she tore that image up. Her hands rising in the air as she ran to discard the confetti of her childish dream. She imagined the pieces of that mental image floating to the ground and disintegrating as they landed on the sand.

When she got to Mark Kosov's house, her body was wet with sweat and her legs and lungs burned, but she kept going. She couldn't stop. If she stopped she would cry, and she didn't want to cry. She wanted to leave and not look back, have her feet carry her far enough away that she didn't need to deal with these things anymore. Anything but crying, not this time.

She kept running down the beach past the expensive houses until she came to the luxury communities that just felt wrong to her. Without stopping she turned around and ran back to Mark Kosov's house. She wanted to keep going but was spent when she got there. She went through the gate, threw herself on the cool green grass and stared up at the blue sky framed in palm trees.

Her breath came in ragged gasps as she began to laugh. It was a high-pitched, manic laughter interspersed with her having to suck air into her lungs. It was all too much. Drawing the living. Silly crushes. A trip to the hospital. A heart condition.

She had stepped out of her comfort zone and wanted nothing more than to crawl back in. She didn't need change in her life. Or adventure. She wished she hadn't left Sedona, had said no to the hand of fate moving her along.

Viki was not sure how long it lasted, but her face was wet with tears and her belly ached when she felt the touch and heard the voice.

"Are you okay, Ms. Dobos?" Alexander asked, his voice and touch gentle.

Viki looked at him and nodded as the laughter continued to escape her.

"Can I get you something?" His brown eyes were kind and he was clearly worried. It wasn't hard to see why with a sweat-covered woman laughing uncontrollably in his backyard.

Viki tried to sit up but felt very light-headed, which scared her and ended the laughter. Her heart condition and the doctor's stern words to "avoid dehydration at all costs" came rushing back to her as she realized she had forgotten to take her bag with her water bottle with her.

Her eyes wide, she looked at Alexander and said, "Juice."

CHAPTER 26

Viki sat up on the lanai watching the ocean. The pineapple juice and coconut water drink that Alexander had brought her had revived her enough to come inside. But now, she felt like a limp rag, drained and worn out.

She was grateful for the insight about Tim, grateful to have let go of any expectations there. But—

She sighed and poked at the bagel and fruit Alexander had brought her for breakfast. Even though she knew what she did was unusual, strange, it still hurt to see how it could engender fear.

She looked inside to the transforming living room. Most of the furniture had been cleared and in the middle of the room was a hospital bed next to the cardiac monitor that would track Mark's vitals as she drew him.

And freak though she may be, she was about to do one of the freakiest things she would ever do voluntarily. And she was doing it for money.

She sighed again and pushed at the soft flesh of a papaya slice, sliding it around on her plate, bumping it against the pineapple and cantaloupe.

Money wasn't enough. Money shouldn't be enough, but she had committed herself to this path, and *that* was enough.

She heard the footfalls behind her but didn't turn until she heard Reg. "What's new, V?"

She took a deep breath, wishing to expel a sarcastic zinger, but instead all that rang out was another round of manic laughter. After the laughter ended, she told Reg everything while he ate the remains of her breakfast. When her tale was over, Reg didn't say a word; he just stood and pulled her into a big bear hug.

In his arms she couldn't laugh any more, but cried. She felt silly and irrational. It's not like what she had been through seemed worthy of crying. A rich man wanting her to do something risky and forbidden. A kind man she was attracted to that she had trouble connecting with. A gift that evoked strong reactions whether it be desire, curiosity, or fear. A heart condition she never knew she had. Her mind said there was no need to cry, but clearly it was out of touch with her emotions. So she cried until her head rested on a wet spot on Reg's shoulder.

When she was done, she took the cloth napkin from the table, blew her nose, and wiped off her face.

"Better?" Reg asked.

Viki nodded slowly.

"What do you need, hon?"

"Nothing," she said as she rose onto her tiptoes and kissed the big man on his cheek. "Thanks, Reg. Sleep, I just need to sleep."

She went downstairs to her room, closed the door, crawled under the blankets, and slept. And while she slept she dreamed, dreamed of her mother.

~ ~ ~

When Viki was eleven, when she had first successfully drawn the dead, and after she came home from the visit to her grandmother's, she felt sick. Her stomach was tight and she just kept crying.

Her cousin Sandy had come alive on the paper. Her cousin Sandy, dead six months from leukemia. Her cousin Sandy, who had lived five blocks away and was one of Viki's best friends.

Sandy didn't say much, except that she didn't want Viki to be sad, and she was having fun being a ghost. She could go anywhere, do anything, and never had to bother with messy things like eating.

Her mother, her long brown hair pulled into a tight ponytail, her dark brown eyes piercing and bright, had asked Viki what was wrong.

"It's my stomach," she had said. "I think I ate something bad at Gran's."

Her mother nodded her head, as if she weren't surprised, and promptly put Viki to bed.

Viki lay there looking around her room. Was Sandy there? Was Sandy watching her? Why was Sandy a ghost? Why hadn't she gone to heaven?

Sleep eluded the girl and after her mother went to bed, and the house was dark and quiet, she got up, got out the paper and pastels that her grandmother had given her, and she drew.

She drew Sandy, just like she had the previous day under her grandmother's watchful gaze. She drew swiftly allowing her small hands to find the right pastels, referencing the small Polaroid of her cousin she had taken down from her corkboard. It showed a smiling Sandy standing in front of a pool the summer before she got sick.

After the drawing was done, she leaned over the paper and blew on it.

Sandy's eyes closed, and then blinked slowly as the image of the blue-eyed girl came to life.

"V-girl," Sandy said with a small smile.

"Where are you?" Viki whispered. "I miss you."

"I'm at my house," Sandy said. "My parents, they are so sad. They keep... they just keep crying."

"Then I will go," Viki said, "I will go draw you for them. Then you can talk to them and tell them you are all right."

"But, your mother..."

Viki frowned, her mother would never let her do it. She had, of course, shared with her favorite cousin what her grandmother could do, what she was learning to do. "Do your parents know what Gran can do?" Sandy was her cousin on her father's side, not her mother's.

Sandy shook her head. "No, Viki. I never told anyone your secret."

"Well," Viki said with a sigh, "I will tell them. I will draw you for them, I—"

The paper Viki held with her left hand was ripped from her grasp as her mother shouted, "No!"

So engrossed in what she was doing, she hadn't heard her mother come in. Her mother stood over her and ripped the paper up, tears running down her face.

"Mom!" Viki shouted, reaching for the paper.

"No!" her mother shouted again. "No... you can't be, you can't have the..." her mother's voice trailed off as she sunk to the carpet.

Viki's anger turned to fear as she saw her mother

continue to rip the paper into smaller and smaller pieces. "What's wrong, Mom? What's wrong?"

"The curse, you have the family curse. I never wanted that for you. I never wanted you to have to live a life filled with death."

"Curse? What Gran can do, what I can do, is a gift. I was talking to Sandy, I miss Sandy. Her parents need to talk to her too. Her parents need me."

Her mother's crying stopped and her eyes grew hard. She rose to her feet, took the trashcan from next to Viki's desk and swept the paper and the pastels into it.

"Mother!" Viki shouted, trying to stop her, but her mother pushed her away so hard that she stumbled back and her head crashed into the wall. Viki fell to the floor and started crying. She watched as her mother took the crayons and the colored pencils and all her drawings, and one by one put them in the trashcan.

Viki had pushed herself up into a sitting position and was holding her head, fighting back dizziness. "You can't do this!" she shouted. "Those are mine. I have to draw, Mom. I have to!"

Viki's pleas went unheard. After her mother was done and before she left the room, she squatted in front of her daughter and gently probed her head.

"You've got a bit of a lump, but you'll be okay." Her voice was kind. "I'm sorry I pushed you, Viki. I shouldn't have done that. But you can't, you can't draw anymore."

Viki's crying intensified. "Why? I don't understand."

Her mother smiled briefly and wiped the tears from Viki's cheeks. "Life is hard, my dear. You don't understand, but you will someday. Life is hard, and it's harder, much harder, when you are different."

"But Gran helps people. I can do it too, I can help people."

"Maybe," her mother said, an edge creeping into her voice. "Maybe you can help some people, but at what cost to you? What cost to your life?"

"But I want to help people," Viki pleaded.

"No. My daughter is no freak. My daughter is not a freak." With that, her mother took the trashcan and left.

Viki lay there for quite some time as the tears flowed down her cheeks.

CHAPTER 27

Viki ran into Mark in the kitchen.

After waking up from her dream-memory of her mother, she had lain in bed not daring to move for quite some time. She wanted to run away, to hide from what was happening, but it was no use. She was committed to the path she was on.

With a sigh, she got up and did yoga, meditated, and showered. She moved slowly, carefully, as if a sudden move might fracture the façade of her calmness.

It was 3 p.m. and hunger had driven her to the kitchen. She could hear a commotion on the floor above, where they must have been preparing for the evening, and that was the last place she wanted to be.

With her head in the refrigerator, she heard Mark say, "Anything good in there?"

Her heart skipped a beat, but she tried to hide it as she pulled out containers with leftovers and put them on the counter. "Well," she began, "we've got cold chicken, fruit, hummus, and some baklava."

"That'll do," he said with a small smile as he pulled out

plates and utensils and started moving everything to the kitchen table.

Viki looked in cupboards until she found some corn chips and joined him at the table.

"I won't be able to eat later," she said, feeling she needed to explain her kitchen raid.

"Me neither," Mark said, looking nervous.

Viki laughed, it was just a brief bark, like an unexpected gust of wind on a calm day. She was relieved that he was nervous, it made her feel better. "You look better." His skin had some color, his eyes were brighter.

He nodded. "The treatments."

"What kind?" Viki asked as she loaded her plate.

"The clinic focused on what goes in and what comes out. Getting nutrition in and getting toxins out. So, stuff like fresh juice and IV fluids going in, and enemas and colonics getting things out."

They ate for a while in companionable silence. There was only the muffled noise from upstairs, the clink of forks against plates, and the soft sound of chewing.

"So," Mark said as he pushed his plate away, "are you ready for this?"

Viki met his blue eyes and shrugged her shoulders. "I guess. I can't say I am completely comfortable with it."

"Understood. Thank you for doing this, I really am grateful."

Viki paused. The question she wanted to ask was like a weight pressing down on her. She couldn't ignore it and couldn't think of anything else, so she asked. "Why are you doing this, Mark? You never told me the real reason."

Mark's lips twitched briefly into a smile before returning

to their normal straight line. "Let's get through this evening's session," Mark said as he rose, "shall we?"

Viki wanted to insist that he tell her the reason. But, after everything that had happened, she didn't feel like she could. She nodded weakly.

He retrieved his cane and left the kitchen. With a sigh, she got up and put everything away.

~ ~ ~

At 5:45 p.m., Viki left her room and slowly walked upstairs to the great room. She had donned her full Madam Valarka garb—makeup, hoop earrings, flowing silk draped on her body in layers. She felt like she needed everything at her disposal for this drawing, and the clothing brought her tradition, her training, and most importantly, memories of her grandmother close.

Her arrival drew stares and surprise, but she ignored it. In the room was Mark, a doctor and nurse, Reg, and Alexander. She felt a brief twinge that Tim wasn't there. Their last exchange hadn't been pleasant, but she still wanted him there. She let her thoughts of Tim go, and went about her business.

She lit a sage bundle and began walking around the room from the door she entered in a clockwise fashion. She waved the feathers and spread the smoke, saying prayers, preparing the space.

Out of the corner of her eye, she saw Reg quietly go to Mark and Alexander. To explain what she was doing, she presumed.

The ritual calmed and centered her, pushing her fear down, lowering the volume of its insistent pleas.

She then smudged Reg, who came to her in the center of

the room. She used the feathers as a fan to push the sage smoke up and down the front of his body and then his back. He then prompted everyone else to go to the center of the room and allow Viki to smudge them.

As she was smudging Mark, the doorbell rang and Alexander left. When she was done with Mark, Tim was there waiting to be smudged. She smiled. Reg had worked the room so well that she hadn't had to say a word.

After she smudged Tim, she whispered, "Thank you for coming." To which he answered with a small smile.

The procedure was not anything her grandmother had taught her, but was something she had picked up in Sedona. The smudging was borrowed from Native American traditions. She used it because, in situations like this, it worked. She had a room full of nervous people—herself included—and needed to calm and focus everyone.

The hospital bed stood in the center of the room, occupying the space where a couch had once been. Mark, dressed in what looked like silk pajamas, sat on the bed. It was positioned so that Mark was sitting mostly upright. To the left of the bed was a machine that monitored his vitals. His heart rate looked a little high to Viki—he must be nervous.

Standing next to the equipment, the nurse looked alert. Sitting next to her was a bored looking doctor.

To the right of the bed was a small table and three chairs. The table was positioned so that Mark would be able to watch the drawing process.

There was a camera set up on one end of the room, recording the proceedings.

Viki took the chair facing Mark, while Alexander and Reg took the seats opposite to her.

The table, festooned with Viki's silks, had her drawing

case on top of it, open and ready. A blank piece of paper and an eight-by-ten color picture of Mark sat next to her case.

Before starting, she pulled out her cards and shuffled them thoroughly.

Mark's eyebrow rose at this and he asked, "Is that really necessary?"

Viki smiled but didn't say anything. This was her space now, her work, she would do it her way.

She walked to Mark and spread the cards on the flat part of the bed next to him. "Pick a card that will tell us something of the journey we are about to embark on."

Mark looked at the cards, his hand darting out quickly and snatching one, handing it to Viki.

Viki returned the single card to the table before sweeping up the deck and returning them to her case and sitting. She turned the card over and heard several gasps in the room.

Alexander sucked in air as his brow furrowed, Reg exhaled in a low whistle, and Mark said, "What? You..."

The card depicted a corpse hanging from a tree, a rope around its neck. It was a nighttime scene with a full moon peeking out from behind a gnarled, bare tree. At the bottom of the card, in white, was the word "Death."

"Death," she began. "This card signifies an ending of some sort. Most of the time it does not indicate a physical death, but more of a spiritual death. The dying of part of ourselves, or part of our way of being in the world. But, given what we are about to do today, it—"

"What is the meaning of this?" Mark said, his voice choked. "What are you trying to do?"

"Excuse me, Mr. Kosov?" Viki said, intentionally being formal with the use of his name. He was just a regular client now.

"You... You..." he sputtered, "You did that intentionally. You are trying to dissuade me from this. You are trying to scare me."

"I am sorry you feel that way," she said as she picked up the card, added it to the deck in the case, closed the case, locked it, returned the little key to her locket, and stood. "I am prepared to draw you, Mr. Kosov, right now. But only if I have your respect and trust. What we are to do requires it. That is the card you drew from the deck. I did not stack the deck or manipulate this in any way." Viki picked up the case and headed for the stairs that led down to her room.

Behind her she heard the fuming of Mark Kosov, and the interjections of Reg, but she ignored it. She was Madam Valarka, she had a gift, and she did things her way or she didn't do them.

CHAPTER 28

It didn't take long. About fifteen minutes later while Viki sat in her room meditating, a soft knock came on the door. Before she could answer, Reg poked his head in and said, "We're ready."

"Good," she said, rising and picking up her case.

Reg held up his hand, "I'm going back in, give it five minutes and then come up. Let them sweat a little."

Viki smiled and sat back down. Reg had a theatrical streak that Viki trusted, or maybe he just knew that she needed more time. It would do them good to have to wait for her. She closed her eyes and focused on her breath. She heard the doubts and fears rumbling through her head.

What if he does die?

It is forbidden to draw the living.

My daughter is not a freak.

She didn't try to chase them away or deny them. She knew that would do no good. She just turned her attention to her breath, focusing only on her breath, not letting her fears and doubts dominate.

When she returned to the room, everyone was quiet

and all eyes were on her. She placed her case on the table, unlocked it, opened it up, removing the deck of cards, and shuffled them thoroughly.

"Do we have to—" Mark began before cutting himself off. Viki caught Reg grinning.

Viki spread the cards on the bed as before, and this time Mark stared at the cards for a time before picking one. Instead of handing it to Viki right away, he looked at it first. "The Fool."

He sucked in air and was clearly about to say something when Viki stepped away from the bed and said. "Go ahead, Mr. Kosov, examine the cards. There is no trickery. That is the card you pulled."

Mark picked up a dozen or so cards before nodding to Viki who swept the cards up and returned to the table.

She placed the Fool card in front of her and said, "The Fool represents innocence, going forward on a path without knowing where that path is leading."

Viki nodded before continuing. "This card tempers the message of the Death card. We are heading into change, change where nothing will be the same, and we are doing it in innocence, with the exuberance of the Fool." Viki looked up at Mark whose expression was inscrutable. "Are you ready to proceed?" she asked.

Mark answered with a single sharp nod.

With a deep breath, Viki began drawing. First sketching the blue eyes and the outline of his face. His narrow nose. His thin, but expressive lips. His long face and narrow chin. His short grey hair, and his well-manicured goatee.

All thoughts of past or present, worries or hopes, were gone as Viki drew. She slid into the well-worn routine of her work, a routine where she was present to the drawing and the energies she was gathering and little else.

When the drawing was done, when the eyes were perfect, Viki indicated for Alexander and Reg to put their left hands on the bottom of the paper as she put her left hand on the top. She inhaled deeply, gathering the energies that had built, and gently blew on the paper.

The image dimensionalized, the eyes widened, a look of surprise as if he were gasping for air that wasn't there. Just as the drawing sprang to life, a sharp insistent tone came from the monitor and the nurse said, "Cardiac arrest."

"Shit!" the doctor said, knocking his chair over in his haste to rise. "Get the crash cart!"

Viki's eyes went from the drawing to Mark unconscious on the bed and back to the drawing.

The drawn Mark's mouth was still agape, his eyes full of fear while he seemed to struggle for breath.

Withdrawing her hand from the drawing, she broke the energy of the connection and pulled the drawing out from under the hands of the shocked Alexander and Reg.

As she did, she saw Mark's eyes and mouth fly open as he sucked air into his lungs. The straight-line on the monitor was replaced by the usual peaks and valleys of a beating heart.

CHAPTER 29

The silence in the room was thick and heavy, as if a fog had rolled in. All Viki could hear was the sound of the waves outside and her own heart clanging in her head. Thump, thump, thump... She loosened her grip on the drawing of Mark Kosov and slowly put it down, not sure what else to do.

Reg pushed his chair back, the sound of it sliding on the floor seemed loud in the silent room. He stood and said, "Well, who's for a drink?" Talk came rushing back in like water in a sinking ship. "I know I need one," he continued. "Alex, do you mind helping me?"

Alexander slowly nodded, his chair scraping against the floor as he pushed it back and stood up.

"Something strong," Reg said. "I bet you have some fine whiskey around here."

The spell broken, Viki went about her usual cleanup activity. The doctor and the nurse talked quietly among themselves while they examined Mark. And Tim, licking his pale lips, said, "I'm going to see if I can help with those drinks."

Viki marveled at how calm her mind was. She had so

dreaded doing this that the reality of it was not as bad as she thought it would be. She was relieved and a bit hopeful that this was over.

As she worked, she glanced up periodically at Mark while the doctor and nurse examined him. At one point Mark's blue eyes met Viki's hazel, and she knew that it wasn't over. The dread she had been feeling came rushing back.

"Here, V, drink this," Reg said, handing her a small glass with a translucent mahogany liquid in it that reminded her of her grandmother's eyes.

She took a sip, nodding to Reg in thanks, and welcoming the burning sensation that slid down her throat into her belly, bringing with it warmth.

She picked up her case and went to Tim who had handed drinks to Mark, the doctor, and the nurse.

"Can we talk?" Without looking back she left and went down to her room.

~~~

"He's going to want to do this again," Viki said, her voice flat. She took another sip of the whiskey.

Tim nodded, sipping his own drink. "Are you willing?"

She nodded and said, "Yes, but not until tomorrow, and not unless he tells me why he is doing this. He has a specific reason, beyond glimpsing the afterlife, that he wants to do this. He's been avoiding tell me, and I'm done with that."

"Okay," Tim said slowly. "Why do you want know this? Does it matter?"

"It does. This is wrong. I should never draw the living. Whatever is driving him, whatever that need of his that is so palpable, knowing it will help me understand him, and understand why."

"Okay, got it. I'll handle the negotiations."

Viki smiled. "Thank you, Tim. It means a lot to me that you are here. That you are my lawyer and... and my friend."

Tim gave her a small smile and nod before leaving the room. Viki sat on the bed, downing the rest of her drink and wishing she had more.

~~~

Tim had come back twenty minutes later and told her that Mark had agreed to her terms and asked her to meet him for breakfast at 8 a.m.

That left Viki with time on her hands. Too much time.

She thought of going to find Reg, he would be a good distraction, but didn't. He would be too much of a distraction, and his form of distraction would probably involve too much alcohol. She needed to remain clear.

Unsure of what to do, she found herself on the beach walking north—her usual route, but at night instead of day. The moon was up and she had found a flashlight in her bedroom. The beach was much like it was in the early morning, but with fewer people and the focus on romance not exercise.

She enjoyed the walk, the crashing of the waves lulling her troubled mind. She just kept walking and soon found herself passing the Kihei boat ramp. This was not her favorite part of the walk. It stunk of urine, and was often filled with locals who seemed to look on tourists as interlopers.

Tonight as she passed she saw a group of men in the dark under the trees smoking and drinking. One of them said, "Hey, pretty lady. Wanna party?"

Her heart and her pace quickened. She didn't reply or

look back. She felt fear, something she hadn't felt on the beach before.

Her feet carried her until she found herself on Kamaole Beach II, right below where Tim and Anela lived. She looked up and saw Tim leaning against the railing of his lanai. She wasn't sure, but she thought she saw the look of recognition on his face and waved. It was the friendly thing to do after all.

Much to her surprise, he waved back and shouted, "Come on up."

Her heart beat hard in her chest again. "Take him at his word, treat him as a friend," she heard Reg's words again. Except her heartbeat was not how her heart beat for a friend. She made her way up the beach, up the stairs to the grounds of the Hale Pau Hana, through the little garden courtyard, up the stairs to the second floor, down the length of the building, to the third floor stairs and to Tim's door.

Her fist poised, she paused. She worried that things would go as they had been, that she would feel herself getting closer to him only to be pushed away. She wasn't sure if she was up for that. She lowered her hand but didn't move away. She was locked in indecision, just standing there, when the door opened.

"There you are," Tim said with a smile. "I was wondering what was taking you so long. Come on in."

He held the door wide and she found herself walking in and thanking him. She seemed to be observing herself do this, but not actually doing it, somehow detached from what was happening.

"Would you like a drink? Are you hungry?"

Viki's feet had carried her to the lanai, to the position Tim was at when she saw him.

She heard herself say, "Yes, now that you mention it, I'm starving. I haven't eaten for hours."

"Great. I'm just finishing up dinner. I made enough for two—Anela's not here, just automatic I guess—so you are in luck. Make yourself at home, I won't be long."

She heard him leave the lanai and stood there, watching the couples below on the beach. She focused on her breath, letting everything else go. Slowly the feeling of disconnection faded and by the time Tim came with grilled fish, steamed potatoes, green beans, and white wine, she was feeling more herself.

They ate in silence until Tim pushed his plate back. "So, do you want to talk about it?"

Viki's heart leapt into her throat and she felt herself becoming distant again. Did he want to talk about their odd hot and cold friendship? Or about what had just happened at Mark Kosov's house?

In her mind's eye she saw herself shrug off the question and lean over and kiss him. That would be just the distraction she needed.

But that is not what she did. Instead she said, "Absolutely, you start."

He shrugged. "Well, it's what you feared would happen, isn't it? Him dying when you drew him."

Viki let the air out of her lungs, surprised to find that she had been holding her breath. He wanted to talk about Mark. "Yes, although I wasn't sure what to expect."

So, they talked about the evening, about what Viki did, and it helped. With the conversation and the wine, she felt herself unwinding and relaxing.

After the conversation had died down, Mark got up and started gathering the dishes. "I'll help," Viki said, quickly standing just as he was leaning in to get her plate. There was a sharp knock as their heads collided. Again.

"Ow!" Tim said, straightening and holding his forehead.

"I'm sorry," Viki said. "Let me see." She took his hand and pulled him into the living room where the light was better. She stood on her tiptoes and had him lean down a bit so she could see his forehead. "Hmmm, it doesn't look too bad, but just in case..."

Viki leaned in closer to kiss his forehead. It was something a friend would do. It was playful. And she had finished several glasses of wine at the end of a very stressful incident.

Just as she moved in, he started to straighten up and her lips caught him on the nose.

"Oh! I'm sorry," she began, "I was aiming for—"

She didn't get a chance to finish; Tim's lips came down and met hers with surprising force. She rose further on her toes and met his force with her own. There were no thoughts of taking him at his word or acting like a friend. There were just lips.

She put her left hand to the back of his head and pressed him closer.

Tim abruptly pulled away and backed up a step, a look of surprise on his face. "I... We..." he stammered, his fingers briefly touching his wet lips.

"Oh shut up," Viki said, closing the space between them and pulling him down to her, their lips meeting again. She felt her body stirring as they kissed, the hormones pumping into her system, demanding action. She pushed him back until the couch was behind him. As they kissed, he slowly sat down and she straddled him, her hands starting to unbutton his shirt.

His hand pressed on the center of her chest forcing them to part. "Wait," he said, his breath coming fast and shallow.

"What is it, Tim?" Viki said, wiping her lips and staring at him.

"This... we..." He smiled shyly. "It's complicated."

Viki laughed and felt more of the tension she had been carrying all this time release. "Yeah it is," she agreed. "So what?"

Tim's mouth moved like he was chewing, but no words came out. Viki leaned in to kiss him again and he put his hand out, this time it connected with her breast and he withdrew it saying, "I'm sorry."

Viki took his hand and guided back it to her breast and held it there. His hand didn't move, but his mouth formed a silent "O." "I know it's complicated Tim," she said. "With what you and Anela and I just went through." She was referring to his dead wife that they had rescued from the bardo. "I know you have doubts about Anela's fascination with what I can do, and what kind of life that could lead her to."

Tim nodded, mutely.

"But tonight, Tim, I need you, and I think you need me. I need to feel. I am sick of death, I need to feel alive."

"I... I haven't been with anyone since—"

"I know," Viki said as she leaned close, a smile playing on her lips. "I'll be gentle."

CHAPTER 30

Viki clutched Tim's hand tightly as they ran, giggles escaping her mouth. It wasn't the wine, it was a much stronger concoction running through her veins.

They had made it into the bedroom when Tim made an announcement, "I don't have any protection."

"What?" Viki had asked, but then added, "Of course you don't. Where is the closest place we can get some?"

"The ABC store is just a few blocks down the street."

They had quickly dressed before starting their mad giggling dash.

Viki felt young, like a teenager sneaking out in the night to buy condoms with her boyfriend. She felt gratitude wash over her at how utterly normal and how utterly exciting it was.

In the ABC store, they stood holding hands in front of the rack of condoms, while a ukulele accompanied by a sweet male voice played on the sound system. "Wow," Tim said.

"There are a lot of choices," Viki added.

"What do you prefer?" Tim asked with a crooked grin.

Viki shrugged.

"Ladies choice, I insist."

"How gallant," Viki said as she grabbed a box randomly.

On the way out, they stopped by the wine section and Viki grabbed a bottle of Up Country Gold. "After all," she said with a grin, "I am sampling the best Hawaii has to offer tonight."

Tim's face was a frozen mask of shock for a moment, and Viki feared she had spooked him. Then the mask broke and laughter came rumbling out.

He paid the cashier, and they laughed all the way back to his condo.

~~~

On the bed, their clothes discarded, they were exploring each other's bodies. The room was silent beyond the sound of crashing waves coming from the window and the sound of bodies finding each other.

"I can't believe you said that," Tim said, as he gently pushed her away.

"Huh?" Viki asked, pushing her hair out of eyes and looking at him. "What did I say?"

"You know. Sampling Hawaii's best."

"Really?" she said, sitting up on the bed. "I can't imagine you minded."

"It's not that I mind," he said, his hand stroking her thigh. "It's just that it's been a long time and now I kinda feel this pressure."

Viki smiled, as she crawled on top of him, her voice sultry, she said, "After two years, I bet there's some pressure."

Tim grinned but didn't laugh. "Seriously, I don't want to disappoint you."

"You're doing just fine," she assured him as her lips came down to meet his.

~~~

In the morning, Viki's cell phone chimed at 6:30 a.m. and woke her. She had set the alarm on it as a precaution. She didn't want to miss her meeting with Mark Kosov.

She turned the alarm off, rolled over, and stared at Tim. His face was slack in sleep, his eyes twitching underneath their lids. With him, she knew it was complicated. But, then again, it is always complicated.

Doubts rose in her mind. Had she been foolish to let their relationship progress? What would Tim be like today? Hot or cold, engaged or distant?

She invited the doubts to assail her.

He doesn't really care, he just wanted sex, like all men.

He is crazy about you and will follow you back to Sedona, upsetting the delicate balance of your life there.

Anela is the female in his life, and you can only ever get tiny slices of him.

He thinks you're crap in bed.

On and on it went. She gave them an airing, let them out. She knew if she didn't they would not abate. And with a nod of her head, ended the train of thought and turned her attention to the day before her.

Not wanting to wake Tim, she quietly dressed, let herself out of the condo, and headed south along the beach to Mark Kosov's house.

CHAPTER 31

"I guess I should tell you," Mark said as he pushed back his plate and picked up his coffee cup.

Viki nodded and smiled. She found herself smiling more than usual.

"Do you know much about my history?" Mark asked.

"A little. You went from wheat in Russia to high-tech in California, and then high-tech in Russia."

Mark nodded. "That's it. Well, I had a business partner for the first two legs of the journey. Michael Pelyovin. I met Michael at university and we hit it off. He was a gifted sales-man, a world-class bullshitter. He was the face of much of what we did, and I was the brains."

Viki nodded, noticing he labeled himself "the brains" without a hint of self-consciousness.

"When I saw the Internet bubble about to burst, I got out of the companies we had invested in, and decided to return to Russia. Michael did not believe the bubble would burst and lost almost everything. Our friendship did not survive that."

Mark went silent, staring into his coffee cup as he stirred in some cream.

"What does this have to do with me drawing you?" she asked.

Mark smiled, it was a small bitter thing. "He was on the island a month ago. He called me and we were going to meet. It seemed like it was time to put the past behind us. But we never did. He died in a car accident on the way to meet me."

Viki was paying very close attention to what he was saying and how she felt when he said it. She didn't think this was a lie, but it was clear that he was leaving something out. "You want to talk to him?" she asked.

Mark nodded, still staring into his coffee.

"Well, I don't have to draw you for that, I can draw him." She stood. "Let me get my things."

"No," Mark said his eyes rising to meet hers. "I need to have a private conversation with him. You see..." he trailed off, his brows furrowing. "You see, he knows some things that I need to know. That would help me before I die. I need to talk to him privately."

"Mark, my service is confidential. This must be business stuff. I doubt that I would even understand."

Mark nodded, "I know. I just want to... I don't know, I don't think I can do what I need to do through a piece of paper."

"Even so, how do you know you can find him? There generally are only a few minutes when I draw. He could be anywhere."

"Oh, he's here. Some things have been happening. Lights turn themselves on and off, and the TV in my bedroom turns itself on every night. I keep hearing his voice at the oddest times, but I can't tell what he is saying."

Viki sighed and slowly brought her hands together several times in a mock clap. She sat back down and said, "Very good, Mark. You almost had me."

"What? I am telling the truth."

"I know you are," she said, "and that is why I almost bought it. You are a practical man, Mark. You wouldn't go through all this *just* for a private conversation with your dead business partner. You would have had me sign a wicked non-disclosure agreement and had me draw him for you. It would have taken a couple of days tops. But that is not what we are doing."

Mark stared at her, his eyes wide. "I... You..." he stammered as his cheeks flushed red.

"I won't budge this time. If you want me to draw you again, I need the truth." Viki stood and left the lanai, leaving Mark Kosov there alone.

~~~

As Viki stared at the waves, her feet buried in the warm sand, Mark slowly and carefully sat next to her.

"I was telling you the truth about Michael. I really do think he has been hanging around, and I do have some sensitive things I want to talk to him about."

"I know," Viki said. She could feel the need he radiated, that he had radiated, since she came here. "But it's not enough."

"Why?"

She sighed, looking at him. He was looking thin and drawn; she suspected he wasn't sleeping much. "You're asking me to do something that I shouldn't do, something that might kill you. So I need more than just money or proving to you that there is an afterlife. Look, Mark, I want to be on your side, I want to help you, but I need to understand."

Mark rubbed his face with both hands, a soft groan escaping him. His ocean-blue eyes caught hers and she saw something she hadn't seen before. Fear. She didn't think it was fear of death or fear of failure, or any of the usual fears. This was something else.

She held his eyes as the waves crashed and people walked past, as the palm trees swayed, and the sun beat down on them. She didn't look away. If this was a child's staring contest, then so be it. She wouldn't budge, not this time.

When he finally looked away, they both sighed. She still didn't know what it was that he wasn't telling her, but she had compassion for whatever it was.

Whatever was causing his fear must be—

"I have a meeting," Mark said, looking at his watch. "There is still much to attend to. Let's continue this over lunch."

Viki helped Mark up and took his arm, like she had when they first met, covertly supporting him and helping him back to the grass and his cane.

CHAPTER 32

Viki heard the sound of power tools when she knocked on Tim's door, a loud grinding noise. The noise didn't stop, so she knocked louder. Still it didn't stop so she got out her cell phone and called him. After many rings the noise finally did end.

"Hi," Tim said, his voice neutral.

"Hi, umm... I had to meet Mark this morning and left you sleeping. I didn't want to wake you."

"Yeah. I knew about that. I figured that was where you were off to."

Viki walked away from the door and down the stairs. She didn't want him to know she was standing outside his door, she didn't want to appear pathetic or needy. "I've got a little time if you..."

"Well, you know, I am in the middle of some things this morning."

"Okay, okay, I just thought I'd take the chance," Viki said, trying to hide her disappointment.

"We're on for six, right?"

"Yeah, six," Viki said, relieved. "I really appreciate you showing up for these, Tim."

"My pleasure. Another voyage into the unknown. I wouldn't miss it."

When Viki hung up she felt the doubts assail her again. What was she, thirteen years old? Can't she just be straight forward? "Hi Tim, had a great time last night, hope we can do it again?" Instead she found herself stammering and talking about what didn't really matter and ignoring what did.

She let the doubts run rampant as she walked down the street to Kamaole Beach Park III and then down to the beach; she wasn't going to walk right in front of Tim's house after that call.

It was like opening Pandora's Box. She invited the doubts in, she let them ping around her head, she allowed the feelings of doubt, fear, and inadequacy to possess her. It was something her grandmother had taught her. "You can't ever get rid of those kinds of thoughts, my dear," she had said once after Viki had failed to make the cheerleading squad in high school. "You are part of the human race. Suppressing them only makes it worse. So let them out, invite them in for tea and tell them to do their worst. And after they've given you all they've got, thank them, turn your back on them, and get on with your life."

By the time she got to Mark Kosov's house, the chattering in her mind had become repetitive and boring. It was the same stuff it always was. She grabbed a towel and did some yoga on the grass.

~~~

Instead of lunch, Alexander ushered Viki into Mark Kosov's office. It was on the second floor of the house and was plain and large. The decorations were minimalistic. Hardwood floor covered by a large rug, with an abstract pattern in various shades of green, several brown leather couches on the rug, a glass desk with a laptop stacked high with papers, and a few bookshelves along the walls.

Mark sat behind the desk, a red pen in hand as he read the documents before him.

"Sorry about lunch," he said, looking up briefly. "I have a lot to get through today."

"No problem."

Mark took a sip of what looked like vegetable juice before looking up again. "Would you like some juice? Alexander is trying to feed me like they did at the clinic." Mark smiled at his butler, and Alexander looked down.

"If it's not a bother," Viki said to Alexander.

"Not at all, I'll be right back," the Englishman said as he left the office, closing the door behind him.

"Have a seat," Mark said, indicating the couches. "I'll be right with you."

Viki sat and studied the artwork hanging on the walls. It wasn't anything she recognized, but they looked like originals, and they looked expensive.

One featured a bleak landscape. A river wound through the right half of the canvas vanishing into the horizon, while the left half showed a rolling hill populated with some odd looking plants. In the foreground a larger plant rose above the rest, looking like some sort of thistle or a weed that had gone to seed.

A heavy grey sky filled the upper half of the canvas with a single bird in flight, barely discernible.

Viki found herself mesmerized by the piece, feeling it opening up as she viewed it, becoming no less bleak, but being somehow hopeful.

"Arkhip Kuindzhi," Mark said as he sat across from her.

"Excuse me?" she asked, pulling herself back to the present.

"Arkhip Kuindzhi. The name of the painter. It's called 'Dnepr in the morning.' Kuindzhi was a Russian landscape artist. He painted that one in 1881."

"It's beautiful," Viki said.

Mark nodded. "But not cheerful."

"No."

"So, how do you like the juice?" Mark asked.

Viki was surprised to see it on the table in front of her. She hadn't noticed Alexander come back in and leave again. She took a sip. She tasted carrots, celery, apple, and ginger. "It's good."

"I felt better at the clinic, so we're trying to reproduce that as much as we can here. There is still much to do." Mark gestured to his desk.

Viki smiled and nodded, sipping more of her juice. She wanted to hear what he had to say but didn't want to push him. "You are lucky to have Alexander."

Mark nodded. "I am."

The room grew quiet, and Viki felt herself pulled back into the painting. She felt calm and peaceful, as if she could fall asleep. And she might have, but Mark cleared his throat, pulling her back into the present. "It really is mesmerizing," she said as she moved herself so she could see Mark but not see the painting.

"It is."

"So, Mark, is it time?"

"I died once," he said. He then crossed himself and bowed his head briefly. "If you recall my history..."

Viki nodded.

"Then you can probably guess what kind of person I was."

"Focused, driven, uncompromising—"

"Yes. All that and more. I was ruthless, relentless, and left a lot of damage in my wake."

Viki nodded, encouraging him to continue.

"I also spent my money nearly as fast as I could make it. Women, parties, drugs. I was a walking stereotype." A wistful smile played on his lips as if he both regretted his past and missed it at the same time.

Studying his face, she could see it. She could see a younger man that was less deliberate, less in control, addictive. With his handsome features and ocean-blue eyes, she was sure he was quite the ladies' man in his day.

"It was fun breaking free. My country was breaking free from communism, embracing capitalism, and some of us went a bit crazy with that freedom. It was an intoxicating time." The smile as he remembered involved his whole face. Not the typically reserved Mark Kosov smile.

"You see," he added, "I've never been good at not working. Give me sixteen-hour days and I am steady as a rock—give me little to do and I am out of control. My lifestyle gave me plenty of sixteen-hour days, but it also gave me lots of free time between the startups, and way too much free time once I had 'made it.'" Mark sighed and drank some juice. "I got to be very fond of cocaine. I had the money, so I had lots of it. I loved it. It made me feel invincible, it made me feel powerful. And one night when I was living in Paris, I had too much, way too much."

Mark leaned forward and struggled to his feet, taking his cane and pacing in slow motion around the office, as if the memories he was sharing were forcing him into motion—as if the ghosts of his past would not let him rest.

"This was about twelve years ago. I was not so young but still stupid. I overdosed. I died. I went straight to hell."

Viki studied his face, a mask of pain and fear. His pacing increased, as much as it could with his cane, as he passed back in forth in front of "Dnepr in the Morning." The painting was a river somewhere in Russia, but it could have been the river Styx with its somber tone. It was the perfect companion to the tale he was telling.

Viki felt relief—she could tell he was finally opening up to her—and she felt compassion for this thing that haunted him, that was driving him.

"What happened that night, Mark?" Viki asked, prompting him to continue.

"I had rented a small villa just outside Paris. I had stocked it with booze and cocaine and invited many friends. I was celebrating. I had successfully gotten out of Silicon Valley in late 1999 and taken those funds and established a presence in Russia as an ISP. Being an Internet service provider was not sexy, but the Internet was expanding rapidly and everyone wanted in on it. I was making a lot of money—I wanted to have a lot of fun.

"It wasn't anything in particular, but I took too much. One moment I was feeling like the king of the world, the next I was on the floor in a pool of my own vomit. The next I was in hell."

"Hell? Why do you say hell?"

"Because it was. There were horrible creatures, demons. They were listing my sins one by one and torturing me. I was in a desolate landscape surrounded by fire and assaulted by the smell of sulphur. I was in hell." He crossed himself again.

"But they resuscitated you?" Viki asked gently.

Mark nodded. "Indeed. Alexander saved my life. He was with me back then and was sober. He never did that kind of thing. He did CPR, called an ambulance, and was by my side when I finally woke up." Mark came back around to the couch and sat heavily. "When I found myself alive, I vowed to change my life—to try to make a difference, to do anything so I didn't end up in hell when I died."

Viki was silent, watching Mark. He seemed deflated after his monologue, as if expressing what he did had taken all the energy out of him. He looked ill and weak and wan.

"Thank you, Mark. Thank you for telling me."

Mark nodded.

"I don't understand. Why couldn't you just come out and tell me why you wanted me to draw you in the first place?"

Mark shrugged and smiled, "I am a business man; I am not used to just laying my cards out on the table. Besides, this is not the type of thing you go around telling people. Saying it aloud is difficult. It... it makes it even more real."

"And are all the cards on the table now?"

Mark nodded, bit his lip, and looked down. "While it is true I would like to talk to my former business partner Michael, what I need to do is make sure that when I die I don't go to hell. I need to know now while there is, at least, a little time left." Mark paused, his head falling into his hands. "And... Well... I was afraid if I told you about this, if I listed my sins, you would refuse me."

Viki smiled gently. "You know, what you experienced was probably just the bardo, like was written about in the *Shuffled Off* book. It may not have really been hell."

Mark looked up at her, his eyes intense. "Does it really matter what it is? If I'm stuck there, does it matter what word you use to describe it?"

"It doesn't," Viki agreed. "My grandmother used to call it *'Beng Rarti.'* Devil's Night. Sometimes a soul gets lost, sometimes we can help them. Listen Mark, I will do everything I can to make sure that doesn't happen to you."

CHAPTER 33

Despite the sound of the waves, the silence in the room sat heavily. The seriousness of their endeavor had become crystal clear the last time Viki drew Mark. The doctor and nurse both stood, watching the equipment, the crash cart at the ready. Alexander, Viki, and Reg sat at the table. Tim stood next to the video camera, watching.

And Mark was asleep on the bed. The doctor had administered a light sedative to try to deal with the problem he had the first time. After much discussion, they theorized that seeing through his physical eyes and his spirit eyes at the same time had been too much of a shock to his system.

Viki took a deep breath, pulled out a blue pastel, began drawing the eyes, and let out a deep sigh. She heard the sigh echoed around the room from the other participants.

She suppressed a laugh at the collective sigh. She was glad some of the tension released, but laughter would not be appropriate. They were venturing into unknown territory and everyone needed to keep their wits about them.

The drawing flowed quickly and easily, and after the eyes were perfect, Viki took a deep breath, leaned down, and exhaled on the drawing.

The room was silent, all eyes on the drawing. One breath, two breaths, three breaths, and the pastel version of Mark Kosov blinked.

His eyes were wide with fear but different than before. His face somehow looked younger as he gazed up. Words with rolling r's, accentuated v's, and hard vowels streamed forth from his mouth in a rapid patter. "*Net, mama, ya ne bral koshel'ka dyadi Valenka. Ya by nikogda etogo ne sdelal...*"

"What is he saying?" Viki asked, to no one in particular.

"He's speaking Russian," Alexander said. "He is saying, 'No Mama, I did not steal Mr. Valenka's wallet. I wouldn't do that; I'm good boy, Mama. Please don't get the stick, please don't beat me. I didn't do it, Mama.'"

Viki could feel Alexander looking at her as the drawing of Mark continued to speak in a desperate Russian. She didn't look but did answer his unspoken question. "He's dreaming. Let's try to get his attention." Viki leaned closer to the drawing and spoke loudly, "Mark. Mark, it is Viki Dobos. You are dreaming, wake up, Mark."

Alexander spoke to him in Russian, "*Prosnis'*, Mark. *Eto son. Prosnis'.*"

Reg, whose hand was also on the drawing, just stared.

"I think he hears us," Alexander said, "but he is scared. He is saying, 'What are those voices, Mama? Do you hear the voices, they are calling my name. What, Mama? *Babaika?* No, the voices can't be him. That is just a fairy tale—he hasn't come for me. I'm a good boy, Mama. I'm a good boy, don't let him take me away.'"

They tried to reach him several more times, but Mark, in his dream, went from scared to terrified. "This isn't working," Viki said as she nodded to the two men across from her. They all withdrew their hands at the same time, and the troubled, child-like face of Mark Kosov faded back into a drawing.

~~~

Viki felt silly, and young, and awkward. She walked Tim out to his car after they had finished. The night was soft and warm with a sea-salt tang in the air.

"So, tomorrow?" Tim asked. He was shifting his feet as if anxious to go.

"It's early," Viki offered. "We could have dinner again."

Tim clenched his jaw, causing Viki's stomach to drop, and he looked at his watch. "Umm. I've got to go pick up Anela. Her grandparents can't keep her tonight. They have a thing early tomorrow."

Viki looked down at the cement driveway and her sandaled feet wondering what he meant. She feared that he no longer wanted her to be near his daughter. She took a deep breath and looked back up. "But, everyone's gotta eat." She felt stupid and pathetic. She was inviting herself to dinner. Her shame started to turn to anger.

Tim nodded. "True enough. But I have to drive upland a ways to get her and was going to grab something on the way."

"Oh," Viki answered, vowing never to appear so desperate to him again. "Well, good night then," she said curtly as she turned and started towards the door.

Just as she got to the door, he called, "Viki." Viki turned as he trotted to her. "Look, it's complicated."

She gave him a look that she hoped was both scathing

and ironic. It did seem to have an effect as he took half a step backwards.

"Umm..." he said, licking his lips. "Do you want to come along? We can stop at this food truck I know of on the way—they've got great coconut shrimp."

Viki wanted to say yes, to jump up and down like a teenager with a crush, but instead she said, "I don't understand you, Tim."

He shrugged and did a nose-wrinkling smile that made her smile in return. "Sorry. Tess knew me better than I know myself. I am out of practice with this."

"How about you just try talking. I know it's complicated, but I really like you, Tim, and I enjoyed being with you last night."

Tim smiled and looked down, red blossoming on his cheeks. "Me too." He looked up and added, "Okay, I'll just try talking. You can come, I'd love you to come, but Anela's been talking about you, about what you did for us. If you come, they're going to want you to draw Tess."

Revelation dawned on Viki's face as she began to see the motives behind his behavior. He was, in some strange way, trying to protect her. Or, was he trying to protect Anela from being around her gift? She wasn't sure. "Thank you," she said. "That's not so complicated. I would be happy to draw for them; let me get my kit."

On the drive up, Tim was a perfect gentleman. He called and talked to Anela's grandparents, telling them Viki was coming and that she was willing to draw Tess. He then turned into a tour guide, telling Viki about the area and answering all her questions. They didn't talk about their relationship, and she found herself wishing he would be less of a gentleman.

~~~

Hani and Jacob Kāne greeted her kindly, but their nervousness was palpable. Anela greeted her with a big hug and said, "Miss Viki, I missed you."

Viki felt her eyes moisten. "I have missed you too, Miss Anela." The girl's face sprouted a large smile at "Miss Anela."

"Mama is here," the girl said. "She wants me to tell you she is so grateful to you for doing this."

Viki squatted down so she was at eye level with Anela. "Good. That will make this easier. Tell her I am happy to do it."

Anela looked up and to her right and said, "She heard you. She also wanted to tell you to be patient with Daddy." Her eyebrows furrowed, and her face turned puzzled as she asked Viki, "Why should you be patient with Daddy?" She then looked up and to the right again. "Why should she be patient with Daddy?" After a moment, she said to the empty air, "I am not too young, Mama."

The niceties didn't last long and after drinking a full glass of water, and having a refill handy, Viki started drawing.

Hani and Jacob looked like all her clients—desperate, hopeful, nervous. They all crowded around a small, round wooden table. The table was set up in the small living room that had large windows facing west. Before Viki started, she had admired the view. The smattering of lights along Maui's western coast, and the silvery moon reflecting off the ocean far below.

They provided her with a different picture of Tess, an eight-by-ten close-up of a younger Tess with long, wet hair, a beaming face, and the ocean in the background. They told

Viki this was from a surf competition Tess participated in the summer after her junior year in college.

Viki had drawn Tess so many times she could have done it quickly. She knew Tess's face, she knew Tess's energy, she knew Tess was close, and at this point anything more than a sketch would have worked. But, she slowed herself. She wanted Hani and Jacob to have a memento, something to root their memories of this night on. So she did her best to accurately capture the young woman's face.

As the drawing progressed and the energies gathered, she could feel Tess's presence. She sensed it to the right of Anela and felt a chill go up her spine.

She didn't need to, but as she drew, she had Hani and Jacob talk about their daughter. Not for her drawing process but for them. She knew that after a traumatic death, or any death for that matter, what is focused on is often the end and the trauma of that ending. What needed to be focused on were the good times, the love, the wonderful memories.

"She first stood up on a board when she was five," Jacob said. "She had always loved watching the surfers and was so determined to do it herself. It was at Hanakao'o beach in October 1976." The man paused, rubbing his face, his fingers poking at his eyes. "I can't believe it was the water that took her. She loved the water, she respected the water."

"What was it about surfing that she so loved?" Viki asked, guiding them, as she did many times, back to the memories that needed cherishing.

"She was a tom-boy," her mother began, nodding her head slowly as her eyes watched the pastels travel on the page. "Anything a boy could do, she wanted to do better. Her cousin, Kyle, who was a few years older than her, had first stood on a board at six. She was determined to do it sooner than he had."

Jacob chuckled, "She was a competitive kid and fearless."

"Too fearless," Hani said. "She took too many chances. She died because she took too many chances."

Tim's face grew tight as he quietly said, "Please. I don't think Anela needs to hear this."

Anela's eyes were wide as she watched the adults.

"Of course, of course..." Hani said, wiping tears from her eyes. "Where were we?"

"When was her first surfing competition?" Viki asked.

And on it went as Viki guided the four of them to pleasant memories as she drew the portrait of their daughter/mother/wife.

When the time came, she put her left hand on the top of the drawing and had everyone else put their left hand on the closest edge of the drawing. She took a deep breath, focusing on the beautiful brown eyes of Tess Unger, and exhaled.

~~~

"Are you okay, honey?" Viki asked Anela. Tim had escorted her out of the room shortly after Tess came alive on the paper, the girl having closed her eyes and covered her ears with her hands.

Anela sat on her grandparents' bed, her hands tucked under her legs. She nodded and bit her lip. Tim sat next to her, his face drawn with concern.

"What happened?" Viki asked.

"It was too much," Anela said, her eyes wide. "I could see Mama standing next to me, and I could see her in the middle of the table in this rainbow light. And her voice echoed; it came from her and from the drawing."

"And that's why you covered your ears and closed your eyes?"

"Yes, but it didn't help."

"Why didn't it?" Viki asked.

"I could see my mama, and I could still hear her."

Viki's brow furrowed. "You saw her with your eyes closed?"

Anela nodded again. "I like it at night, when I go to sleep. I can see her watching over me after I close my eyes. But when you drew her, it hurt my head."

"Well we just won't draw her again, then," Viki said smiling and holding the girl's face. "Besides, you don't need me to draw to talk to your mama."

"Nope," Anela said.

"Is she here now?" Viki asked.

Anela shook her head. "She said she was tired and would be back after she slept." The girl's brow furrowed. "It's kind of funny, why would she need to sleep?"

"Angel," Tim interjected, "why don't you go tell your grandparents you're okay. They are worried."

Anela jumped off the bed and left the room.

"So?" Tim asked.

Viki studied his face—the worry hadn't left. "Are you asking me if she has the gift?"

"I am."

Viki shrugged weakly. "She has a gift, that much is clear. Whether it's the same gift as I have, I don't know. Whether she will outgrow it, again, I don't know."

"Outgrow it?" Tim asked.

"A lot of children see things when they are young but don't when they get older. I could see faeries when I was young, but I can't anymore."

"Faeries?" Tim asked, his jaw slack.

Viki laughed. "Relax, okay. Anela is fine, she's better than fine."

The look on Tim's face made it clear that what Viki had said hadn't made things any better.

CHAPTER 34

"Thank you," Tim said as he drove them back down towards the sea. "That meant a lot to Hani and Jacob."

"My pleasure," Viki said with a yawn, glancing at Anela who slept in the backseat. "I may join Anela there—it's been a long day."

"Feel free."

Viki turned on her phone with thoughts of Reg in her head. She had left so quickly she hadn't told him, or anyone else, where she was going.

Her phone beeped and displayed a text message, "Yo V, where B U? Boss wants you 4 bfast at 8."

Viki smiled and keyed in a reply, "Tell U later. Meet me at 6:30 4 a walk?"

She waited for the reply and laughed when it came in, "No way witch, try again."

"Meet me at noon for bfast?"

"That's my girl."

Viki put her phone away. She didn't like the silence, with only the noise of the car on the road and Anela's breathing in her sleep. It was too quiet for her, things needed to be said.

"Penny for your thoughts," she said.

"What?"

"'Penny for your thoughts,' you know, what are you thinking?"

"Do you really want to know?" he asked quietly.

"I do or I wouldn't have asked." Viki held her breath as she waited for his reply.

"Tess. Anela."

She nodded. He continued to be worried about Anela and the continued signs of her ability. And, of course he was thinking about his dead wife, he had just seen her. Viki could feel a twinge of jealousy but pushed it down. She gently poked him in the arm. "It's complicated."

Tim chuckled, "That it is."

Viki took a deep breath and spoke, the words tumbling out of her rapidly. "I just want you to know that I understand that. That my presence, our relationship, is not making that any simpler. I have only one request of you."

The car was silent for long enough that Viki's stomach tumbled, and she felt like it was going to fall out, as if she were standing on the edge of a high precipice. She felt the old longing for a cigarette latch on to her, and she fidgeted in her seat.

"What is it?" Tim finally asked.

"That you talk to me. That you tell me what you are feeling and thinking, at least in regards to me." Viki's hand came to her mouth after she said it, as if she had cursed in a public place.

"That's all?" Tim said, the sarcasm obvious.

"That's it," Viki retorted as evenly as she could.

Tim took a deep breath and said, "It's complicated."

What had once been a cute catch-phrase between them suddenly felt wrong and out of place.

Viki blinked rapidly, her mouth opening and closing, but she couldn't find any words. She felt anger rising. She had asked for honesty and specificity, and all she got was more generality. Of course it was complicated, life was complicated. Silence descended again, but this time Viki didn't chase it away, but shifted her attention to the dark foliage as they drove down Haleakala Mountain.

~~~

Viki Dobos stood in the driveway of Mark Kosov's house after Tim dropped her off. She was too stunned to be sad. She wanted to be angry and she wanted to be hurt, and thought she should be feeling both of those things. She took a deep breath, smelling the ocean, so glad to be back in its vicinity. Instead of going inside, she walked around to the beach-side of the house, took off her shoes, and walked out onto the beach.

She breathed the air in and let out a slow sighing exhale. On the way down the mountain, she had gone over what she understood about Tim. A wounded widower, freshly grieving his departed wife. A single father, protective of his daughter. A lawyer and an introvert. It added up, under the light of that logic—his behavior, his hesitation, his inability to communicate clearly made sense. It made too much sense. It left her feeling compassion for him which didn't leave much room for anger.

And really, what was she expecting? Her home was in Sedona, Arizona, thousands of miles away. She had made a friend, had some fun, wasn't that enough?

She was standing on the sand, enjoying the water rolling

over her feet when she felt him—that raw need, sharp and palpable. Just like the desert sun, it may not be visible, but when it is around, its presence cannot be denied.

"Good evening, Mark," she said without turning.

"Good evening, Ms. Dobos," Mark replied.

"Really, it's Viki. After what we have gone through I hope we are becoming friends." Viki turned and was surprised to see Alexander supporting Mark as he made his way slowly to the beach. In the silvery moonlight, he looked a bit like a ghost.

"We are," Mark assured her. "Thank you, Alexander, I am sure Viki can help me back."

"Very good, sir," Alexander said with a slight bob of his head. "Will you need anything else this evening?"

"Just set out the bedtime meds," Mark said as Alexander turned to go. "Thank you, Alexander."

Viki watched as Alexander turned back and smiled at his employer. It was subtle, but there was a moment when the assured mask of the professional was replaced by the worried face of a friend.

"He's a good man," Viki commented when he was out of earshot.

"That he is. Too good for me, I am afraid."

"Oh, I don't know about that. Still worried about your past sins catching up with you when you die?"

Even in the dim light, Viki clearly saw the surprise on Mark's face. Death was no stranger to her, and she saw no need to use euphemisms, no reason not to approach it directly.

"Yes," Mark finally said. "We have not succeeded yet."

"We will," Viki said. "I have an idea, but first tell me about your experience."

Mark indicated that he wanted to walk, so Viki took his arm and gently supported him. "I was a boy, back in Russia. I was having this horrible dream about my mother when I saw and heard ghosts... which, I presume, were you and Alexander."

"Yes, but it's progress. Your vitals were fine this time."

Mark nodded. "And your idea to proceed?"

"Sensory deprivation. So you are conscious but not distracted by your physical senses, like you were the first time I drew you."

"Like one of those tanks?"

"No, nothing that complicated. A dark, quiet room should do the trick. I can talk to Alexander in the morning if you'd like."

CHAPTER 35

In the morning, Viki took her usual walk. She was, after all, taking Tim at his word—they were friends, and it was complicated.

She was greeted by a wet and sandy hug from Anela and a terse, "Good morning," from Tim. Anela invited her to help with the sand castle, which Viki gladly did.

Before leaving, and while Anela was playing in the gentle surf, Viki said, "Can you make it tonight?"

Tim nodded, "Her grandparents are out of town, but I have a sitter arranged."

"Thanks."

Tim answered with a nod, keeping his eyes on his daughter as she played in the waves. Looking at him, Viki felt sad; his life seemed so guarded, so small, and it could be so much more. The thought almost made her laugh out loud. It implied that if he would just open up to her, his life would be amazing. And maybe it would, and maybe it wouldn't. Who was she to judge his path and to assume she could make it better?

When the sand castle was done, she said goodbye

to Anela and turned to Tim. "If you want to spend time together, you know where to find me." She walked away without waiting for his reply.

~~~

Viki was late for breakfast. She had gotten back to Mark Kosov's house in time, but because of all the sand she had picked up playing with Anela, she took the time to clean up and change.

When she came up the stairs into the great room, she could see Alexander and Mark engaged in an intense discussion on the lanai.

Mark was seated, leaning back, Alexander was also seated but leaning forward, his hand going to his heart and then briefly touching Mark's knee.

Viki started to turn, she knew this was private and she should give them space, but she couldn't. She didn't know the words, but she could see, could feel, the content. Alexander was telling his employer how he felt about him.

It didn't take long, just the span of a few breaths, but in the end Mark rose and embraced Alexander, patting his back and his head.

After the embrace, Alexander turned, blinking back tears, and took a step towards the lanai door. Viki turned and went back down the stairs a ways, before rushing back up. When she saw Alexander, she said, "Sorry I'm late, I had to change."

Alexander nodded, wiping tears from his cheeks, "Breakfast is all ready for you."

"Thank you, Alexander. Are you okay?"

"Yes," he said, beaming through the tears, "Yes I am."

~~~

Viki spent much of the rest of the day helping Alexander change one of the guest bedrooms over to suit their needs. A dark quiet room for Mark to be in when she drew him next.

"We only have two guest bedrooms," Alexander said as they discussed it after breakfast was over and Mark had excused himself to take care of business. "Do you think your friend Reg will mind if we put him up in a hotel? There is a nice place just a hundred yards down the beach."

Viki snorted. "No, he won't mind. What he will mind is when I go wake his lazy ass up so we can start the work."

"What do we need?"

"Depends. Any budgetary constraints?"

This time Alexander snorted, "No practical ones."

Viki smiled, this was going to be fun. "Okay, we need some acoustic foam, heavy black cloth, and some sort of frame to assemble this stuff on so we don't trash the room."

Alexander nodded, making some notes.

"And we need a handyman or a carpenter to put this together. Can we get one?"

Alexander nodded again. "Let me make some calls, you go wake Reginald."

Later, as they were emptying out the room, Viki asked, "How did it go with Mark this morning?" When she saw the embarrassed look on his face, she added, "I am sorry, I just happened to come upstairs at just the right moment."

Alexander paused and put down the sheet he was folding. "Umm..."

"You don't have to talk about it. I just thought you might want to."

He pursed his lips and continued, "It went... well. He's not going to suddenly start liking men and run away with me to live happily ever after, but..."

"You were very brave to talk to him about it."

Alexander pursed his lips again and nodded. "I knew in my heart there was love between us, but now... now I really know."

"I had no doubt."

"Really?"

"None. I could see it. It's not overt, but it was there. He told me the story of his overdose, and the look on his face when he talked about how you saved his life was telling. I knew."

Alexander wiped away the tears that were forming and said, "Sorry, you've seen me weep twice in one day—this is completely unprofessional."

"And so is this," Viki said as she drew the man into an embrace.

~~~

"He's a dolt," Reg declared as he and Viki walked slowly down the beach. Reg wore a turquoise-colored bathing suit and a loud Hawaiian shirt. It was shortly after noon—morning for him.

Viki smiled, "That's kind of you, but hardly true."

"Okay, he's a moron," Reg offered.

"Not at all."

"Hmmm, how about a coward? Yes, that's it, you can't argue with that descriptor."

She was grateful for what he was trying to do, but didn't think it was really going to help much. She didn't get involved often or lightly, and the state of her relationship with Tim was very frustrating. "I just wish he would talk about it."

Reg snorted, suppressing his burgeoning laughter with his hand.

"What?" Viki demanded.

"The remorseful call of the modern heterosexual woman heard around the globe, 'I just wish he would talk to me.'" Reg lowered his hand and his laughter spilled forth.

A flush crept onto Viki's cheeks as she bumped her body into his. "What?"

"Honey," Reg said, "men, in general, are crap about sharing their feelings."

"I guess you're right, but this particular one is particularly bad." She paused and added, "You share your feelings all the time."

"True, true enough, But," Reg began, holding up a finger, "you and I are friends, good friends, but *just* friends." He held up another finger. "I am unusually comfortable with who I am." A third finger came up. "In general I don't give a shit what people think of me so I can let it all hang out." A forth finger came up, "And lastly, I'm one shallow son of a bitch, so there is not much to see anyway."

"Agreed," Viki said with a smile. Seeing the feigned look of hurt on his face, she added, "Except for that last part, of course."

"But back to my pontificating about your would-be boyfriend. He's a coward. He's hiding from his life, he's over protective of his daughter, and he's afraid to face how you make him feel."

Viki's brow furrowed as she took his arm and they continued down the beach.

CHAPTER 36

The room was all black, with cloth lining all the walls covering the acoustic insulation behind it. Sounds were strange and aborted, as the modifications they made did their work. Viki liked the effect. It felt odd, but somehow comforting. Like a womb.

She pulled back a black, floor-to-ceiling drape to reveal a smaller area within the room. Inside it was all the medical gear and two chairs. "The doctor and nurse will be in here monitoring you, and the equipment will be silenced." She held onto Mark's arm, guiding him further into the room.

"You will be here," she indicated the bed in front of them. It was all black too. "We have an eye mask for you to deal with any light pollution from the machinery." Mark gestured to the bed, and Viki guided him to it. He sat down wearily. "The rest of us will be upstairs in the great room. The doctor will have a muted cell phone and we'll have a call open the whole time so we will know if something goes wrong. We will have a camera setup over there with an infrared light to record what happens."

Mark nodded. "I like it in here. Peaceful."

"That's the idea. We want you conscious, but with no sensory distractions, so you can cleanly experience the event."

"'Event,' that's a nice euphemism," he said with a small nod. "Better than Make-Sure-Mark-Is-Not-Going-To-Hell experiment. Shorter at least."

Viki sat next to him. "Do you really believe that?" Viki asked.

Mark shrugged. "Intellectually, no, probably not. But I was raised Russian Orthodox. There is a lot of stuff, really deep, emotional things, that makes me feel like I deserve to go to hell."

Viki nodded, standing up and offering her hand to him.

He shook his head and took a deep breath, letting it out in a slow sigh. He looked bad, pale and exhausted. "I have a little while before my next meeting. I like it in here. If you will, please tell Alexander to come and get me when it is time." With that, he turned from Viki and lay down on the bed.

~~~

"Hi," Tim said when Viki opened the door. It was almost time for her to draw Mark again.

"Hi," Viki replied, not sure what else to say. They stood there as the seconds drew out. Viki felt silly, like a teenage girl, and just like a teenage girl, she couldn't figure out what to do.

She heard a small chuckle behind her and felt Reg's hand on her shoulder. "I know you're not asking for it, but my advice is: get a room, and then have a long talk. Often works better that way."

Tim looked down at his shoes as she felt her cheeks

flush red. "Reg!" she stage-whispered to him.

"Look, since I've already opened my trap, let me continue. Life is complicated, I get that, I really do. But love is more complicated. If you find someone in this world that makes you *feel,* then go for it, damn the complications."

Reg stepped away and then turned back. "Because you know, kids," he added, sounding like a scolding school teacher, "love is what we're on this big ball of dirt for."

With that, Reg left, leaving Viki and Tim staring at each other. The seconds ticked by again until Tim finally said, "May I come in?"

"Oh?" Viki said, as if woken from a dream. "Yeah, sure, please come in."

Tim nodded and walked passed her. Viki closed the door, shaking her head, her long hoop earrings banging into her neck. She was in full Madam Valarka regalia.

Instead of going into the great room where she would draw, she made her way downstairs to the "black" room, as Mark had termed it. She needed to get her head back on straight before starting.

As she walked down the stairs, she let her insecurities out to play. As she slowly took each step, a new fear appeared in her mind.

You live an ocean apart, for God's sake.

It can't work, get over it.

Tick-tick, your biological clock is ticking, hell, it's past due. If you're gonna have a child, you best do it fast.

Another emotionally unavailable man? Again? Just like Daddy?

He doesn't really care. He was just using you to drag his dead wife out of the bardo.

Condoms aren't a 100 percent you know; maybe the

coward knocked you up—could explain why you keep get-
ting all emotional.

After she got down the stairs, she clenched her jaw, turned her attention from the babbling monkeys in her head, and walked down the hallway.

She got to the black room as Mark, with Alexander's help, made his way into the room. He looked weaker than ever, significantly diminished from the man she had met two weeks ago.

Mark lay on the bed as the nurse applied the electrodes to his chest. Viki watched until it was done, then walked over.

"Ready?" she asked.

Mark nodded, and Viki wondered what exactly he was ready for. She believed his story, or she wouldn't be draw-ing him again, but looking at him... he looked like he was ready for more than just a visit to the afterlife.

She sat on the bed and took his hand. She was sur-prised when he didn't pull back, and in fact squeezed her hand. "It's going to work this time, Mark. You are not going straight to hell."

Mark nodded and licked his lips. "Guarantee it?"

Viki nodded, "I do. Money-back guarantee."

"Okay then, let's do this."

Viki got the mask from the bed stand, helped Mark put it on, then pushed it up so he could see. "I am going to go upstairs and get ready. Alexander here will stay with you until Reg calls him. He'll give the doctor his phone so he can tell us if anything goes wrong, and he'll close everything up. When he does, put on your mask, and take slow deep breaths and don't fall asleep."

Mark nodded, and Viki squeezed his hand before she let it go and got up. "It's going to work," she said.

~~~

Everything was set. Alexander had just sat down across from her, next to Reg and Tim. This time all three men would participate in the drawing.

Alexander gave her a nod and Viki said, "Okay, we are going to do this more like a normal session. Alexander, I need you to talk to me as I draw. I need you to share memories of Mark. Memories of good times, memories that give me a sense of what he means to you."

Alexander nodded and swallowed.

Viki took up a blue pastel and, as always, started with the eyes.

There was nothing in the room but the sound of the scratch of pastel against the paper. No one seemed to be breathing.

"Why don't you start by telling us how you met," Viki said to Alexander.

"Oh, yes," Alexander said with the smallest hint of a chuckle. "That is quite the story."

Viki picked a different shade of blue and continued drawing.

Alexander chuckled again, his hand going to his short-cropped hair. "Well, this was close to twenty years ago now. Mr. Kosov... Mark had just left Russia and was, as he called it, 'playboying his way across Europe.' He was in England looking for what he called a 'proper manservant.'

"I was a graduate of The British Butler Institute in London and had just worked eight years for what you would call a grand old dame. She had passed away, and I was ready for something a bit more adventurous.

"The agency sent me for the interview with Mark. Actually, with him it was more of an audition. I served formal tea, which seemed to delight him to no end. He pelted me with questions the whole time about the history of tea service, the Institute, and the intricacies of high society in England."

Viki finished her first pass on the eyes and outlined the oval face of Mark Kosov. The picture was maybe a year old and highlighted just how much thinner his face had gotten.

"He was demanding and arrogant and brash, but there was this child-like quality to him that was... it was... well, it was appealing. It was almost like he grew up too fast, as if he was making up for lost time.

"After the interview, he offered me a position, but only for three weeks, at three times my normal fee."

Viki looked up and smiled at Alexander as she pulled out grey and white pastels to start in on the hair.

"He didn't want a permanent butler. He was going on a yacht tour of the Aegean Sea with some new, very rich, friends, and wanted to impress. He had more of an accent back then, I remember his exact words, 'Well Alex,' he said, which pulled me up short, no one ever called me that. 'Well Alex,' he said, 'do you think you can make a respectable man out of me?'"

Alexander paused, his eyes far away as Viki continued to work on the hair. "Is that when you fell in love with him?" she asked gently.

The Englishman flushed red and nodded his head. "He was so full of himself, so confident, yet so eager to learn. That and the 'making him a respectable man,' it was... You must never tell anyone I said this," he looked around at the others at the table before continuing. "It was adorable."

Viki smiled, moving on to fleshing out the nose. "And how was that excursion?"

"Oh," Alexander said with a small chuckle, "complete disaster. There were two other couples, Mark and his date, me, and a crew of three. The six of them did way too many drugs, drank too much, and there was not a gentleman in sight. The yacht broke down and we had to wait to be towed back to shore, not that the six of them really noticed."

"And he kept you on after that?" Viki asked.

"He did."

Viki quickly outlined the mouth, a straight line between thin lips. "And…" she prompted.

He blinked, as if Viki's query had yanked him back to the present. "He actually apologized to me. He said, 'Well, I guess making a respectable man of me is a job of more than a week or two.'"

"What are some of your fondest memories?"

"In the beginning it was partying in a new country every week. I remember this time in Paris. We were in the wrong side of the city and got mugged. There were three guys, one with a gun and two with knives. Mark was so casual about it. He gave them what they wanted without hesitation, struck up a conversation with them about French baked goods, and then invited them back to the hotel for a party he was throwing."

"Did they show?" Reg asked.

Alexander nodded, "They did. That speaks to the charisma the man has. He doesn't use it now like he did back then, but if he turned it on, you'd best beware. Those three showed up to the party—he got them extremely drunk and had the police haul them away."

As the stories continued, Viki finished the face, added more detail to the hair, and went back to the ocean-blue eyes. She worked slowly and carefully, making them as life-like as she was capable.

Alexander was sharing a story of learning to ride horses in Spain when Viki interrupted, "I think we're ready, gentlemen."

Alexander blinked, looking startled. Reg nodded and put his left hand on the drawing. Tim avoided Viki's eyes as he mimicked Reg's action.

"Put your left hand on the drawing," Viki gently said to Alexander who blinked again and nodded, putting his left hand in place.

Viki paused, closing her eyes and saying a silent prayer. She didn't ask for success or safety, she prayed, *May the highest good of all be served.*

She took a long, deep breath, gathering the energies that had built up during the drawing, leaned over the paper, and gently exhaled.

Mark Kosov's eyes slowly dimensionalized, coming to life and blinking as the entire drawing animated.

The head turned left and right, an expression of wonder dancing on his lips. "Oh my."

CHAPTER 37

Mark Kosov's blue eyes, wide in wonder, brought memories flooding back to Viki. She had been fourteen years old and was secretly visiting her grandmother and practicing drawing. Her mother hadn't yet forbidden her to see her grandmother, but she had forbidden her from drawing—anything.

"Start with the eyes, Little Sparrow," the woman said, "we always start with the eyes."

Viki stared at the blank paper in front of her and the picture of the young man beside it positioned upside down. He was a year older than Viki, a boy she had a crush on who had recently died in a car accident. She was back here, back with her grandmother, because she wanted to say good-bye, because she wanted, for a moment, to pretend he wasn't really gone.

"Why?" Viki asked, her tone petulant.

"Why?" her grandmother echoed a puzzled look on her face.

"Yes, why? Why don't I outline the face first so I get the

eyes in the right place? Why don't I start with the mouth, which is so expressive? Why the eyes, why always the eyes?"

Her grandmother paused, her lips pressing together as she leveled her gaze at Viki. "I'll make you a deal. I will answer your question if you tell me what happened first."

Viki crossed her arms and pursed her lips. "How? How did you know?"

The older woman just smiled and, with a graceful wave of her hand, signaled her granddaughter to continue.

"Fine," the girl began with a huff. "We had *the* fight again."

"'The' fight?"

"Yeah, 'the' fight. The one fight. The only fight. The fight about this. About *the gift*."

Her grandmother nodded, but didn't comment further.

"It's like, Saturday, and I got up late. When I came down to the kitchen, Mom was at the table knitting a scarf. I was poking my head in the fridge, blood sugar low, when she started in on it. 'What about a musical instrument, honey? I bet you would be great at playing the piano.'

"That alternate creative pursuit is her way of trying to distract me from her denial of the gift, your gift, my gift." Viki went on to describe the fight in great detail. After a few minutes of it, her grandmother stopped her.

"Why do you think your mother is doing this?"

That brought Viki up short. "Why? Because she's a bitch." Her grandmother's eyes widened in surprise at the use of the term "bitch," but she didn't comment. "Because she wants to make my life miserable. Because she doesn't understand me. Because—"

"Close your eyes, dear," her grandmother said gently.

Viki's mouth opened and closed several times before she sighed, crossed her arms, and closed her eyes.

"Good. Now remember, remember what your mom looked like, describe her eyes to me."

"Her eyes?"

"Yes, describe what her eyes looked like when you were fighting. Describe them in detail, enough detail so that I could draw them."

"Okay..." Viki said. "They are brown, a shade of mahogany, not quite as bright as your eyes are. The whites a tad blood shot and the pupils... the pupils are dilated."

"And the eyelids? The lashes? You're doing good, keep going."

"The eyes are wide, so much so that the lids are barely visible. There are some crow's feet on the outer edges. The lashes are dark brown with a hint of moisture on them."

"Good, Little Sparrow, good," the woman said as Viki opened her eyes. "No, keep your eyes closed, we are not quite done."

Viki closed her eyes again.

"Now, in your mind see a blank piece of paper and draw the eyes, just those eyes. Let me know when you can see them clearly."

In a moment Viki nodded.

"Okay, now just looking at the drawing in your mind of those eyes, tell me what emotion those eyes are conveying."

Viki opened her mouth to say "hate" but closed her mouth as she studied the eyes in her mind. "They... Fear, Grandmother, these are the eyes of fear."

"Very good, little one. You can open your eyes now."

"My mom is afraid? She's afraid of my gift?"

The older woman nodded. "This is not an easy road, which your mother knows very well."

The teenager's hand came to her mouth. "Oh. I called her a... I used the b-word. She... She's trying to protect me, isn't she?"

Her grandmother nodded and smiled.

"Why are you doing this? Why are you helping me understand my mother, when she doesn't want us to do exactly what we are doing right now?"

"She's my daughter. I don't want what happened to me and her to happen to you and her."

Viki nodded and was silent for a time, biting on her thumb nail.

"Is she right? I mean, is she right to try to keep me from doing this?"

Her grandmother shrugged. "I can't answer that for you, only you can."

Viki nodded firmly and said, "Okay, grandmother, now you have to keep your end of the bargain. Tell me why we always start with the eyes."

With a small smile on her lips, she said, "I just did tell you."

CHAPTER 38

"Can you tell us what you see, Mark?" Viki asked after a moment of silence.

"It's a bit disorienting. I see all of you like I am in the middle of you. I see the room, the sun going down outside. But I also see me at the same time."

"What do you mean, you 'see me'?"

"Well," Mark began, licking his lips. "I see me. I see my body lying on the bed. There is this silver string going from my belly to my body. It is brighter in here, much brighter than I remember. I wonder if I can move."

"You can, Mark, you can move any way you want to. Walls don't matter. Go ahead and try."

The face on the drawing appeared to be concentrating and then a look of wonder returned. "I can move. I went right through the curtain. I am with Dr. Lane and Ms. Neal. Alexander, remind me to fire them later."

"Fire them?" Alexander asked.

"Yes, they are quite useless with his head buried in her bosom and his hand up her skirt."

Viki looked at Reg, her eyes widening as she nodded

towards the stairs. "Got it," he said, slowly releasing his hand from the drawing and hustling to the stairs.

"Don't worry about them," Viki said. "Reg is going to take care of it. We have limited time, so what would you like to do, Mark?" Viki concentrated on the older man's face, keeping it in sharp focus as she learned when she drew JJ Lynch.

"Okay, I am going to search the house for Michael. How much time do I have?"

Viki shrugged. "A few minutes. We'll keep the connection open as long as possible." She took her gaze briefly from the page and looked at the men across from her. "Alexander and Tim, just focus on his face, don't look away, don't pay attention to anything else. Your focus can help keep the connection open."

Alexander nodded, but didn't move his gaze away from the paper. Tim was silent, his focus steady.

The room was quiet as Alexander, Tim, and Viki focused on the animated drawing of Mark Kosov. The face on the page looked to and fro, his expressions one variant of wonder or another. He looked childlike.

"Can you talk to us, Mark? Just tell us what you are doing."

"I'm moving slowly. I tried to go fast and was yanked back to my body, so I'm moving slowly. I've searched the second guest bedroom and am moving on to the kitchen. Things look different. I can see so well. The colors are brighter, and everything is sharp and clear."

As Mark continued to narrate the tour of his own house, Reg returned with a smirk on his face. "They'll pay attention now," he said. "May I?" he asked Viki, indicating the drawing.

She nodded. "Just go slow."

After a few minutes, Mark said, "Okay, I am coming into the great room. I can see you but…"

"What is it, Mark?" Viki asked.

"There is this glow, this column of light in the center of the table. It's white, and not white, both at the same time. It has these little swirls of color that appear and disappear rapidly. It is so… so beautiful."

Viki looked up from the page trying to see what Mark was describing. She scanned the room quickly, her eyes catching on a shimmering presence. When she tried to focus on it, her sense of it slipped away. It was like a peripheral glimpse of something seen out of the corner of your eye. She purposefully looked away, holding her gaze steady about forty-five degrees to the right. The shimmering form was in the shape of a man, and she could see a sliver cord snaking from his belly into the floor.

"I can see you," she gasped.

"The light, my God it is so beautiful," Mark said, unaware of what Viki had said.

As the shimmering form moved closer to them, it became more defined and what looked like white sparks started to run along the edge of his form.

"Wait," Viki said. "Wait, Mark, don't come closer." As the ghostly form of Mark Kosov moved closer, she could see the sparks along the edge of his form accelerate; she could feel the energy of the drawing grow sharp and insistent.

The three other men—Alexander, Reg, and Tim—had removed their gazes from the drawing as they searched the room for what Viki was seeing.

"I don't…" Alexander said.

"Where?" Tim asked.

"I must see what is in the light," Mark said. "There are

sparks coming off the edges of the column now. It is the most beautiful thing I have ever seen."

Viki felt the energy begin to spiral and fray. She turned back to the paper and saw the look of wonder on the drawing of Mark Kosov's face. She saw that it was starting to de-focus and concentrated on it. "Look at the paper, now! We need to get him back into focus." She didn't look up, but she could feel their energies added to hers as the face snapped back into focus. "Mark! Don't come any closer. I don't know what will happen."

"So beautiful," the face said, his eyes becoming even wider, his mouth forming a beatific smile.

"No, Mark!" she shouted as she felt a prickling sensation on her fingers where they touched the page. First it tingled, and then it hurt.

"Can you shut it down, V?" Reg asked, his voice strained.

She shook her head. "I'm afraid to. I don't know what will happen."

"It feels... It feels so good, so warm. I want to..." Mark said.

"No, Mark! No!" Viki yelled. The pain in her hand had become extreme. Both Alexander and Reg pulled their hands back. It was only her and Tim that still touched the paper. Tim's face contorted and sweat ran down his cheeks. Viki set her jaw and endured the pain, trying to keep the animated drawing of Mark Kosov in focus. His face came into greater focus, looked less and less like a drawing and more and more like Mark.

A long, slow sigh escaped the near-real-looking face on the page, his expression one of bliss. And suddenly it was over.

The picture went back to its original pastel drawn form.

The pain disappeared from Viki's fingers. The form she had been glimpsing out of her peripheral vision was gone. She sat stunned, sweating, exhausted, and panting. She hadn't dismissed the energies, she hadn't let them go, they were just gone.

Viki's hand came to her face as she looked at the three other men. All looked drained, empty.

"Cardiac arrest, he's in cardiac arrest," the doctor said. All four looked around until they remembered the speakerphone, the one that connected them to the muted cell phone next to the doctor. The doctor must have moved away from the phone, because the voice was not very loud. They had to strain to hear it.

Alexander jabbed at the phone, turning the volume all the way up.

"Charging!" the voice on the phone said.

CHAPTER 39

When Viki was five, she first saw her grandmother draw. It wasn't supposed to happen, she was never supposed to see it. At least, according to her mother.

She was spending the weekend with her grandmother while her mother and father were out of town. It was something, even at that age, Viki loved to do. They would spread a blanket in the green grass behind her grandmother and grandfather's red brick house and serve tea.

Viki would be the one to decide how many cups to put out. At least two, of course, one for the woman and one for the little girl, but often several more.

The memories were old and clouded with the silvery light of nostalgia, but they were strong.

"Three more cups," little Viki said. "We have some bold ones today." As her grandmother solemnly put the cups out, Viki pointed to and described each faerie. "Silver wings and long black hair. She has a big smile, she is laughing, and has a purple dress—I want a dress like that, Gran. That one is so sad, one of her wings is damaged, give her extra sugar to help her heal."

They were interrupted by her grandfather, a short man with black hair and bright hazel eyes. It is one of her few clear memories of him; he died several years later in a car accident. "Excuse me, ladies," he said softly.

"And faeries," Viki added.

"And faeries. Excuse me, ladies and faeries, my most humble apologies for disturbing your most auspicious gathering." He bowed and his smile grew wider. Viki didn't understand what "auspicious" meant, but she loved how he was willing to play with them.

His eyes turned to his wife and grew serious. "There has been an accident at the cannery. Young Aaron Gorski. His parents are a wreck. They are here. They need you, Marge."

Her grandmother's eyes went wide as they traveled to Viki. "But…"

"But nothing. Her mother's concerns are not proper. If the girl has the gift, she should use it. Her mother should be using it. Viki's the right age, so let's find out."

The woman's brow furrowed as she covered her mouth with her right hand, and grabbed Viki's hand with her left and squeezed it hard.

Viki didn't understand exactly what they were saying, but she knew it was something secret, and something wonderful. Like a few months ago when Viki had told her grandmother about the faeries in their yard.

"Marge, I'm making the call. I will take responsibility for it."

Viki's grandmother went into the house and disappeared into the bedroom, and her grandfather took her into her grandmother's drawing room. In it were two people with sad, sad faces stained with tears. Viki didn't know who they were, but it made her sad too.

"Go tell them about what you discovered in the back-yard," her grandfather said, gently pushing her towards the man and the woman.

"Hello," she said with a curtsy. "My name is Viki Dobos. I am sorry you are sad. I know something that might cheer you up."

"What?" the woman asked as she wiped tears from her cheeks. She had blue eyes and short blond hair.

"Faeries!" Viki said clapping her hands together. "I can see them."

"That is wonderful," the woman said, her lips moving into the form of a smile, but Viki could tell it wasn't a real smile.

"You need a hug," she said embracing the woman. The woman held her fiercely, and Viki could feel the woman's body shaking.

When the embrace ended, Viki went back to her grand-father who was patting the chair next to him.

"Your grandmother is about to come out. You can stay but you have to promise me you will not move from this chair, and if you have something to say you can only whis-per it to me."

Viki's eyes widened as she nodded.

"I need you to promise, Vik."

"I promise, Papu."

When Viki's grandmother walked in, her breath caught. At first she didn't recognize her with the heavy makeup, hoop earrings, and flowing silk clothing. But then she did. She saw her grandmother behind the makeup, and she recognized the silk scarf around her neck—it was one she often let Viki wear when she visited.

Viki watched in awe as her grandmother drew some

cards and spoke to the man and woman. She then took a bright white piece of paper and began drawing from a picture that was upside down. Viki watched silently as everyone put the fingers of their left hands on the paper, and her grandmother gently blew on the paper. The man and woman inhaled sharply and began to talk excitedly to the paper as they cried. She watched in wonder as the faeries assembled in a circle around the table.

"Papu, Papu," she whispered, pulling on her grandfather's sleeve until the man leaned his head close. "The faeries are here and..."

"And what?" he asked, his eyes sparkling.

"And a boy... no, a grown-up boy. He is standing in the middle of the table."

Her grandfather smiled wide, and she saw tears forming in his eyes. She was curious about it but quickly looked back. She only had eyes for what she was seeing. "What else do you see, Little Sparrow?"

"Light with little rainbows. The grown-up boy is light that is full of rainbow sparks."

CHAPTER 40

"Begin manual compressions," Viki heard the doctor say on the phone, her head spinning from the memory of her past.

She looked around her. She was at the table in Mark Kosov's house. The drawing of him that was recently so alive now sat inert. Alexander, Reg, and Tim sat around her, all eyes glued to the speakerphone.

"Alexander, listen to me," she said. Alexander's eyes moved from the telephone to her and back again. "Alexander, I need to know something, I need to know it now." The man's eyes left the phone and stayed with Viki. "Is he ready?"

"Ready?"

"Is he ready to go? Are his affairs in order? Did he say his good-byes?"

"Charging!" said the voice on the phone. "All clear!"

"I... Ready? I don't think so," Alexander stammered.

"Damn it," she said. "Reg, call 911, now! Alexander and Tim, put the fingers of your left hand on the drawing of Mark. You too, Reg, when you're done." Reg pulled out his phone and dialed, his eyes drilling into Viki. Alexander and Tim stayed frozen, their eyes on the phone.

"Nothing," the nurse's voice said.

"Now!" Viki shouted and the two men moved their fingers to the page. Viki reached over and hung the speakerphone up. "Listen. You have to focus if you want to get Mark back."

"Where is he? What happened?" Alexander asked.

"He's in a good place, but we don't have much time. Focus on the page. Imagine seeing Mark's face come back to life. Give it everything you've got."

When she finished, Reg sat and put the fingers of his left hand on the page. "You sure you want to do this, V?" he asked, his face full of concern.

She nodded her head. She knew the risk she was taking but pushed it down, an ambulance was on the way. After taking a deep breath, she got out her blue pastels and began touching up the eyes. It was only token, it wasn't really enough, but there wasn't time, so it would have to do.

She grasped for the tatters of the energy they had built up. She gathered it together, inhaled deeply, and slowly exhaled on the page.

Nothing. She imagined she could still hear the voices on the speakerphone. "Administer an amp of epi. Charge again." She heard the doubts rising up in her mind.

Gran said never to do this, you can hurt yourself.

Drawing the living, why are you drawing the living? Were you trying to kill him?

This is too dangerous.

The thoughts rattled around her head, but she couldn't give them time to play, as she often did, so she turned her full focus on the drawing.

She inhaled again, feeling the tattered energies come back together. She exhaled ever so slowly onto the drawing.

Something. It wasn't much, but the eyes seemed to move, to widen, just slightly. Viki poured her focus and poured her energy into those eyes, those ocean-blue eyes of the Russian man. She imagined them becoming more real, and they did. It seemed to take forever, but soon the drawing came to life, eyes wide.

"*Krasivaya... chudnaya...*" the drawing of Mark Kosov said.

Viki didn't avert her gaze focusing on the image. "He said, 'Beautiful, wonderful,'" Alexander told them.

"Mark, listen to me," Viki began. "Look around, do you see a silver cord?"

"*Da,*" Mark said. His face looked joyous, like he was happy, or high.

"You have work left to do, Mark, it is not your time. Follow the silver cord."

Mark's brow furrowed deeply as he looked around. "*Krasivaya, sdes' tak krasivo.* It is so beautiful here, so peaceful here. Why do you disturb me? Who are you?"

Viki felt sick to her stomach and was beginning to feel light-headed. Doing this was taking its toll, and she knew there wasn't much time.

"Alexander," she whispered. "Try."

"Mark Ivan Kosov," Alexander said, his voice deep, his R's rolling as if he was speaking English with a Russian accent. "You follow that cord, you follow it now. Do you hear me?"

"*Da, Papa. Da.* But it is so beautiful here, Papa."

"*Mark, pozhaluista. Vernis' ko mne.* Now Mark! Follow it!

It will lead you to me." Alexander's face was hard, but tears were rolling down his cheeks.

The beatific expression faded from the drawing of Mark Kosov's face. First the sparkle left his eyes, next the mouth became a thin line instead of a smile, next the brow furrowed, lips turned down, and the eyes narrowed.

"What? Where..." he said.

"Mark, follow the cord," Viki said. "Follow it now as fast as you can."

"Viki? What happened?"

"I'll explain later, follow the cord as fast as you can."

The face nodded and was silent for a few moments, long moments for those that sat around the table with their hands on the living drawing of Mark Kosov.

"My body," he said. "That's my body. Am I dead? They are doing CPR. They have a defibrillator out and have put some patches on my chest."

"No," Viki said. "Not yet. But I need you to get back into your body."

"But—" he began.

"Please, Mark," Alexander said, "Please, we have more to do. You have more time. Please."

The face nodded. "I will try." A look of concentration came over it and then a look of surprise. "It's not working. I pop right out of my body. What's happening?"

"No time to explain, we're—" Viki said.

"They're shocking my heart now. I... I don't want to... Maybe I should stay this way."

"*Nyet,* Mark," Alexander said. "*Nyet.* We have more to do. The foundation is not ready yet. Please!"

Mark slowly nodded his head. "What do I do?"

"On the count of three," Viki said. She took a deep

breath. She felt spiking pain in her calves, and it felt like her hands were going to cramp. The room was beginning to swim, and she knew she didn't have much time. "On three, you try to get back into your body, and we will release the connection. That should do it."

Viki gathered herself and the energies of the connection as best she could. She took a deep breath—

"One."

The room rippled in Viki's vision. Her left hand remained on the drawing, but she reached down with her right and gripped the chair to prevent herself from falling.

"Two."

The drawing of Mark's face clenched in concentration as Viki pushed down the rising nausea she was feeling. In the distance she could hear a siren.

"Three!"

Mark's concentration turned to a grimace as all four hands flew from the drawing and it returned to its original, inert state.

Viki's left hand came to her forehead as she continued to grasp the chair with her right. She felt a sharp, spiking pain in her head. She twisted to the right and vomited on the floor, and then clutched her chest as that pain eclipsed all the others.

"V!" Reg cried as he surged to his feet, but Tim beat him to her side, knocking his chair over to get to her.

Alexander looked at her, and then at the stairs, and back again. With only a moment's pause, he ran to the stairs and down to Mark.

The last thing Viki saw was the concerned face of Tim Unger. She saw his mouth moving but couldn't understand the words. Her vision was still rippling, and for a moment she thought it was her grandfather.

"Papu?" she said as she let go of the chair and fell into Tim's arms.

"You have a great gift, Little Sparrow," she heard her grandfather say. "Don't ever turn your back on it."

She closed her eyes, clinging to the man holding her. "It's so hard, Papu."

She heard the siren grow louder, then heard voices speaking in urgent tones. She clung to the man she thought was her grandfather and wept as unconsciousness, cold and dark, came to claim her.

CHAPTER 41

"Now you did it," the woman said.

Disoriented, Viki looked around. She was standing in Mark's house, in the great room, but something wasn't right. The woman across from her was a pretty, petite woman with long brown hair and deep brown eyes. She stood with her arms crossed and her hip cocked, staring at Viki.

"Mother?" Viki asked.

The woman's eyebrows came up briefly and her lips formed a thin straight line. "Who else?"

"Where am I?"

Viki's mother looked young, like Viki remembered her when she was a child. She gestured with her hand, palm up, indicating that Viki should look around.

She saw a brown-haired woman lying on the floor. Reg was doing CPR on her, sweat dripping down his face. Tim watched, his arms wrapped tightly around his chest as he paced back and forth.

A table, festooned with silks and covered with her pastels, had a portrait of Mark Kosov on it. Several chairs were knocked over.

"What?" Viki began after she turned back to her mother.

"They're both good men, you know. They would both give you a child and me a grandchild."

"Mother!"

"For God's sake, Viki, what are you waiting for? You don't have much more time. Tick... tick... tick..."

"Is that all you've got to say? Complain about the fact that I haven't had any children?" Viki wanted to add, "Looking at us, is it any wonder?" But she didn't. She bit her tongue, her eyes wandering around the room, back to the woman on the floor.

She looked pale and drawn like she was dead. Her eyes were closed, but Viki could tell that she was pretty enough. Maybe late thirties. There was something familiar about the woman and she found herself moving closer.

The woman had a small mole between her nose and her upper lip. Viki reached to her own face—she had a mole just like that. She sucked in a breath and noticed a silver cord extending from her to the woman on the floor.

"It's me," she whispered.

"You and your damn gift," her mother said right behind her.

Viki jumped, and moved away. "What happened?"

"You over did it. Again. You might have killed yourself this time." Her mother paused, a sneer coming onto her face. "Your grandmother would be so proud."

"Really, Mom? Still? Are you going to help me or just try to make me feel bad?"

Her mother didn't answer but smiled a tiny, wicked smile.

Viki inhaled to deliver a scathing retort, but she held

her breath and slowly let it out as something dawned on her. "But... you're alive, Mom. What are *you* doing here?"

She sighed and crossed her arms, but didn't answer.

"This is not real," Viki said.

"You know," her mother said, "even if you picked that fat one you would be better off. At least he would take care of you."

"Reg and I are friends, Mom."

"Really? Have you seen the way he follows you around like some lost puppy you made the mistake of feeding once? Look at him now. He's going to give himself a heart attack trying to save you."

"Mother!"

"And this one," she said, moving to Tim. "This one has feelings for you too, broken though he may be. See the look of terror in his face as he watches the fat one try to bring you back to life. At least he's not one of those cowboys you seem to keep finding in that wasteland you moved to."

"Wait a minute..." Viki said.

"A broken man is better than no man. At least you know this one is a good father. That is important, so important."

"You're not dead, Mom. This is not real." Viki's mouth opened and her eyes widened as she continued. "I'm in the bardo, my own personal hell."

"About time," her mother said. "You never were the brightest bulb in the batch, were you?"

"You're not real, Mother."

She snorted and nodded. "Not real, eh? Try this on for size." She stepped back, making a grand sweeping gesture with her arms, ending with her right index finger pointing at Viki's belly. "Let's talk about that, shall we?"

"What?" Viki asked, her hands covering her belly and going through the silver cord.

"Your womb, my dear. I want to talk about your infertile womb."

"Mother..." she began, her expression changing from puzzled to scared. "No, Mother. No!"

"You want to know my theory?"

"No," Viki said, tears forming in her eyes as she backed up. "No, please."

"You accuse me of not being real? You try to minimize what I am to you, how much of me is in you?" A smile formed on the woman's lips that scared Viki to the core. "We are going to talk about this."

Viki was crying and continued to back up until she found herself pressed against the wall in the corner of the room, her mother slowly approaching. "I am begging you, please don't."

"I think you ruined it. I think *you* did this."

"Please..."

"I don't think you can have children. And it's God's punishment on you." Viki's mother crossed herself and moved closer to her daughter.

Viki pressed herself into the corner of the room, trying to make herself small. Her mother was so close she could smell her breath. Onions and cabbage and cigarettes.

The older woman leaned close until her lips were brushing her daughter's ear. "I think God took away you're ability to bear children when you ripped the perfectly good one out of your womb."

"No!" Viki cried as she slid down the wall and covered her ears, but she couldn't keep her mother's voice out.

"I think this is punishment for the mortal sins you've committed."

"Please!"

"First you embrace that gift and then you deny your heritage as a woman. No wonder you are alone, no wonder you are sterile, no wonder you are a miserable, dried up husk of a woman."

Viki's breath came in ragged gasps. She was shaking her head violently back and forth, banging it against the wall. All thoughts of being in the bardo gone, she was trapped by the words her mother was pouring down on her. They burned her as badly as if they had been molten lead.

Her mother was close again, her words a sinuous whisper. "You deserve this lonely, loveless life you are leading, my dear. You deserve it."

Viki surged to her feet, pushed her mother aside and bolted from the room.

A blast of cold hit her, and she looked around. She was standing on a vast expanse of ice. The cold bit into her, and her teeth began to chatter. She tried to cover her body and found she was naked.

In the distance she could see her mother approaching. She turned to run, but everywhere she turned she could see her mother approaching. There were thousands of them and each one had the same cruel look of condemnation on their faces.

Viki screamed.

CHAPTER 42

Her mothers paused in a dense crowd around her, leaving a circle ten feet in diameter. Viki shivered from the cold as she spun around facing the same look of condemnation over and over. There was nowhere to run, no escape. Just her and her mothers in this frozen wasteland.

Viki was lost to the bardo; she didn't know that her heart was in fibrillation and her soul had separated from her body. She only knew she faced the cold of the elements and the frigid judgments of her mother.

She wanted to sink down to the snowy ground and roll up into a ball. Why fight when she couldn't escape? Her mothers must have sensed her weakness because they took a collective step forward and silently watched her.

"Go away!" Viki shouted. "Leave me alone."

One of her mothers stepped forward and spoke. "We are your mother, you need us." When the one mother spoke, her words were echoed by the thousands of doppelgangers that stood on the frigid plain. The words assaulting Viki so that she covered her ears.

"No, I don't need you!" Viki shouted.

"Yes you do. You should have listened to us. You should have ignored your grandmother and the family curse. You should have kept your baby like we told you too. And, after that tragedy you should have stayed in Boston."

The scene changed and gone were the thousands of mothers, and only the one remained. Frozen walls rose up around them, and furniture formed out of the ice. Viki was in her mother's living room the day she had told her about the red-headed boy.

"I didn't know," Viki said after telling her what had happened, how she had tracked down the boy's friends and what they had said.

Her mother paused, her eyes narrow, her lips forming a frown. "But you did, Viki. How many times did I try to stop you from doing what your grandmother does? How many ways did I try to change the course of your life? You knew this thing could end in ruin, because I told you."

"What?" Viki said.

"Each time I tried to guide you, tried to be your mother, you turned your back on me and ran to your grandmother. You... you chose her every time. And this is what it has gotten you."

Viki studied her mother. Her arms crossed, her jaw locked. "This isn't about you... this is about a boy who died, who I..."

"Who you killed. Just say it, Viki. You killed that boy. You drew someone who was living, and now that person is dead. You killed him." Her mother's voice was as cold as ice.

"But..." Viki slowly sank to the couch, her head going into her hands.

She felt her mother's hand on her shoulder. "I can help you, honey. It's finally time for you to turn your back on that curse. For you to come home to me. I will help you get over this."

Viki looked up and saw compassion in her mother's face, but it just made her mad. Her mother seemed glad that this had happened. It had brought her daughter back to her.

"But I help people, Mother. It changes their lives when they to talk to their departed loved ones."

"I know," her mother said, sitting on the couch besides her. "You'll find another way. You are a wonderfully compassionate person. There are many ways to help people. You could go back to school, study to be a social worker."

"Are you saying I shouldn't draw anymore?"

"Never again. Ever. It must be clear now that it's too dangerous."

"No," Viki said, shrugging off her mother's touch and standing. "I can't let the gift die. I can't turn my back on my—"

"Grandmother?" Her mother's face turned angry.

"She told me not to give the gift up. She told me I had done my best."

"You drew her?" Viki's mother said, her voice becoming shrill. "After this tragedy, you drew her?"

Viki nodded.

Viki's mother began to pace, circling Viki. And as she did, the walls and the furniture sunk back down into the frozen landscape and her thousands of mothers returned, all of them walking around her, their voices one terrible roar.

"You choose her over me, every time," her mothers shouted. "When you got pregnant, you listened to her and ripped the fetus out of your womb. When it was time for you to go to college, you listened to her and began doing that blasphemous drawing for people. And now, when the family curse has claimed a life, you summon her back from the dead and listen to her."

"No..." Viki said weakly, falling to her knees.

"You know what I wish, Viki. I wish you had never been born. You aren't my child. You're a freak."

Viki knew what came next. She would run from her mother's home weeping and leave Boston. But she wasn't in her mother's home; she was kneeling on a frozen plain shivering, vitriol raining down on her from thousands of her mothers.

The cold began to take her over, and she could no longer move. A thin part of her knew that the frozen plain wasn't real, but the coldness creeping into her body was. She knew that she was dying.

CHAPTER 43

Viki took a slow, deep breath. It was all that she had left
to her. She felt the cold, burning air enter her lungs, she
felt her chest expand, she slowly let the air out, feeling the
rush of it at the back of her nose, the warmth of it tickling
at her frozen cheeks.

Breathe in, breathe out.

Perhaps it was time to die. She felt the press of her mothers around her, their thundering condemnations banging
into her, battering her. She had nothing left to give them,
what did they want beyond her life?

Breathe in, breathe out.

The cold continued to creep into her body. She felt like
a statue outside in Boston in the middle of winter. Unable
to move. Hoping for spring.

Breathe in, breathe out.

And then a thought occurred to her, that chilled her
even further. If she died now, the gift would die with her.
If there were others with the gift, she didn't know of them;
her grandmother had never mentioned them.

Breathe in, breathe out.

Her head bowed, she felt a whisper of heat on the back of her head. It wasn't much, but it was noticeable. She found she could move her head, the warmth having thawed it. She slowly looked up and then opened her eyes. In her peripheral vision she could see her mothers, but she ignored them. Not so much out of an act of will but because she had nothing more to give them. Her life was all she had to give, and it was clear to her that she was giving that.

Breathe in, breathe out.

Above them in the leaden sky was the tiniest break in the clouds. A pinprick of warm, yellow light shined on her face, warming her. Somehow she heard a whisper coming down that beam of light. "You are worthy of love," the whisper said. The voice was male and kind. Full of emotion and urgency. She knew the voice, she knew who it was: JJ Lynch. The ghost.

"I am?" she whispered back, but there was no reply, only the honey-colored column of warmth in her frozen world.

Her mothers sensed what was happening and charged. They grew claws and fangs. They became louder, until Viki could not even hear her own thoughts. They attacked.

~ ~ ~

Was there flesh left on her body, or was she only bones? Her mothers, with their claws and their fangs had bitten and stabbed her over and over. They had piled upon her until there was only darkness, and cold, and their voices.

"You've only gotten what you deserve."

"When you embraced that curse, you embraced evil."

"You should have listened to me."

But, maybe she was still alive because she still had a sense of her breath.

Breathe in, breathe out.

Was she worthy of love? Was she worthy of the gift her grandmother had cultivated in her? Was what she did a good thing? Would she ever get to pass the gift along?

"No!" the haranguing voices of her mothers shouted back at her.

The cold, sharp and unforgiving, bore down upon her until there were no voices, no claws, no fangs, only the cold and the pressure and darkness.

She knew that she was dead, that she was buried in the cold ground, and soon the worms would come to eat what was left of her body.

And what was she to do about it? Rage against death— that which all women must face? Or, accept it gracefully and go quietly into the darkness.

She laughed, it was a tiny thing. Like the time her grandmother had slipped and fallen on the ice when Viki was just a girl. The laughter had slipped out, and she covered her mouth in surprise. She knew the laughter was not appropriate; she knew her grandmother might be hurt. But soon the older woman joined her in laughter.

In the cold darkness she smiled. If she were dead, then maybe she could find her grandmother. If she were dead maybe she could help people like JJ, Jesus, and Banquo.

When she thought of the ghosts, the words she had heard came back to her. *You are worthy of love.*

And when she remembered those words, she felt that tiny shaft of warmth again. It unfroze her and she began clawing at the earth around her. At first she could hardly move, but she strained and struggled and started to dig in the direction that felt like up.

The dirt clogged her mouth, stuck to her naked flesh,

but still she fought. Alive or dead it was time to live. Time to take control of her life. Time to—

She wasn't in the cold ground anymore but on the frozen plain, her mothers descending on her again. Except they looked a little different, with their brown hair in ponytails and their hazel eyes sharp and accusing.

It wasn't her mothers descending upon her, it was herself. Thousands of Vikis shouting the words her mother said, the words Viki had continued to say to herself throughout her life.

The Vikis told her that she wasn't worthy of love. That she shouldn't pass on the gift. That it was a good thing she had never had a child.

Viki stood naked weeping on the ice. How long had she dragged her mother's condemnation along with her? How long had she pushed her gift away while at the same time holding it tightly?

"No," she said in the quietest of whispers. "Not anymore."

Her body shook, not from the cold, but from what it took for her to say those words.

She turned her head and looked up, the only direction she couldn't see her selves coming towards her. She saw the honey colored shaft of light, but it was getting small, the opening in the leaden sky closing.

All that she had, all that she was, she gave to that shaft of light. She focused on it, ignoring everything else. She felt that warmth enter her third eye, in the middle of her forehead, and flow down her spine, warming her frozen body.

She could feel her doppelgangers press against her, clawing at her, yammering on, but she ignored them and let the warmth flow through her.

"I am worthy of love," she said back to the light as tears ran down her cheeks.

A sharp pain blossomed in her chest as the warmth expanded and consumed her and she felt herself flying upwards to the nearly closed hole in the clouds.

CHAPTER 44

The woman lying on the ground appeared to be dead. Viki wondered who it was. Her blouse had been opened and large pads adhered to her chest. Two paramedics attended to the woman. Was she dead? Was she dying?

Reg stared at the woman, his long grey hair coming loose from his ponytail. Tim was there too, he paced with his arms hugging his chest. Both men looked devastated as they watched the paramedics attend to the woman.

Viki looked closer. The woman was dressed in silks and had heavy layers of makeup on. She looked like a gypsy.

She then noticed the silver cord that ran from her to the body as she hovered in the air looking down at the body.

She knew it was her body, but she wasn't scared. Life and death, she knew, were not that far apart to her, not that different to her.

Viki felt a warmth against her back, like she had felt on the frozen plain. It cleared her mind, it made her feel happy. She didn't turn around, but somehow she knew that JJ Lynch was there filling her with that warmth just like he had described doing in his book.

"Clear," the brown-haired paramedic said.

She watched her torso rise as they shocked her heart, trying to restore a normal rhythm. After her torso rose and before it came down, everything froze and she felt a question. The question wasn't in words, but still it was clear. The question rode on the warmth she felt. It was a whisper, but louder than all the shouting of her mothers and her selves: *Do you want back in your body or do you want to be a ghost?*

Live as a woman or live as a ghost.

Live or live.

The activity froze in the room as she considered, the four men she hovered above frozen in action. She pondered what her life would be like if she reentered her body, reentered her world.

She would have to change. She would have to grow. She would have to let go of the fears that had kept life so small for so many years. The thought scared her.

Or she could stay a ghost. She knew JJ was there, she looked around and saw Banquo watching. They could help her, teach her how to be a ghost. She felt excited at the possibility.

She turned back to her body. Should she go to what scared her or to what excited her?

Viki smiled and chose what scared her.

~~~

Searing pain in her chest as her torso fell to the ground after the shock to her heart. Her body cold and heavy. Sucking air into her lungs in a long, drawn out gasp. Light, sharp and bright, assaulting her eyes.

Her head hurt and she tasted vomit in her mouth, but she celebrated it. She sucked air into her lungs again and thanked it. She heard talking and saw shapes moving in her field of vision, but she couldn't focus on them. She could only focus on the life she felt. Pain, air moving in and out of her lungs, the sound of the ocean, the feel of the gurney under her as they loaded her onto it.

She celebrated it all. Each sensation. Each feeling. Each moment.

As her eyes focused, she saw Reg, his face drawn and exhausted, looking down on her. "Reg," she croaked. "I saw my mother. I was in the bardo."

"It's okay, honey," he said. "Just rest. Everything is okay."

She wanted to tell him that she knew everything was okay. She wanted to tell him what happened, but she had no more energy for words.

She saw Tim with a strained smile on his handsome face. "I'll be there when you wake up," he said.

She felt fatigue pull on her, making her body feel even more heavy. With a sigh, she surrendered to it, her eyes fluttering close.

CHAPTER 45

Viki woke slowly, her return to consciousness escorted by the beep-beep of her vitals and the biting smell of antiseptic. She wanted to wake up, and wake up quickly, but she couldn't. She sought consciousness like a swimmer who has been under water for too long. She wanted an escape, even if it meant escaping to another hospital room.

She remembered what happened with Mark. She knew what she had done to put herself in the hospital.

The lights were dimmer than the last time she woke in this hospital. Her eyes adjusted quickly, and she saw that she was not alone.

Slumped in a chair, his ponytail undone, and his grey hair spilling out over on the chair and his shoulders, was Reg. Asleep, with his head on her bed, was Tim.

Viki felt her heart pounding in her chest as several questions raced through her mind: Was it really a dream? Is Mark alive?

She swallowed hard and tried to sit up, but her body wouldn't obey. It felt dense and foreign, like it wasn't her own. Her muscles felt heavy, her head had a spiking pain going through it, and her tongue felt dry and swollen.

"Now you did it," she heard her mother hiss, the words reverberating from her dream.

"Tim?" she croaked, poking at him with her right hand. "Tim!"

The sandy-haired man moaned and slowly began to move.

"What happened?"

He raised his head blinking rapidly and rubbing his eyes. "Viki?" he said as his eyes slowly focused on her. "Oh, thank God. You're okay."

Viki nodded and tried to smile, but she aborted the attempt when she felt how dry her lips were. She was afraid a full smile would cause them to crack and bleed. "What happened?"

Tim rubbed his face again, stifling a yawn. "You died, Viki. You were gone when the EMTs arrived. They had to shock your heart."

"I died?" Viki asked.

Tim nodded solemnly.

Her time in the bardo with her mother came back into focus and Viki gasped.

"What?" Tim asked, looking at the machine that was monitoring her vitals.

"Bardo, I was in the bardo. And it was not good."

They were both silent for a few breaths. Viki with a look of intense concentration on her face, Tim with a look of tired puzzlement.

"And Mark?" Viki asked, the words coming out slowly, reluctantly.

"He's alive. They released him earlier today."

"Released him?"

Tim nodded, "You've been out for two days, Viki."

"Two days? What did they say happened to me?"

"Severe dehydration and electrolyte depletion. Your sodium and potassium levels were low. They had fancy names for that, but I can't remember. Because of that and the long QT thing, the doctor said the electrical activity in your heart went crazy and your heart stopped pumping. If that ambulance hadn't been on the way... If Reg hadn't done CPR..." Tim trailed off, his eyes going to his hands.

Viki reached out and took his hand. "I'm here. It's okay."

Tim nodded and Viki saw his brow pinch together and his eyes moisten with tears before he blinked them away.

"Where's Anela?"

"She's with her grandparents. She's very worried about you."

Viki inhaled deeply, letting out a long, slow sigh. "Tim, I..." she began, but found her throat too dry to speak much more. "Water," she croaked.

She slowly sipped the water Tim presented. The straw took her back to her childhood when she and her grandmother would sit on the porch on hot summer days drinking lemonade out of tall glasses with straws.

"I'm sorry I pushed you... pushed you away."

Tim paused before speaking, his face revealing pain. "No. No, you didn't."

"Yes I did," she said.

He nodded in agreement. "Okay, maybe a little. But I needed to be pushed. I'm... It's... It's been a hard few years."

Viki sipped some more water out of the straw and said, "I am sorry I complicated things for you." She remembered her mother pointing at him and calling him a broken man.

"No. Please. Don't be. We... I think we—"

Behind Tim, Viki caught movement and heard a loud yawn and groan. Tim cut himself off and turned to look.

"V!" Reg said as he pushed himself into a standing position. "Praise be to the Goddess. You are back among the living." Viki smiled at him and almost laughed. His long grey hair was in disarray making him look like a crazy homeless man.

"And glad to be, Reg. So glad. My mother, thousands of her, were the star of my bardo experience."

"Tell me everything."

~~~

"He wouldn't leave, you know," Reg said. They were alone in the hospital room, Tim having excused himself, saying he needed to pick up Anela.

"Who? Tim?"

Reg nodded his head.

"I thought you said he was a coward," Viki said, adding a smile to balance out the bitterness she heard in her voice.

The big man shrugged. "Yeah, maybe, but he does care."

Viki nodded. "Well that's something." She was silent, studying the concern in the older man's face. "Tim told me you did CPR on me."

Reg nodded and looked down.

"Thank you."

Reg nodded again, his eyes meeting hers. "But no more of that crazy stuff now, okay?"

"Okay," she agreed.

~~~

Viki spent another twenty-four hours in the hospital while they kept her under observation. She found it annoying. The constant checking of vitals, the constant interruptions. She needed rest and couldn't get very much of it there.

As she lay in bed, she reviewed her time in Hawaii, thought about what she had experienced, thought through her feelings for Tim. It was complicated, all of it.

Why hadn't she had a baby? Was it about her relationship with her mother souring her on the idea? Was it just the lack of a viable partnership? The years were passing quickly and forty was not too far away. If she was to have a baby, it needed to be soon.

And what of Tim? Viki didn't think of him as broken, but there was no doubt he was damaged. Not that Viki didn't view herself, and every adult she knew, as damaged. It was just that his damage, his grief, made it very difficult to be in a relationship with him. He had been, seemingly, devoted to her to the extreme while she was unconscious, but now that she was awake, he hadn't been back, or called, or—

And with him living in Maui and her living in Arizona, how was that even possible? Why did she even start with him?

Mark was frequently on her mind too. She really wanted to talk to him, but he didn't come visit her in the hospital either. She wanted to know what his experience was like, if he got what he needed, if she could finally be done drawing him.

It was complicated.

During the hours she was awake and Reg wasn't there to distract her, her restless mind dwelled on problems it couldn't solve. She was happy when they released her and Reg took her back to Mark Kosov's home.

CHAPTER 46

"I'm going home in the morning," Reg said as he walked Viki to the house. She was weak and needed support but had refused the offer of a wheelchair.

Viki nodded. "I bet you're dying to get back on the private jet."

"Nope, they're flying me back commercial. First class, but commercial."

"Really?" Viki sighed dramatically. "Treated like royalty on the way in, but on the way out..."

"It's not like that. Alexander told me they sold the jet. The funds are being used to buy mosquito netting in Africa. This Kosov guy is serious about cleaning up his act."

"Welcome back," Alexander said as he opened the door for them. "Can I get you something? Are you hungry? Or thirsty? How about some fresh papaya or pineapple juice? Or do you need to rest? I've got fresh linens on your bed and can draw the shades for you."

Viki laughed and said, "I'm glad to be back too, Alexander."

"I... We were so worried," the Englishman said.

She smiled and kissed him on the check. "Some juice would be great. With ice."

Alexander nodded happily and scurried off.

"Where to?" Reg asked.

"The lanai."

Viki and Reg found Mark Kosov sitting at the table on the lanai, papers spread out in front of him, glasses on his face. Viki thought he looked a bit better than the last time she had seen him.

He stood, with some effort. "So glad you are back, Ms. Dobos." He added a smile and bowed towards her with his head.

"So glad to be back, Mr. Kosov. Glad to see you among the living."

Reg guided Viki to a chair at the table across from Mark and left.

Mark's eyes brightened, and his lips turned up briefly. He seemed far away. His lips pursed, and his eyes refocused. "Well, I wasn't quite ready for *that* yet. Thank you, Viki."

"You're welcome, Mark," she said. "If you don't mind, I would like to hear more about what *that* was."

Mark gathered his papers up. "I do want to talk, but there is more to do today, so much more. How about dinner?"

Viki nodded, stifling a yawn. "That would be great."

Alexander came out and put a glass of juice in front of Viki. It had a pineapple wedge on the rim and was a lovely pinkish color. "Papaya-pineapple," Alexander said.

"Thank you."

"Alexander," Mark said, "can you help me into my office? I think Ms. Dobos has earned some quiet time on the lanai without watching me do this endless paper shuffle."

After they left, Viki gingerly moved herself to a more

comfortable chair facing the ocean. She leaned back, enjoying the lulling noise of the surf and the fresh smell of the air. She was soon asleep.

~~~

"I hope you like lobster," Mark said as Alexander pulled the covers off her and Mark's dinner. "I thought, considering the circumstances, that some sort of celebration was in order."

"Circumstances?" Viki asked. "You mean that we are both still in our corporeal form, both still alive?"

"Indeed," he answered with a smile that was somewhere between genuine and ironic.

Alexander popped the cork on the champagne and poured before leaving them.

They ate slowly, talking of many things, but not what they had been through. They talked about the weather, about Viki needing to return to Sedona soon, about the foundation Mark was creating. Viki enjoyed the dinner and enjoyed Mark's company, but over cheesecake, she asked, "So, Mark, what happened?"

He smiled, wiping his lips with his cloth napkin. "You know," he began, "when I told you the story of my overdose, that I went straight to hell?"

Viki nodded.

"Well this time, when I entered that column of light, I went straight to 'rai'... to heaven."

Viki nodded, enjoying the creamy, coconut-laced flavor of her cheesecake. "Can you back up? Start from the beginning."

"One moment I was lying in darkness, the next I was standing there looking at my body with that silver cord going from my belly to... to... well I guess you would say it went to the belly of my body." He paused and chuckled. "It is a very interesting experience to have a sense of yourself that doesn't include your body."

"Did you notice anything else?" Viki asked.

"I could see. That room was pitch dark, except for the UV light on the camera, but I had no problem seeing myself, my body."

Viki nodded, encouraging him to continue.

"So I slowly searched the lower floor of the house looking for Michael. I wasn't walking, more like floating. I went right through doors and walls, which was a bit odd."

"Odd?"

"Yes. My sense of space, my vision, would pop from one room to the next. I didn't see inside the wall, but experienced a brief period of absolute darkness, which was a bit disorienting."

"And your cord?" Viki asked. "Did you ever feel like it was pulling you back to your body? Like JJ describes in his book?"

Mark nodded his head. "Once, at first, when I moved too fast. As you know I soon came upstairs and saw..." Mark's voice trailed off as his eyes became distant.

"What did you see, Mark?"

"Like I said, it was the most beautiful thing I had ever seen, at that point. There was a column of light going up and down, centered on the drawing you made. The light grew a bit dimmer along its edges, which encompassed all of you at the table. The light was pure white with sparks of all hues and colors dancing along the edges. It was beautiful. But..." Mark's voice trailed off again as he rubbed his head.

"Is something wrong?"

"That whole time I had this kind of dual vision. I was seeing from my—what do they call it in the book—my spirit 'form,' but I was also seeing things from the perspective of the drawing. I could see you and Alexander and Reginald and Tim. It was quite disorienting but not as much as you might expect."

"What do you mean?"

"It wasn't like being cross-eyed. I could see through both sets of eyes clearly, but it was... it was, well, it was distracting, and intense, and took a lot of concentration to manage."

"That's good for me to know. I would expect that most of the souls I draw experience something like that."

Mark had grown quiet with that faraway look on his face again. Viki let the conversation stall as she enjoyed several bites of the cheesecake. This was the first time she had been able to talk with someone she had drawn. She found his experience fascinating.

"You were talking about the column of light," she said quietly.

"The light..." Mark continued. "The light..." He took a deep breath and let it escape his lungs slowly. "It was so beautiful. I said that already, didn't I?" Viki nodded. "It was so beautiful, and the closer I got the more coherent my dual vision became, which I liked, but moreover, the closer I got, the..." Mark paused, taking a long drink of water and staring out at the ocean. "It became so I didn't just see that light. I began to hear it, and feel it, and taste it. It took over my senses. Calling it beautiful is like calling the Grand Canyon a little ditch, or the Taj Mahal a nice building, or the walk of a beautiful, confident woman interesting. Words fail... they just fail.

"As I got closer to the light, it just took me over. My dual vision converged and this beauty took over my senses and I had no choice but to enter it. I heard you speaking, like you were very far away. I heard the words, I knew what words you were saying, but they had no meaning.

"I entered the light and... and..." Mark lowered his head and covered his mouth as he silently wept.

Viki gave him a moment. She watched as he took a deep breath, wiped his eyes with his napkin, and straightened, meeting Viki's eyes but not speaking. "What?" she finally asked.

"It was heaven, Viki. It was heaven. Only not what I had ever imagined or ever heard of. It wasn't streets paved with gold or people running around with wings playing harps. It was..." He took another deep breath. "I'm sorry, words fail me even further here. It was peace, pure peace. So much so that I no longer had a sense of myself, of who or where I was.

"When you drew me... You did draw me again?" he asked.

Viki nodded.

"I got a sense of 'self' back again. But not a sense of myself that I had ever had. I was an individual again, but I was so utterly at peace, so completely satisfied. If you hadn't contacted me, I am sure I wouldn't have left."

"Should I apologize?" Viki asked, as she stabbed another piece of cheesecake.

Mark smiled. It was small, but genuine. "No. No apology necessary. To tell you the truth, I wasn't really ready for that yet."

"That?"

"For heaven, for bliss, for no longer having a sense of self. I'm not ready for that yet."

Viki nodded, relief washing over her. As she listened to

his tale of peace and bliss, she had grown more and more worried that she had made a mistake.

"Really," Mark said. "Thank you for bringing me back. You did the right thing."

"You're welcome." After a moment she asked, "What was it like, leaving?"

Mark paused before answering, "Hard. Very Hard. The hardest thing I have ever done. But once the decision was made, it happened very quickly, and I was back in the room with my body.

"And I wouldn't have done it. But, hearing Alexander's voice. I... I came back for him."

"He's a good man," Viki said with a smile.

CHAPTER 47

Viki's Hawaii routine resumed, if a bit reduced. She rose with the sun and walked on the beach. But she didn't walk down to Kamaole II, she stayed in front of Mark's house.

The first morning after she returned from the hospital, she barely made it to the beach. She had a sharp realization of empathy for Mark. Who she was physically was gone. For her, she knew it would come back, but not for Mark.

She found herself surprisingly content to tarry here. It was Hawaii, after all, but she found herself in need of some healing. Both Mark and Alexander encouraged her to stay, told her that she could stay as long as she wanted, but she knew it was only a matter of time.

As she sat on the beach, the rising sun just striking her back, she realized she was waiting for two things. She was waiting to be strong enough to travel, and she was waiting for Tim.

She knew he cared, but she didn't know if it was enough. She wanted to reach out to him but didn't. She needed someone strong enough to reach out to her. The whisper of her bardo-mother calling him a "broken man" echoed in the back of her mind. She didn't agree, not in her heart, but the voice would not let her be.

Lost in these thoughts, she heard someone clear his throat. She turned and saw Alexander standing next to her.

"Good morning, Alexander."

"Good morning, Viki. Mark is up early today and has requested your presence at breakfast."

Viki's brow furrowed. Her first thought was he was going to ask her to draw him again. She dismissed it as ridiculous, but then, pondering her experience with the man, knew that it wasn't.

"Ms. Dobos?" Alexander prompted.

Viki shook her head trying to banish the thoughts. "Breakfast sounds good, Alexander. But really, call me Viki. We've been through enough that you never need to call me by my last name."

Alexander smiled, helped her up, and offered her his arm. Viki gratefully took it as they made their way to breakfast.

~ ~ ~

Breakfast was different. It was clear that there had been a shift in the Kosov household since Mark was last drawn.

The difference was dramatic—there was a third person at breakfast. Alexander. He still set the table, brought the food, and cleared the table. But for the first time that Viki had seen, he sat and ate with them.

Viki didn't comment on the change but watched both men closely. Alexander seemed to be an equal mixture of delight and discomfort. Mark, on the surface, seemed as at ease as he always had, but as the meal progressed she could see something below the surface. He was delighted too.

She couldn't help herself; she had a smile on her face for most of the meal.

The conversation was companionable. Mark and Alexander talked a lot about the foundation they were forming. Mark asked Viki quite a bit about Sedona; he had never been, and it was clearly his belief that he would never go at this point.

After breakfast was cleared, Alexander brought them more coffee and left them. As if on cue, the conversation shifted.

"I understand that your heart stopped the other evening," Mark said. His delivery was very casual, but it was easy to see there was a lot going on under the surface.

Viki nodded casually in answer.

"What was that like for you?"

Viki smiled widely and laughed. "Reg has been talking, hasn't he?"

Mark paused briefly before nodding. "He has. And I very much would like to hear the story directly."

Viki shrugged, took a sip of the Kona coffee and told him.

~~~

The rest of the day Viki spent sleeping, walking on the beach in front of Mark's house, and doing yoga. She felt the weight of the unanswered questions in her life. Tim—what, if anything, should she do about him? And Mark—she was sure he was going to ask something else of her, she just didn't know what it was.

She was on the freshly cut grass of Mark's yard, having finished a yoga set, when Reg ambled up.

"Well, it's time, V," he said. Gone was the tacky Hawaiian shirt and back was his usual jeans and silk shirt.

"Time to say 'aloha'?" Viki asked.

He lowered himself down to the grass next to her. "It's going to be time for you to go soon too."

"I know. I am going to talk to them tonight. Day after tomorrow should work fine. I am getting better fast, I..."

"Tim?"

"Yes. And Mark, he's got something up his sleeve yet. I'll tell him tonight that I'm leaving. I suspect that will chase it out."

The big man crossed his legs awkwardly and took a deep breath. "You know, I am starting to think I owe you an apology."

"Apology?" she asked.

"Yeah, an apology. I really encouraged you into this because—"

"—of the money," Viki mocked.

"Because of the money. Yeah. And it has been awfully hard on you."

Viki put her arm around his neck. "Well, the money is good, isn't it?"

His eyes widened and he smiled. "I'll say."

"And I've been thinking, what with Mark being so generous with giving away his wealth, forming his foundation and all, that we've gotten paid a little too much."

Reg's eyes widened, his mouth forming an "O," and then a smile. "You're kidding, right? Please tell me you're kidding."

Viki turned solemn and shook her head, no. "You were about to tell me how sorry you were for getting me into this. Let's just say you donate half your fee back to the foundation and we'll call it good. I'll do the same."

His mouth silently opened several times to speak before

he looked into Viki's unwavering eyes. "Okay," he said quietly. Viki's eyebrows came up and he said louder, "Okay. Yes, I will donate half my fee to the foundation."

Viki smiled and patted him on the back. "Now doesn't that feel good?" she asked, a mocking smile upon her face.

"Oh yeah, that feels so good. I am a changed man. I am going to give half of everything away from now on."

Viki punched him in the shoulder. "Shut up, Reg. Even half is a big payday."

Reg slowly rose to his feet, a smile spreading across his face. "You know, you probably could have gotten me to give back, 65, maybe 75 percent. You're always asking for too little."

Viki, from her seated position, took a swipe at his legs. The big man danced back.

"Aloha, darling, V," Reg said with a casual salute. "See you back amongst the red rocks soon. Now that we've got you out of your shell a bit I have plans for us. Boy, do I have plans."

~~~

Viki was pleased that Alexander sat and ate with them again. He didn't look entirely comfortable, but she was glad he was there, glad that the two men's relationship was growing.

Over dinner Viki told them of her plans to leave, and Alexander said he would make arrangements in the morning.

After dinner, over coffee, with Alexander there, Mark broached the subject Viki had been anticipating, "I've been thinking..."

Viki kept the frown and worry from forming on her face

and smiled at him. She felt a need from him, similar to the need he exuded when they first met, but it was a bit different. It was quieter and smaller. The last drawing they had done had changed him.

"I would like to... This is a bit awkward, Viki, but I have something I want to ask you. A favor, really. A huge favor."

Despite her best efforts, Viki felt her face fall and her eyes widen.

"It's okay," Mark continued holding up his hands, "I am not asking you to draw me again, at least not while I am alive."

Viki let out a sigh of relief. "That, I am glad to hear."

"I hope you understand how truly grateful I am for what you have done. What respect and awe I have for your gift. What—"

"Mark, please cut to the chase. I am still recovering from the last thing you asked me to do, and I just can't take the suspense."

Mark nodded. "Very well. I apologize. I would like to propose a pact." He paused and looked at Alexander, the other man was looking down. "It was Alex's idea, really. I was going to throw money at you, but he felt we could enter a pact for our mutual benefit."

"Mark," Viki said, her sharp tone prompting him.

"Okay. Here it is. If you will agree to monitor me after I die and do your best to make sure I stay out of the bardo, I will promise to do my best to be there when you die and make sure you stay out of the bardo."

Viki's jaw dropped, and she reached for her wine glass to cover the reaction. "What about heaven?" she asked when she recovered. "What about the light? Don't you want to go back?"

Mark's facial expression was complicated. First a trace of the bliss she had seen when he was approaching the light, then a furrowing of the brow and pursing of the lips, followed by a small nod of the head. "I'm not ready for it yet. As appealing as it is, I am not ready. There is more to do that concerns this world, and since it looks like I will have a chance to do it, I would like to try."

Viki nodded slowly as she absorbed the information. "So you plan on being a ghost, for a while, at least until I die?"

"Yes. I am prepared to do that. You are young and healthy. By the time you die, I will have had a lot of time to learn my way around. I will help you and teach you. Provided, of course, that you don't move on right away. Given how you are in the world, that would not surprise me."

"And how, exactly, would this look?" Viki asked.

"Well, about once a month after I die, you will draw me to check in on my well-being. If I am in the bardo, you will take steps to remove me from that state. Alexander here will provide you with any resources you require to do that."

"And me? How will you know when I die?"

Mark paused, his hand rubbing his chin. "I've been thinking about that. In that book, the one with JJ and Jesus and Banquo, they talk a lot about traveling, how they 'pop' from place to place. I will make it a priority after I die to learn how to do this. Once I can, I will check in on you at least once a month."

She paused, looking at Alexander who nodded encouragingly. "Okay, from the book it sounds like that kind of traveling is hard. How will you learn?"

Mark shrugged, "The way I learn everything. I will find a teacher. If I have to, I will get on a flight to Tucson and find the graveyard JJ writes about and ask Banquo to teach me."

Viki smiled and slowly shook her head. "You've got it all figured out, don't you?"

The older man seemed taken aback, his blue eyes drilling into Viki. "From your tone I gather you think I am missing something."

Viki licked her lips and nodded. "Life, and I guess death, is usually not simple. It's messy and complicated. What you are proposing, I am sure, will be much harder than it sounds."

"I suspect you are right. But, what do you think of my proposal? This pact?"

"I think I need to think about it," Viki said. "Do you have some contracts for me to look over?"

Mark looked to Alexander, who nodded encouragingly to him, and then back to Viki. "No. No contracts. A handshake and your word is all I am asking for."

CHAPTER 48

It was another beautiful morning in Hawaii, and Viki drank it in more than usual; it was her last. She felt her strength returning, and it was time to go. There were only a few things left to do.

Just as the sun was rising behind her, she heard some shuffling in the sand and some labored breathing. She turned and saw Mark Kosov slowly making his way across the beach, supported by Alexander Wells.

She smiled. "Good morning, gentlemen. It's a beautiful day."

Alexander smiled warmly, but Viki could see the strain there. When she had first arrived on the island, Mark could make his own way to the beach. Mark nodded, doing his best to keep the grimace of effort off his face.

"Good morning, Viki," Mark said as they made their way to the firm wet sand next to her. "I have a favor to ask of you." He smiled slyly and added, "A small favor. Alexander needs to prep for the parade of suits—we are being overrun by lawyers today—and I wanted a few moments with you. Would you take a walk with me?"

"Of course."

Alexander reluctantly removed his support from Mark as Viki got his arm over her shoulder and supported him. "Take good care of him," Alexander said.

"I will." Viki guided the older man slowly down the beach.

Their progress was slow, which suited Viki. She didn't want to rush anything today. "I've been wondering," she began, "why did you settle here? Why Maui? You could have moved anywhere in the world."

Mark's face grew distant for a bit and a small smile crept onto his lips. "The ocean, of course. But when I was a much younger man, flush with cash for the first time, I came here and fell in love with a native woman. It didn't last, but she was my first real love, and I associate this place with her."

"Where is she now?"

"She lives up *mauka*, up on Haleakala. She has a grandchild now."

"Do you talk?" Viki asked.

"We didn't, not for decades, but now that..." Mark sighed and stopped his progress. "Now that my time is coming we have talked a few times."

Viki nodded. "Do you want to sit?" The house was still in sight, but she could feel his energy fading.

Mark nodded and she helped him onto the sand.

"I wanted to thank you and Reg for your donations to the foundation."

"Of course," Viki said. "Your payment was way more than generous."

"In terms of value, it wasn't. You have lifted a tremendous burden from me. I know there are difficult and frightening things about death, like the bardo, but I don't fear it anymore. I... I don't fear it." His eyes became moist as he spoke. After a time, he said, "I am sorry it was so hard on you physically... that you had to give so much."

"You have given me a great gift too, Mark. For so long I carried the burden of what I thought I did to that young man in Boston. That weight is lifted. It is clear now that drawing the living can be a trauma to them, a big trauma, but it doesn't mean death. I still wish it hadn't happened, but it doesn't haunt me anymore."

Mark nodded and smiled. "I am glad for that."

"And something else," Viki continued. "I feel different. I feel like most of my life has been passive, waiting for life to come to me, waiting for clients to come to me. In some ways afraid of who I am and what I can do..." Viki trailed off, her eyes growing distant.

"And now?"

She leaned over and kissed him gently on the cheek. Mark looked surprised and Viki giggled. "And now, my friend, and now... Well, I don't know. But I do know that I will not be nearly so passive. I will be more like you."

Mark blinked back tears, staring at her. When he spoke, he spoke slowly, each word formed in his mouth with great care. "I am so glad I could be of service."

Viki stood. "I am grateful for you, Mark, and for this," she threw out her arms and spun around, her smiling face drinking in the sunshine, her ears soaking in the sounds of the ocean, her feet brushing against the warming sugar sand. "Now, how about breakfast? I am starving," she said, as she extended her hand.

Mark did not accept her proffered hand, but asked, "And our pact?"

"You know," Viki began as she squatted in front of him. "One good thing about my little bardo experience. Hearing those things from my mother, feeling so horrible about myself. Fighting my way out of it. It's like I faced my worst fear. The rest of this, of life, seems less daunting."

"I agree, provided the bardo experience does not become endless." He raised an eyebrow pointedly.

"You are a persistent man, Mr. Kosov. More lessons for me there." She paused, letting her face go serious as the seconds ticked by. She could see the surprised annoyance on Mark's face but didn't let it last too long. "Yes, Mark Kosov, I accept your pact. I agree to monitor you after you die and do everything I can to keep you out of the bardo in exchange for you helping me when it is my time if I am an earthbound spirit." She extended her hand and shook Mark's firmly.

CHAPTER 49

Viki was nervous, her palms sweating. She rubbed them on her shorts, her fist coming up for the third time to knock on the door. She paused, hand frozen, and chided herself. She had survived her mother in the bardo and she couldn't knock on Tim's door to say good-bye?

To be fair, there was plenty to be nervous about. He had showed such concern in the hospital but hadn't made any effort to contact her since. And, she hadn't either, but what she needed was for him to reach out. She knew it was going to be awkward and uncomfortable, but now that she had mere hours before Alexander took her to the airport, there was no more time to wait.

She took a deep breath, and this time, with her eyes closed, she knocked. Her fist hit harder than she meant it to. She withdrew her fist, smarting from the blow, and knocked with an appropriate amount of energy with her other hand.

She waited, breathing deeply, doing her best to ignore the voices of doubt, shame, and recrimination in her head. She had known what she was doing. She had chosen to do what she did.

She raised her fist again and as she brought it down to knock, the door opened, throwing her off balance and she stumbled into the doorway.

"Umm, hi Tim," she said as she corrected herself and stepped back out.

"Hi," Tim said, his face unreadable.

Viki smiled, not to put him at ease, not because she felt happy or anything, but because his un-reaction was typical. In some ways, it made what she wanted to do seem easier. If he had been suddenly warm again that would have made it hard.

"Can I come in?" she asked.

He nodded and stepped back, giving her room to enter. She picked up the two packages she had put down and handed the larger one to Tim.

"That is for Anela. It is drawing supplies and some DVD instructions aimed at her age group. They should help her art move along."

"Thank you," Tim said. "Would you like to sit on the lanai? Can I get you something? I just made some iced tea."

"That would be lovely," Viki said as she went out, keeping the second, smaller, package with her. She sat at the table and stared out at the beautiful ocean. The usual mix of tourists and a few locals were in attendance. Kids played in the surf, screaming with delight. Adults lounged or walked. She knew she was going to miss the ocean.

"I'm sorry I haven't been in touch," Tim said as he set a glass of iced tea in front of Viki and sat across from her with his own.

"It's okay, Tim." She saw the puzzled look on his face and continued, "Really, it is. I am not here to talk about you and me."

"Oh," he said. She couldn't tell if he was disappointed or relieved.

"I'm here to say good-bye. I am leaving in a few hours."

"Oh," Tim said again with the same expression that could be relief or disappointment.

Viki brought the package to her chest and sighed heavily. "Actually, I am here to talk about *you* and to give you a gift."

Tim blinked several times and nodded uncomfortably. As if she were a dentist about to drill out his tooth.

"First the positive," Viki began. "You are a good man, Tim. Down to your bones, you're a good and caring man. I am glad I got a chance to spend time with you." Tim didn't speak, he just listened. "And I would love to spend more time with you..." Viki trailed off, losing her nerve.

"But," he began tentatively as if he might have forgotten how to speak, "you're leaving, and the Pacific stands between my home and yours."

Viki smiled and took a sip of tea. "I know. And that is not that big a barrier. I bet my talents would go over big in a place like this with a lot of tourists. Not all that different than Sedona in that way."

"I'm sorry, Viki. I just can't... I wish I could, but I can't."

Viki reached out and put her hand on top of his. "I told you, I am not here to talk about us. It can't happen, and I am fine with that."

"What did we need to talk about then?"

"Like I said, you."

"Me?"

"Yes, Tim, you." Viki saw him swallow uncomfortably, but continued. "You've been through a lot, are going through a lot. Tess's death. Raising Anela on your own. What we just went through with Tess and the bardo. Me and my frequent trips to the hospital. It's a lot, Tim."

Tim's eyebrows pinched tightly, and his eyes looked on the verge of tears as he nodded.

"I care for you, I do. And I am not saying this with any personal agenda. But, Tim, you need help."

He opened his mouth to speak, his eyes going from misty to angry before he looked into his lap.

"You need someone to help you to deal with these traumas. A counselor, a close friend, someone you can talk to and get these things out." Viki's heart was beating fast, her palms sweating again. This wasn't the kind of thing she ever did. "You've got to let it out, Tim."

The silence that filled the space between them was dense and thick and uncomfortable. Tim stared at his hands for some time before meeting Viki's eyes. She could see the pain in them, she could see the need. She wanted to be the one to help him, to love him out of this, but she knew that wasn't possible. She knew that couldn't happen. She knew it wouldn't be a healthy thing for either of them. It made her very sad.

He nodded slowly, his lips pursing briefly before he said, "I know."

Viki let out the air she had been holding and sighed noisily, the escaping sound turning into a strained laugh. "I was so scared to say that. I was so worried you would be angry."

"I know it's been hard for you," he offered.

She nodded but didn't speak. Giving him room to talk.

"I thought my life was set. That Tess and I would grow old together. That we would raise Anela and retire here on Maui. That our life would be simple but beautiful. It was my whole world and..."

Viki put her hand on his again. She wanted to do more, but that didn't feel right.

"I care for you, Viki. But..."

"You're scared of me," Viki said. "You're afraid to love again. You're frightened by Anela's attraction to my gift and the unusual abilities she has displayed since I came."

He nodded, his face a mask of guilt.

"It's okay, Tim. As much as I can, I understand."

"Thank you," he said, his relief evident.

They sat and chatted for thirty minutes. Mostly about Anela, Mark, and Viki's plans once she returned to Sedona.

"I'll probably be back before too long," she said. She paused, the fear in her belly coming back. "Can I check in on you if I do come back?"

"Of course."

Viki let out another sigh of relief and laughed. "This is becoming quite the sigh party we are having."

Tim nodded, standing and picking up their glasses. "More tea?"

"Oh, no thank you. I really should go." Viki rose, her foot bumping into the package she had set on the floor. "Oh, I almost forgot. I have a gift for you."

Tim accepted the bag, gingerly peaking inside before pulling the bathing suit out. "A bathing suit? But I don't wear—"

"I know, Tim, you never wear a bathing suit. But it is time you did."

"I..."

"You used to surf, you used to love the ocean until Tess's accident." Tim nodded but didn't speak. "If you can find your way back into the ocean, somehow, I think you'll be better for it."

CHAPTER 50

As she walked back down the beach to Mark Kosov's house, Viki wept. It was a silent affair with the tears rolling down her cheeks, salty as the seawater her feet touched.

She was grateful that she had been able to say what she needed to say. She was relieved that it was over, that she didn't need to wonder about Tim or about her and Tim. But, mostly, she was sad. She cared for him and wanted to see him happy. It was clear that he wasn't. His burdens were too great.

But that is not why she cried. She cried because she was grieving. Grieving the loss of what might have been, grieving the loss of who she had been. Grieving the fact that it was time to leave.

As she walked, slowly, down Kamaole II, she cried and said good-bye. It was the wrong time of day to see Howard with his white military cap and his cantaloupe-sized belly. She wished she had a chance to say good-bye to him. It was the wrong time to see Baxter the dog and the woman who cared for him. She even felt a twinge at not being able to see the Ex-Pat Businessman with his watermelon-sized belly one more time.

She walked slower than usual, but soon she was back at Mark's house and it was time to leave.

The Russian man didn't say much, they already had said it all. He thanked her, hugged her fiercely, and kissed her on both cheeks.

She offered to take a cab, but Alexander wouldn't have it. As they pulled away from the house, Viki turned back and saw Mark Kosov standing at the edge of the driveway leaning on his cane, smiling and waving.

They were stopped at the edge of the driveway as Alexander waited for a break in the busy traffic. She watched the iron gates close, with the griffin on them, and through them saw Mark turn and make his slow way back into the house.

It was the last time she would see him alive but not the last time she would see him.

Epilogue

Three months later.

Viki was dressed in her Madam Valarka outfit, with silks, full makeup, and hoop earrings. Her client, the man that sat across from her, was not desperate, hopeful, or nervous, like most of her clients. No, he was excited and impatient.

Before him sat the card he had drawn. Coyote. It was a playful archetype, representing the trickster, one who distains the status quo and conventional behavior, and loves to break the rules.

Viki looked away from the eager face of Alexander Wells down to her blank sheet of paper and the upside down picture of Mark Kosov. She took a deep breath, slowly letting it out as she relaxed her body. Her hand reached for and found an ocean-blue pastel and she began working on the eyes.

The drawing went quickly, Mark's face being so familiar to her. The eyes first, then outlining the face, drawing the nose and mouth and ears, filling in the hair, and then back to the eyes. Always back to the eyes.

As she drew, she sipped from a drink that Alexander had made for her. It was slightly sweet, tasting of pineapples.

It was one of the things Alexander had insisted on and had required her releasing her medical records to Mark's personal physician. The doctor had studied her charts and determined that the contents of the drink would help prevent the dehydration and other problems she had experienced.

It wasn't tradition but Viki welcomed it. It was time for her to make her own traditions.

She had Alexander put the fingers of his left hand on the bottom of the page, while Viki did the same on the top. She inhaled deeply and breathed out onto the page.

The ocean-blue eyes of Mark Kosov snapped to life. He blinked and looked around. "Oh my," he said.

"Shall we get right down to business?" Alexander asked.

The drawing of Mark shook its head. "I need to talk to Viki a bit first."

Alexander looked surprised but nodded.

"What is it, Mark?" Viki asked.

"This... this afterlife, it... Well, it hasn't been as simple as I had hoped."

Viki smiled gently. "It's okay, Mark. You have me for thirty minutes twice a day for the next twenty-one days. We have time. We'll work it out."

Mark nodded, looking childlike.

"Alexander has some urgent foundation business to discuss," Viki said. "Let's start there and we'll spend some time on your questions after."

Mark nodded and Alexander began his questions.

~~~

Later, after dinner, they lingered on the lanai, watching the stars come out. Neither talked, but Viki knew they needed to. She excused herself and came back with a thick three-ring binder. She carefully handed it to Alexander.

"What is this?" Alexander asked, picking it up and flipping through the pages.

"After I got back to Arizona, I took a trip down to Tucson and tracked down the people in the *Shuffled Off* book. Tamara Watson, who is in the book, showed me around the facility, showed me the chamber JJ used to write the book. This is his next book, *To Be a Fool.* In it JJ documents his side of the two times I drew him, and how he helped me after the final drawing of Mark."

"We are in it?"

Viki nodded. "That we are... and a whole lot more. I brought it so you can read it while I'm here."

The Englishman slowly shook his head. "All of this... It's just too much."

"You said it, my friend. It's just crazy. Other ghosts are communicating now, and Tamara wants me to work with a writer up in Flagstaff to tell my part of the story."

"This... I..." Alexander chuckled. "This is going to be big."

"Huge, my friend. Huge. Reg is going crazy trying to figure out how to capitalize on what he is calling the 'Ghost Boom.'"

Alexander's face darkened and he put the binder down. Viki breathed a sigh of relief. She knew she wasn't here just to draw Mark. She was here to help Alexander too.

"Do you think you can help Mark?" he asked.

Viki shrugged her shoulders. "I suspect, but I'm not sure. It has been less than a month, so maybe this isn't all that surprising."

Alexander nodded. "He seems most distressed about not being able to leave the house and not being able to find a way to communicate with me like in that book. He hasn't been able to find Michael yet, either."

Viki nodded. "I really think it will just take time." Viki paused, letting her eyes go out of focus and slowly moving her head from the left to right so the entire lanai was seen from her peripheral vision. "He's here," she said.

Alexander straightened up and looked around.

Viki pointed to one of the empty chairs at the table. "Don't be surprised. Where else would he be?"

Alexander nodded. "You can see ghosts now?"

She shrugged. "Sometimes. When I was very young I could. I could see ghosts and faeries. I remembered it when I was here last time, and I have been trying to do it again. I don't see much, just a flash of light in my peripheral vision. We can check with Mark in the morning and see if I'm right."

Alexander's nostrils flared as tears started to run down his checks. "I miss him. I miss talking to him and seeing him. Twenty years I worked for him. I... I don't know how to do this." He took his napkin and blotted his eyes with it.

"It's okay, Alexander, it's okay. It's normal for you to feel this way."

"Normal!" he said loudly. "Normal? Normal for me to cry every day with the object of my grief looking on?" He pointed at the empty chair that Viki had indicated earlier.

Viki smiled gently and shook her head. "Maybe, Alexander, maybe. Perhaps the dead watch the living grieve more than we know. And don't forget the dead are grieving too."

Surprise registered on Alexander's face. He put the napkin down. "Of course. Of course they are grieving too. But... I wonder what it is like, what the dead feel as they watch the living grieve them."

Viki shrugged her shoulders, "I don't know, but we can find out next time I draw Mark."

Alexander nodded slowly.

Viki got up. "It's been a long day. Good night, Alexander." She turned to the empty chair. "Good night, Mark. I'll be seeing both of you in the morning."

~~~

The sun wasn't yet up, but Viki was out on the beach, her body-clock still on Arizona time. She walked slowly north from Alexander Well's house—she had to keep reminding herself that it wasn't Mark's anymore—on the walk she had grown to love when she was here the previous winter.

It looked the same. A few locals fishing, a lot of tourists walking, palm trees, soft sand, the beautiful blue of the pacific. She took her time and breathed it all in.

She was nervous to go too far. If she walked as far as she used to she would run into Tim and Anela. They hadn't spoken since she left the island and returned to Sedona. It seemed better that way.

But they were friends, right? What would a friend do? She thought back to that advice Reg had given her, to take him at his word. Well, she wasn't sure what his "word" was concerning her. On their last visit he had admitted that he cared and that was as much as she knew.

She stopped on the tongue of land that preceded Kamaole Beach II. She peered out and thought she saw them. The small brown girl with flying black hair and the erect man with short blond hair.

She breathed deeply and let out a long sigh. She knew this might be hard, she knew this could lead to more heartache, but she also knew that if she didn't take action she would be wondering about this for the next three weeks until she returned to Sedona.

She checked her appearance. It was a bit embarrassing, but she had primped. She wore a new, black, one-piece bathing suit with a blue sarong. She had lost a few pounds recently and she knew she looked good.

After returning to Sedona she had cut her hair. Her whole life her brown hair had been long, almost always pulled back in a ponytail. When she had returned she felt different, and marked that difference by cutting her hair. Today her shoulder-length hair flowed freely in the gentle breeze, and a plumeria flower was behind her right ear.

She took another deep breath and put one foot in front of the other and made her way towards the father and daughter.

It was Anela that spotted her first. "Miss Viki!" she cried. The brown-skinned girl kicked up sand as she ran towards Viki. She squatted and met the girl's wet and sandy hug.

"Anela, I am so happy to see you. You have grown."

"I knew you were coming, I knew it!"

"You knew?" Viki asked.

The girl pulled away and nodded vigorously. "Mama told me. She said you were coming back to help the man in the house with the turquoise roof." Anela pointed back down the beach towards the house. It did have turquoise tiles on the roof and, to her knowledge, Anela had never been there.

"That's right, Anela. You did know."

"And you can give me more drawing lessons. I watched all the DVDs you left. I loved them."

"She did," Tim said with a smile. "She watched them over and over."

Viki slowly stood. "Hi, Tim." He looked the same, his

kind eyes framed by crow's feet, his blond hair short with a few grey hairs, his slim frame dressed in a polo shirt and—

She did a double take. Instead of the shorts he habitually wore when she was here last, he wore a bathing suit.

He wore *the* bathing suit that Viki had given him on her last day here.

"Don't be so surprised," Tim said with a laugh.

"But..." she gawked, she couldn't help herself.

"He doesn't go swimming yet," Anela said, her nose raised and her eyes rolling in a surprisingly grown-up gesture. "Want to see some of my drawings?" the girl asked as she took Viki's hand and began tugging her up the beach.

She looked to Tim who smiled and nodded.

Viki paused, a vision passing before her eyes. She saw a blue silk scarf in her hands, and she saw herself wrapping it around Anela's head. The girl appeared to be a few years older and looked up at Viki and smiled nervously.

"Are you okay?" Tim asked.

The vision fled and Viki smiled at Tim. She wasn't sure what she had seen or what it meant. What she did know is that it didn't scare her, it excited her. "Yeah, I am good."

AUTHOR'S NOTE

Thank you so much for reading. What follows is an excerpt from *Shuffled Off*, the first in my "A Ghost's Memoir" books, and then acknowledgements and a bit about me.

But, before you proceed, I have a favor to ask you. If you've enjoyed this book, then do me the honor of spreading the word. Write an honest review on Amazon (just a few sentences is fine), loan the book, or tell your friends. Word of mouth is the best endorsement a book can get, and only you can do that. Thank you!

If you want to know as soon as new books come out please sign up for my email newsletter. Go to RobertJMcCarter.com, you'll see the signup offer on the home page. As of this writing I am giving away ebooks of the first episode of my Superhero/Love Story series.

The Following is an sample from
Shuffled Off: A Ghost's Memoir, Book 1

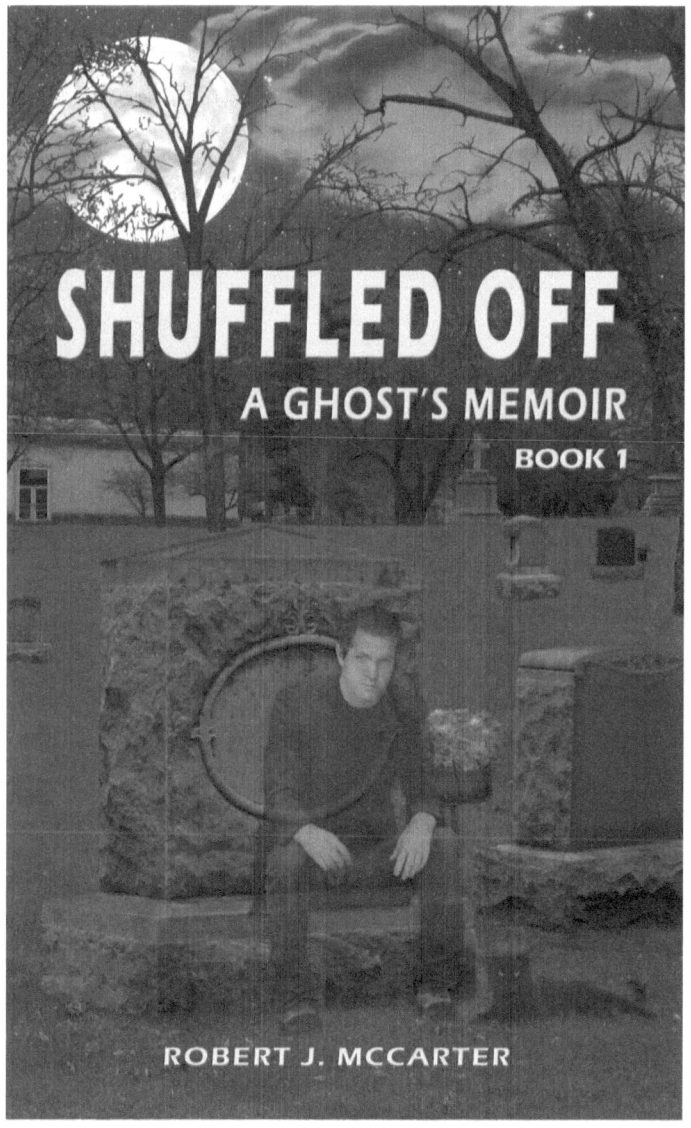

SHUFFLED OFF

A GHOST'S MEMOIR

BOOK 1

ROBERT J. MCCARTER

Transmission #1

Received 2010/10/19 03:14:03

WHEN SOMEONE DIES, THE WORLD DOESN'T STOP. IT seems like it should, but it doesn't. Sure if it's a famous person, or a grisly murder, there is a period of piranha-like activity on the part of media. But that's not stopping, that is just business as usual in the land of the twenty-four hour news cycle. Even then it settles down quickly and everyone gets back to their shaky, unsure life.

It would be useful if it did stop. You know, take a moment, get your bearings, and deal with the practical and emotional details that engulf a death. But no, no stopping, no break, you just gotta continue your drunkard's walk down the path of life.

When I died, the world didn't stop, not a bit. I wasn't expecting it to, but it would've been nice, you know?

The death effect is kind of like throwing a stone into a pond: a famous person is like a rock—it stirs things up; an everyman, like me, is more like a tiny pebble—it effects the immediate surrounding but has no discernable effect on the whole. In the end neither one really changes things much; the world doesn't stop. Life goes on.

My ma was a mess, it rocked her world—"a parent shouldn't outlive her child," and all that junk. My sister Jean spent about three days contemplating her own mortality and just went back to business as usual—the college social scene is all consuming. Nate, now he was ripped up. We've been joined at the hip since junior high, and my exit really sent him spinning.

I used to wish there was a sign that a person was going to leave soon. Like a light over their head that they can't see, and no one tells them about, but everyone around them sees and can act on. You know: be nice, spend time with them, tell them what you've got to tell them. My dad died quick, a heart attack, and it left me devastated, wishing I had said and done things different towards the end. You know the end is gonna come, but when it arrives it arrives so damn quick.

But now that it was me, I would want to have seen the light over my head too. I would have liked to look up Rhiannon and told her how sorry I was. I would have ditched work and taken a good long vacation. I would have slept a lot less, and lived a lot more.

So now you must be thinking who's the mouthy guy writing from beyond the pale. Woooooooooooo. At least that's what I would be thinking, I have no idea what you are thinking, I ain't no mind reader.

OK, so my name is Joseph Jeffery Lynch, JJ to my friends. I am twenty-nine years old, and I am dead. Well mostly dead. Actually I don't really know. The body is gone, but I seem to still have a sense of myself, of who I am, even without it. Is that alive, or is that dead? Is that un-dead? I guess if you had to choose a word for my condition, you would choose the word "ghost." Wooooooooooooo.

Scared yet? I would be if I were you. What I have to tell has its scary parts, its happy parts, and its sad parts—just like life. Is life scary to you? To me it was, sometimes, and I can now say the same thing about death.

Wonder how a ghost can write? Good question. I am using some new technology here at the University of Arizona (UA) that allows me to "type." Part of the SECI program. Never heard of it? It stands for the Search for Extra-Corporeal Intelligence. What SETI is to aliens, SECI is to ghosts.

Don't be surprised if you haven't heard of it. It is kind of a ghost project (pun intended) running underneath a more respectable project studying lightweight electromagnetic (EM) shielding. Now I don't fully understand the technology, but here I am the first beta tester.

I graduated college (barely, and with a liberal arts degree at that), but because of circumstances, that I imagine we'll get into later, I never moved on from my college job. I worked as a janitor at UA and among other things, I cleaned up the small lab that Jin Shi and Tamara Watson run the SECI program out of. They would often be there late and we would talk about things: about ghosts, and death, and the nature of life. The basic theory is this: consciousness exists outside of the body, the body being an amplifier for that consciousness. Jin and Tam were trying to figure out another type of amplifier—so was born SECI.

"Look," Tam told me once, "every religion in the world believes consciousness goes on beyond the corporeal form, exists separate from the corporeal form. They can't all be wrong; we are just trying to find a way to communicate with that realm."

Tam, she was always good to me, and she was cute, so I kinda had a crush on her. Big lips, lots up top, but not much of a butt (but I wouldn't kick her out of bed for that!). She also had this vulnerability, this deep need; it was clear she was doing SECI for very personal reasons.

"Imagine it, JJ," Jin said, he always had this glint in his eye when he talked about this part. "How much would this be worth? Talk to the dearly departed; solve murders; find out the secrets of the great beyond." Clearly the monetary ramifications were what got him going.

"So how does it work?" I asked.

"Our theory revolves around detecting non-random, patterned EM fluctuations in a highly EM shielded space," Tam explained. "Our SECI Chamber will theoretically shield all external EM radiation, so that any EM it picks up will have to be from within the chamber, from an extra-corporeal. The chamber will have in-depth instructions for the earth-bound extra-corporeal entity so they know what patterns to create to communicate with us."

"Huh?" It was all beyond me; I'm just a janitor with a liberal arts degree.

I lived about a mile south of UA, in a little studio apartment. It was old, not in a good part of town, but serviceable. Couldn't do much better on what I made.

I mostly used my skateboard to get around. Yeah, I know, a man of my age—what can I say? I was without four-wheeled motorized transport.

About two months ago—give or take, time is tough to measure right now—I was headed home on a blistering August night at about 2 a.m. I was kicking my way south when a black Audi A4 plowed into me.

The car, full of drunk undergrads, veered to avoid something (or nothing, they were seriously altered), hopped the curb, hit me and plowed us all into a Mickey D's. I was out quick, and my body expired some minutes later pinned to a kiddie jungle gym.

That undergrad's car was equipped with airbags leaving the passengers relatively unharmed. I, on the other hand, was smushed like a bug against a windshield.

The EMTs tried to revive me, they tried hard. They got me out and hauled me back to Saint Mother of the Weeping Virgin (or something like that), but it was no use.

It wasn't bad, dying that is. I've had headaches that hurt more. What was hard was watching it all. As soon as the car plowed into me, I popped out and kind of floated (I guess) along and watched the whole bloody procedure.

One plastered, Barbie-blond co-ed stumbled out of the car, looked at what was left of me and said, "Oh my God, that is so gross!"

The driver, a GQ pretty-boy, called someone, Daddy I presume, and said, "It wasn't my fault, you've got to get me out of this." His voice shook and his face was pale.

There were people screaming, others with broken bones and injuries, weeping women, and one patron barfing up their recently consumed meat-like-substance.

As the firemen pulled back the car, it was surreal watching my body slide to the floor like a wet rag, my eyes open and vacant, my limbs bent at odd angles. So quick, so sudden, one moment alive, the next dead and all that is left is the meat body I used to inhabit. Like a candle being snuffed out, like a marionette getting its strings cut, like the air rushing out of a balloon, like a... Too many metaphors?

Maybe, but man was it sudden, and that suddenness was bizarre and hard to accept.

The paramedics went right to it, following their procedures: mobilizing my neck; shocking my heart; pumping me full of meds; hauling me off in the ambulance. I was attached to my body by some sort of silver cord. When the body was moved, I just got dragged along.

The ambulance was cool; I had never been in one. All that gear, and it was fast. We tore through the streets, sirens blaring, weaving around what little traffic there was. Kind of made me wish I had been an ambulance jockey instead of a janitor. What a ride!

Transmission #2
Received 2010/10/20 02:15:26

Sorry about that, got tired I guess. This is hard work: forming the shapes clearly enough to be translated into letters.

Jin, you called it. The feedback system works well. If I couldn't see the result of my efforts this just wouldn't work. Sorry if the prose is a bit rough, it's just too much to go back and edit it into something prettier.

I can't think that it matters to you though. I bet there was jumping for joy when you saw the first intelligible bit come in. Did that bottle of champagne finally get opened? Sorry I wasn't here to witness it.

So where was I? Oh yeah, death by car at the Mickey D's.

When my dad passed, I got my head shrunk for a while and the shrink, she told me about the five stages of grief. As I recall they are: Denial, Anger, Deals, Depression, and Acceptance. I think that is it, normally I would just look it up, but that's not going to work right now.

JJ's Things That Suck About Being Dead (JJTTSABD)

#1: *Can't use the net to look stuff up and pretend you are smarter than you really are.*

So I think there are stages, similar stages, to dying; at least for me.

Stage 1: Shock, aka Denial, aka wtf just happened?

So watching myself die, the self-absorbed bleating of my killers, the wild ride to Saint Mother of All That is Virginal, watching the heroic efforts to save me—was Stage #1: Shock, and shock is just one variant of the larger (much larger) area of Denial.

There was this weird detachment. It was me, but it wasn't me. As I watched those doctors and nurses trying to pummel my body back to life, I kept trying to talk to them. I said, "Hey, I'm right here, it's OK. I'm not really dead." Shattered hip; broken ribs; lacerated bowels; punctured spleen; blood loss; head trauma; and on and on it went. One at a time they accessed and tried to stabilize my injuries. They got the heart going a few times, but never for very long.

After a while I started getting worried—what if they succeeded? I didn't want back in that thing, man that would just be hell. So I kept telling them that it was OK, that they should let me go. Eventually they did. The process, though, was gratifying. It was amazing seeing my life cared for to such a degree by a room full of strangers.

At this stage I was attached to my body—I went where it did, just got dragged along. After the heroics were over I was left there for some time, just me and my body. Just me and me.

I don't remember much of that time, but I developed a little mantra that pulled me through: wtf, wtf, wtf, wtf, wtf... For how long I have no idea. How could this have happened? That might have been crossing tentatively over to Stage 2:

Anger. But believe me, it was way more shock than anger. When anger came there was no denying it.

The morgue was next, a cold sterile room where my body was shoved into a drawer. There were three others there with me. I guess you would call them ghosts, but I was still having a hard time with that. All three were wispy floating forms with silver cords leading to a drawer. Two were completely out of it, looking gape jawed and stupid, just wandering around. The third's name was Jesus.

"Hey fresh meat, what happened to you?" he asked.

I would have jumped out of my skin, if I had skin. I don't know why, but I just wasn't expecting that.

"Huh?" I mumbled.

"Oh man, not another bardo-brain," he said.

"What?"

"What a waste of space. Can't you bring me someone to talk to?" He looked up as he said this.

"Are you talking to me?"

"Praise be to Guadalupe! Yeah man, I'm talking to you." With a big smile on his face he added, "My name is Hey-zeus."

"Hey-zeus, you mean as in Gee-zus?"

"Difference in pronunciation. If you would be so kind, please call me Hey-zeus. Although I am a mighty handsome guy, I don't want to be confused with the big fellow." He pointed up.

I am not sure if he was handsome or not: his dancing eyes were brown; his face was plain and kind looking; and he had a big full mustache wiggling above his smile.

"Oh yeah, sure. My name is JJ." I would have extended my hand, but it wasn't quite like that. I had a sense of form, but it wasn't steady, especially regarding limbs. Jesus's face was clear, but the rest of his body came in and out of... hmmm... focus I guess, depending on what he was doing. I suppose it was the same for mine.

Turns out Jesus had been there a while. He was an illegal and as such his body had not been claimed yet. Jesus was a bounty hunter that had snuck across the border chasing a murderer. He wasn't like a normal bounty hunter, at least not what I thought normal bounty hunters did; he also tried to "show them the light of the divine Mother Mary" before he turned him in.

Next came, what I have come to know is, a standard ritual among the dead.

"So, how'd you die?" Jesus asked.

"Pinned to the jungle gym at a Mickey D's by a car full of ripped college kids."

"Nice! Wow." He seemed to be impressed.

"How did you die?" I asked. It only seemed polite to reciprocate.

"Ice pick to my left eye," he answered pointing to it. "I had the perp caught and cuffed, not sure how he came up with the pick."

There was a period of awkward silence for a while after that. I mean, what do you say? So sorry we're both dead; what the hell do we do now? I guess I must have started to glaze over.

"Don't go bardo on me man!" Jesus yelled. "Just keep moving man, and keep talking. That will help you settle in to... well you know." With that he walked to the other end of the room and right through the doors.

I tried to follow him, but after I got about two feet further I was snapped back all the way into my drawer. I got out of there quick; I didn't want to be in there with my body.

JJTTSABD #2: *Being attached to a dead chunk of rotting meat really sucks.*

When I got out, Jesus was back and he just chuckled. "You've got to keep practicing. I met a fellow a few days ago that could move independently of his body; he didn't have the silver cord."

"Really?"

"Yup, you might see him too. He likes to come down here and mess with the bardo-brains, they're easy to scare."

"Bardo-brains?"

"Yeah, those poor suckers," he pointed at the two others wandering around gape jawed and unaware, "are stuck in their own private hell—can't get out and move on. Banquo, that's his name, says he is doing them a service, trying to shock them back to this world. Me, I don't know, just kinda looks like he is scaring the shit out of them."

"Banquo? That's a weird name," I said.

Jesus shrugged, "Well he's a *strange* fellow."

We talked a lot about everything, and when that got old we would turn to trading insults. I would give him shit about his name, and he would say: "At least I didn't die at Mickey D's kiddy land." I would come back with: "And what kind of bounty hunter were you? Getting ice-picked by some coked-up, handcuffed perp." He would then call me a redneck, and I would call him a wetback. It was good natured and it was fun. Until it wasn't, that is. Eventually someone would hit pay-dirt sending one of us close to going bardo and the other would have to pull them out while staying in safe conversational territory.

Transmission #3
Received 2010/10/21 04:23:15

So Jesus really saved me there. Kept me from going bardo, which I guess I would have done if he hadn't been there. I was with him for maybe a day before I got transferred to the mortuary.

They pulled the body—yeah, I wasn't calling it mine anymore but "the," trying to view it more as an anchor—out of the drawer onto a gurney and into a meat-wagon. I guess you could look on this as the first whisper of Stage #5: Acceptance. I was starting to accept the fact that hunk-o-meat was not "me."

As I was being dragged along with the body I shouted to Jesus, "Thanks Jesus, you really saved me!" Pronouncing his name as Gee-zus.

That made him grin as he floated along besides me, "Just keep talking, keep moving. Stay out of bardo-land and you'll be OK."

"You too bro. Thanks, I owe you."

Jesus hit his limit and couldn't go any further. As we parted I shouted, "Jesus saves!"

THE MORTUARY SUCKED. I WAS STUCK, ATTACHED TO THAT which used to be me, watching this weird guy with thick old fashioned glasses work on my body.

He first checked for a pulse (yeah bub, I am seriously dead), stripped and washed the body, flexed and massaged the arms and legs until they would lie flat, sewed up the injuries, and injected fluids into it. Then came trying to make it look like it wasn't dead. Only problem was, he was making my meat-face look scary as shit. Some sort of android version of what I once was.

I can't believe my mom was going to do the open casket thing. I guess it is good for some folks: seeing the dead chunk of meat helps them let go. Me, I never wanted that. Just burn me quick and dump the ashes somewhere. Nothing left, no place for folks to go and cry.

I slipped briefly into Stage #4: Depression, but thanks to Jesus I was good at catching the signs. See, depression leads to bardo-brain, and I was more scared of that than I was of being dead. Without Jesus here to save me I had to keep myself on track.

So when I felt that depression coming on, I just started singing as loud as I could, the song *Don't Fear the Reaper*.

The worse it got, the louder I sang, and I marched slowly away from "the meat that used to be me" stretching out the cord. When I got there I could only move four feet away. After a few hours of singing and marching (and making up really lyrics staring your's truly). I stretched it to eight feet.

I was trying to break the record, went too far, and got snapped right back to my body. My head, such as it was, was taking up the same space as the spectacled embalmer dude. He was applying rouge (yeah, rouge!) to my cheeks. It freaked me out and I felt the bardo approaching fast, so I started singing louder than ever.

Embalmer dude—let's call him Ed for short—jerked up and looked around, scratching his head. Did he hear me? Not sure, so I got right next to his ear and shouted as loud as I could, "Don't fear the reaper, JJ is the man!"

Sure enough, Ed jumped, just a bit, and looked around. "What was that?" he whispered.

I was ecstatic, and started running around with my hands in the air as if I had just won an Olympic gold medal. I wasn't really watching where I was going and popped out into the next room where another piece of meat was laid out in a coffin with folks lining up to pay their respects.

Not only had I communicated with someone, I had extended my leash! As I found out later, feeling good made things work better on this side too.

The situation in the room was tense: folks in small intimate knots talking quietly; a small line of people parading past the body muttering their goodbyes, most crying or with tears in their eyes; and one older lady, the wife I presume, wailing in a corner, awkwardly comforted by what I assume were her children.

That is another tough thing about grieving. The one with the greatest loss is the one that receives the comfort, kind of like a pecking order. The wife lost the most, so the children comforted her, when they were ripped up inside too.

There were also a few mortuary suits standing there: impeccably groomed, good posture, and appropriately dour expressions on their faces. How do you do a job like that? To be surrounded constantly by other people's grief and yet retain a shred of your own joy, or sanity at the very least.

Yup, I woke up happy today, smiling with a spring in my step. Then I went to work and had to transform myself into a conciliatory zombie. Yuck.

And then, finally, was the ghost. Hovering around the coffin was a bardo-ed, gape mouthed extra-corporeal. From what I heard folks saying he had a massive stroke and went fast.

I walked up (OK, hovered) to him and said, "Hey pops, how'd you die?" His expression didn't change, those eyes hollow and far off. Then I had an idea: since he was still closely attached to his body, maybe…

"Look at this old fart. I bet he has a mouth full of crowns in there, probably some of them gold. I love gold!" I glanced over but nothing had changed. "I'm just gonna reach in here and see what I can find." I gingerly stuck my hand into his mouth and made a good show of it.

That did it, his eyes popped into focus, and he said "Hey!" He swooped towards me, passing through those that were standing there looking at the meat that was him. One of them shivered, and I felt what I can only describe as a cold breeze rushing past.

I pulled my hand out and said, "No harm pops, no harm. My name is JJ. So how did you die?"

He stopped, looked around and moaned, "Dead, I'm dead? How can I be dead? I'm not dead!" A look of horror came over his face and, pop, back to bardo-land for him.

I left; he just didn't seem to be ready for what had happened to him, thoroughly engrossed in the denial/shock stage. I spent the rest of the day just outside the building. I tried to go further, but couldn't. So I loitered near the entrance yelling in people's ears seeing how many I could reach.

Not many, but a few seemed to sense something. Not what I was saying or anything, but they sensed something. One old biddy shivered, a man with a hearing aid twiddled with it like it had squealed or something.

Not much of a way to pass time, but at least I wasn't stuck in there with my meat.

When I went outside, I discovered this was not just a mortuary, but a cemetery too. That freaked me out a bit, probably lots of ghosts around here. And you know, just because you are a ghost doesn't mean you want to run into a bunch of other ghosts. The bardo-brained newly dead were bad enough, but what must it be like for a spirit stuck in a place like this for a decade or a century?

This place was on the corner of Miracle and Oracle. You think the roads were named that way when they built the place? Seems like two strange names. With tall trees and green grass it was surprisingly lush for Tucson. At least it was a lovely place, and peaceful at the moment.

I hung around outside, and poked around inside, carefully avoiding my meat, but not much exciting happened. I did learn a few things.

First of all those mortuary suits got pretty weird when they were on break and no one (but us ghosts) were around.

The tall one, Hal I think, did a dead-on impression of the grieving widow for his coworkers, complete with crying, carrying on and a grief soaked east coast accent.

Alice, the only chick on duty, was a foulmouthed, chain smoking witch when she was out of sight of the patrons. She kept going on about how much she would drink at night, and how sick she would get. Later in my stay I caught her and Hal getting it on in the embalming room—sick.

Ed, my embalmer, started to regale them with the gruesome details of just how messed up I was. I got out of there fast, planning to stay outside until everyone had gone home and the place was locked up.

I didn't take it personally. I've just got to imagine with a job like that you've got to blow the steam off any way you can.

Transmission #4
Received 2010/10/22 02:56:21

I HAD TO TAKE A BREAK, BUT I THINK I AM GETTING BETTER at this; it is going faster at least.

One weird thing that happens; when I get really exhausted, I just go away. I have no idea what happens to me or where I am but some time later I come back and feel all groggy. Kind of like a deep dreamless sleep. It is referred to as "fading," I have seen other spirits do it, and that is what it looks like—they just slowly fade away.

I often wake up somewhere different from when I went to sleep, often not in good places. The other day I woke up in the middle of I-10 with a wall of traffic descending on me. I would have died, if I had not already been dead.

JJTTSABD #3: *Waking up at some random location and getting the shock of your life... err death, ... sucks.*

I don't like "fading," I just don't trust it. I guess I am afraid that I won't come back, that it will be the end. I think I went through a phase like that when I was a kid. I would fight sleeping as long as I could—I didn't trust it, I didn't want to miss anything, and I was afraid of not coming back.

That evening things got really interesting at the mortuary; I had a series of visitors.

First up was Marilyn. She arrived just as the sun was going down, the sunlight filtered through the dust and pollution bathed everything in a warm glow. She was well formed, wearing last century's fashionable clothing over her bulbous body. She was so well formed that for a bit I thought she was meat. That is until she walked right up to me and said, "Have you seen my cat?"

"You can see me?"

"Of course I can sonny," she said. "Have you seen my cat, Motor? He got himself lost again; he must be around here somewhere."

"So, how did you die?" I asked. Standard greeting, right? Just like in prison—hey bub, whatcha in for? Her face got pinched, her form started to break up, and her eyes got vacant. I scrambled, "Cat. Yeah, I saw a cat, just a little while ago." That snapped her back a bit, her hands reforming out of the vapor.

"You saw my cat?"

"Not sure if it was yours, but I did see a cat," I lied. "Hey lady, what's your name?" I backed up a bit, forcing her to follow me. Following Jesus's lead and getting her talking and moving.

"Marilyn. My name is Marilyn. I really need to find my cat." She paused and thought for a moment. She was fully back now. "Was it a black cat with lovely green eyes that you saw?"

"Yeah, I think so. I saw it run into the trees over there."

She waddled off and I didn't see her again until the same time the next day when we went through a similar routine. She didn't appear to recognize me; it seems like she was running the same track on repeat.

Shortly after Marilyn left, right after the sun went down, the noise started: stirring, rattling, whispers, mumbles, and more shocking noises. This place was surrounded: graves on two sides, and crypts on the other two.

At first I was curious, but when the moans turned into screams I started to get scared. I was really wishing Jesus was with me, and just when it was getting bad, I thought I heard him say, "Just keep talking, just keep walking."

I had no one to talk to, so I started back up with my butchered rendition of *Don't Fear the Reaper* and started running. At first I ran around the building, but the crypt sections just creeped me out too much so I kept to the front, running back and forth singing as loud as I could.

The red of the sunset deepened, and then before I knew it the light was gone. The night was moonless and the darkness dropped fast and heavy. As things darkened I saw shapes moving out in the cemetery. Perhaps my singing attracted them or perhaps they marched onto the mortuary every night, but either way they were coming closer and closer.

So I ran faster and sung louder—what else was I to do? I had no idea what they wanted, or how to defend myself. In retrospect I thought of them as "them." Not the same as me, but somehow separate and scary. Ghosts are scary, right? I didn't know what they could do to me, and that unknown was keeping me tottering on the brink.

I think he must have been yelling at me for a while before I noticed him.

"Boy! Boy! Screw your courage to the sticking-place."

He was the most well-formed spirit I had seen, although not an impressive form. He was short, bald, with a heavy belly.

I slowed down, and he repeated the phrase again: "Screw your courage to the sticking-place." The phrasing was odd, but his delivery resounding. I got the drift, and stopped long enough to look around.

The spirits were indeed moving into the mortuary, but they had given me, and this fellow, a wide berth. After I stopped, they moved in and took over the path I had been running, and I had no choice but to move closer to the man.

"So," I said, trying to insert some swagger into my voice, "how'd ya die?"

"Better, boy, better. My name is Banquo and I died in a plane crash." His void was deep, resonant, and calming.

"My name is JJ; I died pinned to a jungle gym at a Mickey D's."

"I thought I would find you here. Jesus told me that you might need some help."

"Jesus saves!" I couldn't resist pulling that one out again.

Banquo chuckled, "Indeed he does."

"Those... Those..." I stuttered, pointing towards the mortuary where the gang of spirits had gone.

"Just curious, for the most part. It is a small community, visitors are always an excitement. Come, we must talk."

Banquo guided me, much to my dismay, to the embalming room where my body, now dressed and fully "restored," was laid out. There were a few of the cemetery spirits examining my body, sticking their faces into my abdomen, fingers into my head.

"Hey!" I shouted. Just like the old fart that I messed with, I felt proprietary about that piece of meat. It was *my* piece of meat.

"JJ, until you accept what happened, accept that you are dead, and that *thing* is no longer *you*, you will be chained to it."

Shuffled Off: A Ghost's Memoir, Book 1 is available now. Go to ShuffledOff.com for more information.

ACKNOWLEDGEMENTS

Writing a book entails the author sitting alone for many, many hours imagining, planning, writing, and editing. It is not, though, done alone. I had a huge amount of help on this book.

First to my amazing wife, Aleia. The basic premise of this book—drawing the dead—is based on a dream she had that just stuck with me. And beyond that, her love and support for me and these stories is what makes this possible.

This book is dedicated to VTara Ruscher. When I conceived of the character Viki Dobos, I thought of VTara. She was a wonderful artist and a gentle, loving spirit. While Viki is not VTara, there are pieces of her in there. When I started writing this book, VTara was in remission from colon cancer and doing well. When I was finishing up my first round of edits, she was entering hospice. So, I rushed a version to her (she was the first person to read it). The last time I saw her we chatted a little bit about the book. I am happy to say she loved it, and I'm glad she got a chance to read it.

The fantastic cover art is by Barry Miller (BTBArtist); you can see more of his art at www.btbartist.co.uk. I needed to find a piece of pastel artwork with compelling eyes. I almost fell over when I found Barry's piece that graces the cover. It fits so well with how Viki draws and the eyes are amazing.

Many thanks to my fabulous beta team who schlep through my words first and help me find my way. John Bifano, Roni Hornstein, Chris Kalinich, Michele Lytle, Gary D. McClellan, O. Nazhmetdinova, Aleia N. O'Reilly, Eliot Schipper, and Janine Schipper. I thank you guys often, but it is never enough.

Special thanks to O. Nazhmetdinova for doing the Russian translations and making sure Mark's character felt real to his culture. I can't tell you what a relief it was to have her reviewing this one.

Thanks to my editor, Joshua Essoe (www.joshuaessoe.com) and my proofreader Diana Cox (www.novelproofreading.com)—you two make me look good and help me get across what I'm trying to say.

Jordyn Redwood (www.jordynredwood.com) helped out with the medical scenes and helped make them real.

And thank you for reading and taking this journey with me. I hope it was enjoyable and maybe made you think just a little. If you would like to read more of my ramblings (there are some more in-depth discussions about this book), check out my blog at RobertJMcCarter.com.

ABOUT THE AUTHOR

ROBERT J. MCCARTER IS VERY COMFORTABLE WRITING about characters as long as one of those characters is not himself. Actually, Robert is anything but comfortable speaking (or writing) of himself in the third person—he finds it pretentious and silly.

So, let's drop all that usual bio crap.

Hi, my name is Robert, and I make things up and write them down. As a reader you may be interested in knowing something about me, so here goes:

I am a computer programmer by trade and have been for a very long time. I wrote my first program over thirty years ago and never stopped. I found the dramatic arts in high school, which got me through that rather daunting rite of passage, and fell in love with the arts. After high school, I started writing really bad poetry about how lonely I was and how clueless I was about the opposite sex (which, fortunately for all of us, I burned). After that my writing turned towards fiction.

I have written sporadically for several decades, and in what is, in all probability, part of a mid-life crisis, I started writing seriously (i.e. regularly) a few years ago. I have always been drawn to the arts (acting, photography, fractal art, and writing) and find that I am most happy when I am being as creative as possible. Thus, all the sitting alone at my computer making things up.

My writing is colored by my technical (i.e. geek) past as well as my age. I'm no youngster, so themes of death, grief, and change tend to creep into my writing (Okay, that's an understatement). Also, having been trained as an engineer, I like things to make sense and do my best to keep the hand waving to a minimum.

If you asked me to succinctly say something to summarize my writing style, I would tell you to go buzz off. But then, after profuse apologies, I would say: "I write humanist-geek, character-oriented sci-fi with heart."

I live in the middle of a Ponderosa Pine forest in the mountains of Arizona with my beautiful wife and my ridiculously adorable dog.

If you'd like to get a hold of me, use the contact form on my website (RobertJMcCarter.com/contact-me/). I'd love to hear from you, really I would.

Oh, and if you want the inside scoop on my writing, sign up for my newsletter (I won't share your name and emails are infrequent—around once a month). You can sign up using the blue box on the right of my website at RobertJMc-Carter.com.

Books by Robert J. McCarter

Novels in the "Ghost's Memoir" world:
Shuffled Off: A Ghost's Memoir, Book 1
Drawing the Dead
To Be a Fool: A Ghost's Memoir, Book 2
Of Things Not Seen: A Ghost's Memoir, Book 3
  (Coming soon)

Books in the Neutrinoman and Lightningirl Series:
Meteor Attack!
  Lightningirl and Neutrinoman, A Love Story. Episode 1
Toxic Asset
  Lightningirl and Neutrinoman, A Love Story. Episode 2
Protocol X
  Lightningirl and Neutrinoman, A Love Story. Episode 3
Season 1 (Omnibus edition of Episodes 1 - 3)
Off Book
  Lightningirl and Neutrinoman, A Love Story. Episode 4
  (Coming soon)

Short Stores and Collections
Life After: Stories of Life, Death, and the Places in Between
Probability: Resolve
The Turing Test Will Be Televised
Ghost Hacker, Zombie Maker

For a complete list, go to RobertJMcCarter.com

www.ingramcontent.com/pod-product-compliance
Lightning Source LLC
Chambersburg PA
CBHW031555240626
47153CB00002B/520